THIRD
KILL

BOOKS BY JOHN RYDER

GRANT FLETCHER SERIES
First Shot
Final Second

THIRD KILL

JOHN RYDER

Bookouture

Published by Bookouture in 2021

An imprint of Storyfire Ltd.
Carmelite House
50 Victoria Embankment
London EC4Y 0DZ

www.bookouture.com

ISBN: 978-1-80019-286-7
eBook ISBN: 978-1-80019-285-0

Grandad. You were loved more than you were ever told and will be missed more than can ever be said.

PROLOGUE

The Mantis has a ten-minute window in which she can kill the head of a Las Vegas casino empire. If things go as planned, she'll need no more than six of those minutes to enter the building, kill him and make her escape.

A rear door that should be locked, isn't. A security camera that should be pointing her way, isn't. A guard who should be patrolling this area every ten minutes has been distracted. The Mantis hasn't been distracted. She has her focus. She has to have this focus, as she knows she'll face a slow, agonizing death if she fails her mission.

The Mantis wasn't ambidextrous by birth. Her left hand had always been dominant and more assured than her right. This was something she worked on until she could shoot with equal accuracy regardless of which hand held the gun.

She walks along the passage, ignoring the first four doors. A keycard-activated lock opens when she swipes the master pass card she's obtained.

A set of stairs lead down. Most casinos count and store their money below ground level.

Cash is a bulky thing to steal in any great quantity. A couple grand can be stuffed into a pocket, but the risk versus reward involved in stealing less than a six-figure amount is prohibitive. When there are millions, though, as most casinos have, the reward becomes far greater. As many are owned by those involved in organized crime, lots of Las Vegas casinos have far more than their actual takings in their vaults. They act as laundromats for the money the gang has raised from other criminal activities, and those who control the books of the casinos are some of the smartest accountants in the country.

Unless the target has deviated from his routine of having dinner in his penthouse at nine, the Mantis knows exactly where he'll be.

To get to the penthouse, she has to get her way to the private elevator that only goes between the penthouse and the suite of offices used by the target.

It sounds simple. It isn't.

To get to the elevator she has to enter a place where her presence isn't expected or welcome. Even without the fact she has a silenced pistol in each hand, as soon as she's seen, guns will be pointed her way.

She has a way to deal with such issues.

Two of the syndicate's henchmen round a corner as she makes her way to the inner sanctum. Both are hit with a pair of bullets from her pistols before they can react. Neither man is alive when his head thumps against the plush carpet.

As she makes her way to the elevator another henchman-cum-guard appears. Her pistols spit more death, and the man falls to the ground.

Two more guards are patrolling the area by the elevator. These are higher quality and one of them actually manages to get his hand inside his jacket before the Mantis shoots him. His buddy even releases a muted shout, although it dies on his lips as a bullet rips into his chest.

The Mantis is where she needs to be, so she pushes the button to call the elevator, then swipes her magic pass card.

Elevators are a risk when assaulting a building. They confine you. Cocoon you in metal walls.

To launch an assault from an elevator is to gamble on the unknown. When the doors open you can face a platoon of enemies or nobody. It's a roll of the dice and for all the Mantis is operating in a Las Vegas casino, she's not the gambling type.

When the doors open, the target is waiting for her. Brendan Aurier is mid-sixties and known for his utter ruthlessness. He holds a machine pistol at waist height, as do the two men at his side. They are his right-hand men, and they run the other two casinos in town owned by the syndicate. All three of their muzzles are aimed chest high, ready to shred whoever is riding up the elevator uninvited.

The Mantis may be trapped, but she has one advantage—she knows whoever is in front of her is a foe, whereas the three gangsters have to take a microsecond to see who's in the elevator before they start shooting.

Her silenced pistols spit bullets with muted coughs. The first shots put a bullet into the hearts of the two men flanking Aurier, and then she adjusts her aim onto Aurier. The gang boss is quick to react to what's happening, and his machine pistol barks a deadly hail of bullets into the elevator.

The Mantis has time to put a bullet into his chest before he can get his gun pointing her way. Even as he reels back from the bullet's impact, she puts a second round into his left eye.

She stands and puts a bullet into the left eye of Matty Canton and of Serge Pires. They were on her list of targets as well as Aurier, so after observing their routine and learning of their weekly dinner in the penthouse, it was always her intention to go for the three-fer.

The penthouse is the best room in the hotel above the casino, although to call it a room is akin to calling the Pacific Ocean a puddle. The Mantis pays her opulent surroundings no heed as she prepares for her escape. To go back down the elevator will see her met with a host of enemies, as her trail of destruction is sure to have been discovered by now. To escape she has to use another way down.

A long rope lashed to a stout piece of furniture would allow her to rappel down the building, but she knows the windows are made from bulletproof glass. That little gem of obstruction was unearthed in her research when she was considering a high-powered rifle as the tool for this mission.

The elevator is sent back down. The Mantis expects that as soon as it reaches the bottom, it'll come back up filled with gun-toting goons. That doesn't matter. She'll be long gone by then. She's confident enough in her escape plan that she allows a part of her brain to wander… towards the next target.

CHAPTER ONE

It was a typical winter evening for Grant Fletcher. He'd finished work on the construction site when it got dark, came home and cooked dinner for himself and his daughter, Wendy. The dishwasher was loaded and he had no plans to do anything more strenuous than watch a couple episodes of a Netflix series with Wendy once she'd done her homework. Their nightly interactions were diminishing as she developed her own social life, but on at least three nights a week they made time for each other. To Fletcher it meant his week had three highlights, because his only daughter was his world.

Fletcher turned on the television and called through to Wendy, who was clattering things in the kitchen. "Honey, I'm starting it now! What are you even doing in there?"

Wendy shouted back, her teenage voice layered with fond exasperation. "Can you not wait two minutes, Dad? I'm just grabbing some nachos. Do you want the chili dip or the salsa?"

"Both, please." Fletcher gave a sad smile at how much Wendy reminded him how her late mother had been, from her sassiness right down to the need for snacks every time they sat down to watch television.

A ring from the doorbell made him look up. No visitors were expected, and Wendy's face, as she came through from the kitchen, showed puzzlement. Their little Shih Tzu, Wilson, did his usual thing of barking up enough of a storm to warn them of a nuclear holocaust, when it was probably some innocuous caller.

Fletcher opened the door and saw a face he'd hoped he'd never see on his doorstep. Special Agent Zoey Quadrado.

Fletcher wasn't naïve enough to think this was a social visit. Nor had he ever harbored any illusions that Quadrado didn't know his home address, even though he'd never given it to her.

Quadrado's presence meant only one thing though. She had another mission for him. Since he'd helped out a friend whose daughter had gone missing, a mysterious government figure known only as Soter had been blackmailing him into conducting black-ops missions, and using Quadrado as the conduit between him and Soter. His handler, of sorts.

For all they were friends, their friendship was forged in adversity and they still always called each other by their surnames. He'd saved her life, and she'd kept him off death row. It was enough for him. And a sweetener in Soter's deal had also been a promise that Wendy would be guaranteed free tuition at any college of her choosing.

All the same, he didn't like that Quadrado was at his house uninvited. The violent side of his life was one he kept separate from his domestic set-up.

"Quadrado." He opened the door wider to allow her into the house.

"Fletcher."

There was something in her eyes that spoke of guilt and stress. She'd know she was breaking unwritten rules by arriving here, and he surmised that her presence wasn't her idea.

"I'll get you a coffee."

"Thanks. Nice place you have here."

Fletcher didn't know if she meant it or was being polite. A single father, he'd done his best to make the house a home for Wendy. To not have it as a sterile, masculine place. He saw Quadrado's eyes linger on the pictures of Rachel, his late wife, whose death still lay heavy on his conscience, and the marks on the back of the kitchen door where he'd measured Wendy's height as she grew.

Those marks were a fabric of his being and he could no more paint over them than slit his own throat.

"Hi."

Fletcher had heard Wendy's footsteps and knew she'd be getting herself a can of soda or something else to eat. She seemed to be able to eat twice what he could these days, although he'd enough parenting experience to recognize a growth spurt when he saw it.

"Wendy, this is Zoey Quadrado."

"Hi. Your pop has told me a lot about you." Quadrado's hand extended to Wendy.

Wendy's hand took Quadrado's and gave it a firm shake. Fletcher caught the way Wendy was looking at him and read the unasked question from her expression. "Quadrado is a colleague. You know how I sometimes go away for a few days? Well, Quadrado here works with me then."

Wendy's face bent into a scowl. "Oh. I thought maybe you were dating her." The scowl got aimed at Quadrado. "You're obviously not very good at what you do. Every time he goes away, he comes back looking like he's been kicked half to death." With her piece said Wendy left the room.

Fletcher made to follow her and call her back, intent on making her apologize for her rudeness, when he felt Quadrado's hand pull at his arm. "Leave her be. It's to be expected that she won't like me. Let's face it, she's right, every time we work together you return home looking like you've been run over by a whole fleet of trucks. Her animosity to me is an echo of the love she has for you."

"I guess. I'm not happy with her rudeness though."

"Drop it. In her position I would have been a damned sight ruder at her age. So far as I'm concerned I got off easy. I expected far worse if I ever met her."

"Really? I thought I was the cynical one?"

"You are." Quadrado's smile robbed her words of any offense they might carry. "But you've told me you haven't dated since your wife died. Yet you've just introduced her to me, not as her first fear, a date, but—far worse—as the person who takes you away and sends you back beat-up. Not only will she be worried about me bringing harm to you, I'd also hazard a guess that I'm the first woman to significantly feature in your life." Rather than continue speaking, Quadrado paused to sweep her eyes over the room. Fletcher knew the action was to give him time to process what she was saying. "So even though you've told her we're colleagues, she's going to be wondering about our relationship, both professional and personal. She'll think I'm either going to get you killed or am somehow here to try and replace her mom. That's a lot to deal with. Trust me, she's handling it a lot better than I would have in her position, and I was hardly a wild child."

Quadrado's admission about how she imagined she'd have behaved if she was put in Wendy's position was enough to show Fletcher a different side to her. He was used to her being matter-of-fact, and while she hadn't been disrespectful towards Wendy, it was clear that she'd expected to get a hard time from his daughter. Quadrado was a good person with a warm heart and the fact she had potential for a rebellious streak was news to him.

On reflection he realized he shouldn't have been caught out by her. The deal he had with Soter went against so many legal and ethical rules, and if Quadrado was as morally sound as she acted, there was no way she could condone it. He put Wendy's behavior aside for the time being; there was a more pressing matter.

"So. You're here. What does Soter want from me?"

"I don't know. My instructions were to come here and then email him when we were somewhere private."

Fletcher led Quadrado to his den. It was a place he drank beer and smoked cigars with buddies, as well as the room where he stored the various pieces of household paperwork.

Twenty seconds after Quadrado pressed send on the email, Fletcher's cell rang. There was no number displayed on the screen and he figured that if there had been it would belong to an untraceable burner phone.

He thumbed the screen and tapped the right button to activate the speakerphone.

"Mr. Fletcher?" The voice was distorted by some kind of electronic software. Fletcher had expected no less.

"That's me. Are you Soter?"

"I am. I have a mission for you. It requires someone of your talents."

"What is it?"

"You may have heard about some shootings in Las Vegas. Someone has been picking off the top men from various crime gangs and syndicates who own the casinos there. So far there have been thirty-one murders of known gang leaders, their associates and their lackeys. Normally this wouldn't bother me in the slightest, but the crime syndicates are blaming each other and there's been a few skirmishes in what we're expecting to escalate until it's a full-scale gang war. Again, one set of criminals killing another wouldn't be something that worries me too much, but so far twenty-two innocent members of the public have been killed simply because they were in the wrong place at the wrong time. That isn't acceptable on any level."

"When did this happen? I heard about some killings in Las Vegas, but not on the scale you're saying."

"Fifteen of the victims were shot today. Another five were yesterday. This whole thing is escalating out of hand. So far we've been able to keep something of a lid on it for the sake of Vegas's tourist dollar, but it's going be national news when the press learn of today's event."

"What is it you want Fletcher to do, sir?"

Fletcher pulled a face at Quadrado's use of the honorific. For all the pact with Soter meant Wendy could get the finest education available, he was still a ruthless blackmailer who expected Fletcher to risk his life whenever he deemed it necessary. Soter's comments that he wasn't too worried about criminals being killed fit with what Fletcher knew about him, though it didn't match his self-appointed moniker of the Greek god of protection.

"We learned there's an assassin picking off the crime bosses. We have intel on who it is. A female killer known as the Mantis. I want her stopped, and that's why I'm talking to you two. I also want to know whose payroll she's on, as one of the very few things we know about her is that she doesn't work for free."

"Do you know what she looks like?"

Fletcher heard the sigh before Soter spoke. "We have pictures of her, but her face isn't visible."

"What about known associates?"

"There's none we know of. She's a wraith who lives off the grid. Her name had been touted around for a couple years, but there'd been nothing but rumor and myth known about her. Until it came up in the investigations into the Las Vegas assassinations. The kills are typical of others attributed to her. She gets in and out without being seen. All her victims are killed the same way: a bullet to the heart then a shot to the left eye."

"That figures. And you want me to go up against this deadly assassin you know nothing about and kill her when nobody even knows what she looks like?"

"That's right." Even through the distorting software, enough steel to build a supertanker filled Soter's voice. "And you're to find out who she's working for and neutralize them as well."

"It sounds like a suicide mission, provided I can even get close to her."

"I understand any concerns you might have. But this is a killer who has to be stopped. It's not public knowledge yet, but the first Las Vegas hit attributed to her was on Hoon Sung Chang; nine people were shot dead and two of them were civilian innocents: a housekeeper who'd stopped in on her day off to deliver a birthday gift to Chang's cook—she and her son were both killed." He paused, taking a breath before he continued. "Her only little boy, Frankie, was eight years old and had Down syndrome. He was the Mantis's third kill in Vegas."

The revelation about a child who'd been gunned down painted a snarl on Fletcher's face and fueled a murderous rage in his heart that had him gripping the phone hard enough to whiten his knuckles. Fletcher was no longer in his den. He was back in time and was his fourteen-year-old self, standing beside the grave of his sister and failing to hold back the tears. Issy was the daughter of his adoptive parents—a girl with Down syndrome and an infectious joie de vivre. He'd yet to meet a sweeter, more innocent person than Issy, and as Soter continued talking, Issy's smiling face was stuck in his mind's eye. For all he recognized Soter was manipulating him with this revelation, now he knew the Mantis could kill someone like Issy, it was personal. He wanted to stop her more than he wanted anything else, to end her reign of terror as soon as possible, to prevent more innocents dying. Fletcher rested his gaze on a picture of him and Issy that was one of his most precious possessions. "Okay, I'm in. But surely the FBI are better suited to finding the Mantis and stopping her than I am."

"Normally you'd be right, and believe me, I'd love the FBI to catch her. It would be a banner day if they could. Sadly, other than the name she goes by, they have nothing to go on that's likely to get them anywhere. And they're taking too long. That's why I'm bringing you in. You don't look like a cop, and nor do you think like one. You're a killer and can think like her. *That's* what's needed here. Special Agent Quadrado, you are to liaise between Mr. Fletcher and the Special Agent in Charge of Las Vegas. Whatever Mr. Fletcher needs, he gets, no quibbles. If you meet any resistance, or need a line of support unavailable in Vegas, email me and I'll fix it. Good luck and good evening to you both."

As the phone clicked off, Fletcher cast a look at Quadrado. She didn't look confident, and he could see her mind whirring from the blank look in her eyes. He passed over the thoughts about her and turned his mind to the practical.

First of all he had to inform Wendy she and Wilson would be going to stay with Rachel's parents again. It was where they always went when he was on a mission, whether it was one of Soter's or the out-of-state construction jobs he took from time to time.

But as he left the den, he found Wendy in the kitchen already packing up Wilson's feed, bowls and dog toys.

"When are you going?" The fact she wouldn't look at him tore at Fletcher.

"As soon as possible." He didn't say anymore. Didn't need to. Wendy didn't know the full story about the missions he went on, as he knew she'd be horrified at what kind of man he really was. He'd told her that he helped out on certain government projects that needed a soldier's input and that he was well paid for it. Not the brutal details though. He knew she'd just tell him not to risk his life so she could go to a better college. But Fletcher wanted the best for her, and he'd stop at nothing to get that. Not to mention, Soter had things over him that would see him jailed, things he never wanted Wendy to find out.

He pulled her into a hug as Wilson jumped up at their knees. "Don't worry, I'll be back before you know. If you're lucky, I'll pick myself up a new joke book when I'm away."

"You need it. Your jokes are older than Grandma and lamer than a two-legged dog." She pushed herself free of his embrace. "I'm packed and ready to go, and I've got Grandpops picking me and Wilson up in half an hour. Go do your own packing."

As Fletcher turned his mind to what he had to take with him to Vegas, he recognized that Wendy had gotten him out of the room before he could see how scared she was for him.

She had good reason—if what little they knew about the Mantis was true.

CHAPTER TWO

The Las Vegas FBI office is a long, modern building on Lake Mead Boulevard that could easily be mistaken for a random company's headquarters were it not for the white stone portico emblazoned with the words "Fidelity Bravery Integrity."

Once he'd been admitted and given the security pass that was waiting for him at reception, Fletcher followed the aide who'd met him and Quadrado as he led them to the Special Agent in Charge's office.

The name on the door was Eric Thomson, and when a voice answered the aide's knock, it was gruff and commanding. That was no surprise to Fletcher. Thomson would be under intense pressure to keep order and with twenty-two civilian homicides as well as the thirty-one gang members who'd been murdered, everyone would be looking at him for results.

When Quadrado opened the door, he saw Thomson was a squat, powerful man in his mid-forties. His hair was tight curls of what Fletcher suspected was once bright red but was now softened by the graying process.

"Sir, I'm Special Agent Zoey Quadrado and this is Grant Fletcher, a specialist who's been drafted in to help find and catch the Mantis."

"I'm quite aware of who you are, Quadrado. I've received word from on high that you're to get whatever help you ask for and access to any of our files that you want."

Fletcher hadn't been expecting a red carpet or a ticker-tape parade, but he'd not expected to be met with bitterness. A few ruffled layers of professional pride were on the cards, but not this level of animosity. Thomson's office was neat, too neat for its occupant to be achieving any real work. It may be that this was where he did his managerial stuff, and he led the investigation from the office populated by the agents on the case, but to Fletcher's thinking, there ought to be something on the desk to show that he was actually doing something. It could, of course, be that Thomson had OCD and couldn't help but keep things neat, but there was a randomness to the angle of his laptop, desk phone and the pair of files in front of him that suggested otherwise.

"That is correct, sir." Fletcher was happy to let Quadrado do the talking. She was far more diplomatic than him, and he was sure it'd be easier all round if they kept on Thomson's good side, narrow as it appeared to be. "We appreciate that it may seem like we've been parachuted in because someone in the Hoover Building doesn't have faith in you, but so far as we're concerned, you're on the same side as us and we'll be happy to share what we find with you. I will personally make sure that regardless of who catches the Mantis, the credit is given to you."

"You sound confident that you're going to find something. Someone in Washington doesn't think I can catch the Mantis, and they've sent you here to wipe my ass. I don't like them for their assumption, and I don't like how you've just strutted in here and assumed that all the hard work my team has put in is just going to be handed over to you. As for your promise of us getting the credit, that's a crock and don't you go thinking I don't see that. The way you said it sounded a lot like you expect to solve this case and then give me and my team a pat on the back for not getting in your way." Thomson made a visible effort to rein in his temper and reached for the water bottle on his desk. "Oh, and yeah, if you're trying to pass your friend off as a specialist, best not give me a shopping list that looks like it was written by Rambo or a character in a Dwayne Johnson movie. Two pistols, a hunting knife, one submachine gun, one sniper's rifle, flashbangs and grenades, and don't get me started on all the tactical gear on your list. Damnit, Quadrado, your man isn't any kind of psychologist or person with special insights. He's a soldier, I could see it in the way he walks. The way his eyes scan things. Look at him now." Thomson flapped a hand Fletcher's way. "He's standing ready for action. Hands loose at his sides, up on the balls of his feet ready to move fast."

"With respect, sir, we're here to do a job, and that's what we're going to do. Now if you'll tell us where we can get the information and items we requested, we'll get out of your way."

"There's a desk in the next office. It has a computer and the files are all on there." A gesture towards the door. "I won't take up anymore of your time."

Quadrado's mouth pursed as she moved to the door. Fletcher got there first and blocked her from opening it.

"Wait a minute." Two long strides had Fletcher in front of Thomson's desk. "Listen here, Thomson, you might be the top man around here and used to getting away with treating your people like trash, but that's not going to happen to us. Whether you like it or not, you're going to have to treat us with respect. Sending us off to an office to pore through files we haven't compiled will waste days of our time. This is your town, your patch. The innocent civilians who are getting caught in the crossfire might not be from Las Vegas, but when they're in your city, it's your job to protect them." Fletcher cast a glance Quadrado's way to involve her in what he was about to say. "I understand you're a busy man, but I want one of your most informed agents to give us a proper briefing so that we're up and running as soon as possible."

"Yeah, that's what you want. I want to flap my arms and fly and that's not going to happen either. The files are on the computer, and my agents are all busy."

"Fine. If that's how you want to play it, we'll play it your way."
Fletcher moved to the door. "I'm going home."

"What? That's your threat, Mr. Tough Guy? That you're going
home?"

"Absolutely. Think about who told you we were coming here? It
was someone from D.C., wasn't it?" Fletcher gave a shrug. "When
they ask you why I left before I'd even gotten started, be sure to
them the truth."

CHAPTER THREE

"Who the hell do you think you are threatening me like that?" Thomson's arm extended, a forefinger jabbing Fletcher's way. "You're a goddamn asshole as far as I'm concerned. This is an FBI matter. I don't care who you are, nobody threatens me like that. Now get out of my office before I have you arrested and thrown in jail."

"On what charges?"

Quadrado knew Fletcher well enough to be certain of two things: one, he wouldn't ever back down when he felt he was in the right, and two, the way he was staying calm and relaxed didn't bode well for Thomson's immediate well-being, if he planned on making good his threat of arrest.

With both men in the room butting heads, it was up to her to instill some perspective on proceedings. "Can we all take a moment here? Sir, I understand that you probably aren't happy about us being parachuted in like this." As she spoke, Quadrado moved forward until she was between Fletcher and the desk. "That's out of the control of everyone in this room. We didn't ask to be here, and you didn't ask for us to come. However, we are here and the reason we're here is to help. As Fletcher pointed out, this is your city, your domain. Surely it's not too much to ask that you extend a little professional courtesy to people who are here to help you restore order in Las Vegas."

"Restore order? This isn't the Wild West anymore, you know. Sure there's been a spot of trouble with some of the gangs, but it's nothing we can't get on top of."

"A spot of trouble? You've got fifty-three people dead. That's got to be the understatement of the year. No wonder they called for us if that's your attitude."

As much as she agreed with Fletcher's take on things, Quadrado knew it wasn't in their interests to continue butting heads with the deluded Thomson.

"Hey." To accompany the shouted word, Quadrado slammed her hand on Thomson's desk hard enough to make the photo frame jump. "That's enough. Both of you need to take a look at the bigger picture here. People are being killed and it's our job to stop it." Her hand lifted from the desk and pointed at Thomson. "You. It's time to face facts. We've been drafted in and whether you like it or not, we're here to stay. We need your cooperation and if we don't get it, we have enough pull to send an email that will result in you clearing your desk within an hour." Quadrado turned to face Fletcher, her expression as hard as she could make it. "And you, you need to leave the office politics to someone who has more than your tiny fragment of tact."

"You can't threaten to have me sacked or relocated. I outrank you in every way."

"I know that you outrank *me*, sir. But the FBI got us here from Mr. Fletcher's home in Utah via helicopter, and then a private jet that was hired just for us. I think it'd be fair to say that the person who made that happen has more pull than you." Quadrado fixed Thomson with a glare she hoped was harsh enough to make him reconsider his position of blunt obstinacy. "So, over to you. Are you going to do the right thing, or do I have to send that email?"

The look Thomson fired her way was savage enough to make Quadrado realize she'd made a lifelong enemy, but she held his stare as he reached for the phone on his desk and stabbed a finger at one of the buttons. "Forbes, get your ass in here and bring your notes on the Mantis case."

Now it was a case of maintaining the right facial expressions. Quadrado didn't want to show relief at having made Thomson back down, as that would only piss him off further. She hadn't wanted to send the email to Soter complaining about him. For her that was a last resort, as it would make Soter think they couldn't cope, and there was never anything satisfying about telling tales on people.

She cast her eyes Fletcher's way to see what he was doing and was pleased to see he was in the same place, with his face arranged to give as little away as a poker player bluffing on a pair of threes.

The door opened and a man she presumed was Forbes entered. He carried a thick file and a bookish air.

"Forbes, I want you to bring this pair up to speed on the case. They're specialists and I want you to show full cooperation. Am I understood?"

If it wasn't for the gritted-teeth tone, Thomson's choice of words would have made it seem like bringing them in was his idea.

"Sir." Forbes turned to her and Fletcher. "What do you want to know first?"

"Elsewhere, please, I have work to do."

Quadrado knew Thomson's dismissal was designed to piss them off, but she'd rather get a straight briefing from Forbes without Thomson butting in, and she was sure Fletcher would want the same.

The office they'd been allocated was neither spacious nor terribly clean, but it gave them somewhere to receive the briefing from Forbes and work out their own theories without interference.

"Okay, Forbes, I'm Zoey Quadrado and he's Grant Fletcher. Can you take us through the assassinations in chronological order to start with? I don't mean to sound callous here, but our focus is on the gang members rather than the civilians. Until we stop the Mantis, the gangs won't settle down."

Forbes pushed his glasses up to the bridge of his nose. "Agreed. The first hit was seven days ago, on a Korean gang who owned the Mandalay Bay Hotel and Casino. They're one of the smaller operators but rumor has it they were looking to increase their assets in Vegas." Forbes gave a sigh. "Mind you, that could be said of any of the gangs. The hit took place at the top man's house on the edge of town, and the total number of gang deaths was seven."

"Any witnesses, CCTV footage, anything like that?" Fletcher beat Quadrado to the question, but that didn't surprise her. For all he wasn't a cop and had no detective training, he possessed a sharp and perceptive mind and could think outside the box.

"None that we know of, but that doesn't mean they don't exist."

Quadrado got what he meant. Crime syndicates and all levels of organized crime were never forthcoming with information the police or feds wanted. Holding things back from law enforcement was the norm for them, and they would rather exact their own brutal revenge than see their enemies locked up.

"Who was the target?"

"Their top man was one Hoon Sung Chang. Suffice to say his reputation went before him. Unfailingly polite and utterly deadly."

"Okay. Can you move on to the next target? Then we can go back and dig into the specifics on each one individually." Fletcher's pen hovered above the notepad he'd grabbed as soon as Forbes started talking.

"Fair enough. The next was two days later. Top man was Ken Beltzer. This was a biker gang who have been astute and vicious enough to elbow their way into a position of owning two casinos. Four of his men died with him, and the hit took place at their flagship casino, Smoking Wheels."

"Okay, and the next one?"

"The third and final attack was yesterday and took place on the head, or I should say heads, of a firm who originated from Denver. They had three casinos, and the hit went down when the three were having dinner in the top man's penthouse above the Golden Chance. Their names were Brendan Aurier, Matty Canton and

Serge Pires. Four of their men died that night, too, which brings the Mantis's tally up to nineteen gang members plus the housekeeper and her son. The other twelve gang members who died were the ones killed in the gang wars that also killed the twenty civilians."

Quadrado gave an approving nod to the quiver of outrage in Forbes's voice when he spoke of the innocent civilians who'd died.

Fletcher echoed her nod. "Okay. This Mantis woman. What about her? We've read the files on her and at best they offer slim pickings. I've served with women who were as hard as nails, as ruthless as any man, and that's fine. There's no reason why they shouldn't be. What I do question, though, is that a woman is operating as an assassin. At the risk of sounding sexist, aren't assassins predominantly male? Has there been a psych profile drawn up on the Mantis and if so, what does it say?"

"Very little is known about her, except that she's deadly and utterly ruthless. I take it you've heard about her third kill? The little boy called Frankie? That's as bad a thing as I've ever heard. The psych profile we've got on her says a lot without saying anything worth listening to. It suggests a possible traumatic event in her childhood, a broken home. She's between twenty-five and forty-five and is likely to be promiscuous."

Quadrado saw the tightening of Fletcher's jaw at the mention of Frankie. She'd seen the picture of him as a child that was in his den. He'd had an arm around the shoulders of a girl with Down syndrome, and both were pulling faces for the camera. She'd not asked him about the girl in the picture, but it was clear she meant a lot to him, and she knew Fletcher well enough to know that he'd tell her about the girl when he was ready to.

"What about training? Surely she's ex-military on some level. I don't believe that she could be as good as she is without being properly trained."

Forbes jerked his head. "That seems to be the consensus, but as we don't know who she is, there's no way of knowing who trained her. She could be one of ours, or she could be from any country you care to name."

"Why promiscuous?" Quadrado couldn't get her head around why a female killer would be thought of as being this way. "How does that fit into her profile?"

Forbes gave a shy smile. "The profilers say it's to do with power. To do with control. For someone as cold-blooded as she is, control over others as well as herself will be a compunction. For a female killer, sex is just another weapon in their armory, and they think she's the type to have honed every one of her skills."

"Tell your profilers they're a bunch of idiots." Fletcher's tone was mild, but the look on his face was one of disgust. "Whether she's promiscuous or not, she's here on a mission and she's a professional. She won't be hitting the sack with anyone in Vegas unless it's necessary for her mission. Sure, you might feel like it after a near-death experience, but this is a cold and calculated killer, not some bimbo trying to sleep her way to stardom. Trust me, she'll be celibate until she either leaves town or we catch her."

Back and forth for the next hour the questions flew at Forbes as both Quadrado and Fletcher picked his brain. Their notes were copious and lengthy, but she could see Forbes was beginning to flag; his eyes were drooping and there was the odd stammer as he tried to get a tired brain to communicate properly. The time was well after nine, and there was a good chance he'd been at his desk since long before dawn.

When Forbes gave a third yawn that threatened to dislocate his jaw, she decided to show him some mercy. As much as Forbes was giving them solid information, she could tell Fletcher was being guarded around him, as he'd bucked his usual trend of theorizing as he went and had instead spent his time making notes. "Thank you, Agent Forbes. You're clearly beat and we've a lot to assimilate with what you've told us before we even start drilling down into the minutiae."

"Thanks. I'll get you some copies of the files we've produced. Everything we get is copied in triplicate so there's plenty of paper copies around."

Ten minutes later he returned to their small office with a trolley bearing four boxes of files.

Quadrado's heart managed to both plummet and dance in the same movement. At best it would take them days to fully go through all the files.

CHAPTER FOUR

Fletcher carried the last box of files up to his hotel room and stacked it on the two that Quadrado had yet to open. The other one she'd already delved into, and she was arranging reports in various piles on the bed. He let her do her stuff, knowing she'd be categorizing the reports in a way that made sense to her.

He'd picked up a map of Las Vegas in reception, so he taped it to a wall and then marked the locations of the three hits. He'd explained to Quadrado on the journey from the FBI office to the hotel that he wanted to start by getting an overview of the whole situation before digging into specifics.

He'd also wanted to get out of the FBI building as soon as possible. His thinking was that the eyes of the crime gangs may be watching the building, and he didn't want to be seen coming and going by anyone he might want to get information from.

Another reason to get out of the FBI building was that he didn't trust Thomson not to have bugged the office he'd allocated them. He knew it was a cynical thing to suspect, but he'd seen the resentment Thomson had displayed at their involvement, and it wasn't much of a leap to imagine him listening to their plans and then claiming them as his own. Or worse, having his agents interfere.

"What are your initial thoughts?" The question from Quadrado was punctuated by the rustle of papers as she continued with her task of collating the files into her own order.

"There's escalation. Each target had a larger portion of Vegas's casinos. I'd anticipate the next target would have four or more, but there's also a case to be made for the fact that in terms of tackling the gangs who run Vegas, the Mantis is picking off the wounded gazelles at the back of the pack rather than targeting the front runners. It could be that the gangs' assumption that one of the big hitters is picking off the smaller players before they become a real threat is on the money."

"I'd agree with the general theory of escalation." Quadrado's back was to him, but she had the sense to raise her voice a little to compensate. "I'd also agree on the other point. One consideration I'd add is that if it is the big hitters behind it, why are they bringing in the Mantis when surely they'd have their own men who could carry the fight to those they're attacking?"

"Deniability would be my first thought. Vegas might be a sizable place in geographical terms, but when it comes to the various gangs, it'll be a relatively small community and I'd bet your 401K they will all know each other. If it is them, bringing in a stranger like the Mantis would make it look like outside forces rather than a local job. That's what I'd do if I was them. Create distance and deniability and then pounce when things have calmed down. All the same, my first thought is that it's someone else, but I'm not discounting the theory."

"You could be right. And why would you bet my 401K and not your own?"

"I'm not a gambling man. There's something else to consider. Remember what Forbes said about the smaller casinos having to pay fealty to the larger guys? That's racketeering by any other name. Why would the big player upset that particular applecart when they'll be making good money for little hassle with the status quo?"

"You make a fair point. On that thought, do we know if the affected casinos are all paying fealty to the same gang? Or are they paying to different ones?"

"We don't, but we'll need to find out. The attack on the gang that killed all the civilians, was that the three affected gangs hitting back at their fealtors for not protecting them? Or returning the insult by attacking those they felt were behind the hits?"

Fletcher didn't give an answer to the question Quadrado had posed, about the affected casinos and where their loyalties lay because finding out the information would be more than answer enough. Instead he turned his mind onto the next part of the puzzle.

"It's good that we're getting this overview of things but I think we're going over the same ground as all the FBI agents. As Soter said, instead of thinking like the cops, we need to think like the killer. In short, we need to get inside the Mantis's head and work out just what she's thinking and her thought processes as she's making these hits."

Quadrado emptied her hands of papers and turned to face Fletcher as she sat on the bed. "I get what you're saying, but how the hell do we do that? You heard what Forbes said about her. There's no footage of her getting into and out of any of the places where she killed her targets. The last one is the most complicated of all, as it's as if she vanished once Aurier and the others were dead. The only reason we're so confident it's the Mantis at work is because all of our sources are saying it's her. Not one of them is saying anything different or pointing the finger elsewhere."

"I agree, it does look like she vanished, except she can't have. Look at what we know about that hit. She went in via the back door, eliminated anyone who got in her way then went up the elevator to the apartment. The position of the bodies suggests that Aurier and co. were waiting for her as she went up the elevator and she shot them from there. The bullet holes in the back wall of the elevator and the missing rounds from Aurier's machine pistol tells us that he got some shots off before he was killed. The bullets recovered from all the people she's killed are small caliber and that suggests pistols to me. In her position I'd use a SIG Sauer or something of a similar size."

"How did she avoid getting herself shot, though? If you were in her position, what would you do?"

"Good question." Fletcher scratched at his nose and looked at the ceiling as he thought about how he'd approach things. "First off, I'd put myself in the shoes of the people I expected to be there when the elevator doors opened. They wouldn't know who was coming up and would have to react accordingly. The fact they wouldn't know if it was friend or foe would mean they'd have to react when they saw who was there. That would hand a slender advantage to the Mantis, but all three were found by the elevator with guns beside them. One of those guns was fired, so that tells us they were expecting and prepared for a foe. They were standing ready, most probably with fingers on triggers when the elevator doors were opened."

"Agreed, but you've not said anything that's not in one of the reports."

"That's because you interrupted me before I was finished." Fletcher kept his tone light to alleviate the rebuke in his words. "Think back to your weapons training: where were you taught to aim?"

"Center mass."

"Exactly. The torso is the biggest target on the human body, and it's jam-packed with important organs that all of a sudden stop working when hit by a bullet. If I was expecting someone to shoot at me, that's where I'd expect them to aim. Now that we know where their aim is going to be, it's simply a question of how you make sure you're not where they're aiming. Yes, you'll have the element of surprise and it's possible you can get bullets into everyone before they start shooting, but you have to prepare for them being quick to shoot or death spasms making fingers squeeze triggers. And then you're back to not being where they're aiming. You've seen the pictures of the elevator. It's compact, maybe six feet deep by four wide. There's not enough room at the sides to offer proper concealment, and hiding at the sides limits you to only having one arm free to shoot with and a limited field of view. That leaves the floor."

"The floor? So what are you saying? That she was crouched down in a corner?"

"No. She wasn't crouched down, she was lying on the floor. Feet towards the door would be my guess."

"How do you know she was lying down and not crouched?"

"The bullet holes in the back wall of the elevator. They're in a more or less vertical line. My first thought was that Aurier had started off aiming low, as machine pistols tend to kick up when they're fired, but then I realized he'd started at center mass and was adjusting his aim down when he was killed. If the Mantis had been crouched in a corner, the bullet holes would have veered on a diagonal instead of going straight down. We haven't read the autopsy reports yet, but I'm confident they'll show the trajectories of the bullets as having been fired from below the victims."

"That's pretty ballsy doing that, isn't it?"

"Definitely. This Mantis certainly has a pair of lady cojones on her."

"So we know how she got in, but the reports from the staff say that she didn't come back down the elevator, so how did she get out? You heard what Forbes said, there's no other way out of that apartment. No windows open. There's no fire escape. As I said earlier, it's like she vanished."

"There would have to be a fire escape. It'd be in the building code. Fair enough it may have been built up for security reasons, but it'd be there. Forgetting that for now, the elevator is the only way in and out of the penthouse, so it stands to reason that the Mantis got out via the elevator shaft. At the bottom there would only be a pit big enough to receive the lower parts of the elevator itself, whereas at the top there will be winch mechanisms, motors and, more importantly, an access hatch to allow maintenance crews in. If she pegged the doors open, sent the elevator down and then went upwards, removing the peg as she went, she could have been up out of sight long before the elevator returned up."

"Surely it's too far to climb." Quadrado shook her head. "Scratch that, the penthouse is on the top floor; she'd only have a few feet to climb."

"Exactly."

Quadrado rustled some of the papers she'd laid out on the bed until she found the one she was looking for. Her eyes flickered across the page for a moment until she jabbed a finger at it. "Hang on. It says here that the door on the elevator shaft opens out on the same side as the rooftop pool. There are no witness reports of someone coming out of that door."

"Of course there isn't. The attack happened at night. It's January. Only the hardiest or drunkest people would have been at the pool then."

"That doesn't matter, Fletcher. The agent who checked this out says the door is triple locked and only the hotel manager has keys. The locks can't even be seen from the inside. The door is also alarmed."

"Forget about the alarm on the door; other security systems would have been circumvented too. What else is accessible from the top of the elevator shaft?"

"Nothing. It's a sealed shaft."

"In that case, the Mantis either came out of that door or she's still in there, and I don't think it's the latter. My guess is she accessed the door earlier in the day and unlocked it, ready for her escape."

Quadrado pulled a face. "You're probably right, but I'd like to take you back to your earlier point of thinking like her rather than like me. All this is ground for the FBI to cover, not us."

"I need to get a feel for her methods. She's resourceful, brave and damned good at what she does. If I'm going up against her, I need to know exactly how good she is so I can make sure I'm better, otherwise I'm toast." He pointed at the many files that were scattered across the bed. "Do any of them give a list of all the casinos and say who they're owned by?"

"I'm sure Forbes said that he'd included such a list. Why do you want it?"

"Because I want to put us in her shoes. We're going to go and reconnoiter a couple of what we deem are her most likely targets."

"And how are you going to know which are her most likely targets?"

"I've been thinking about what I'd do in her position." Fletcher had thought of plenty else, but he'd always circled back to this point. "She's escalating, right? If we follow that pattern, her next target will be someone from an organization who owns four casinos. Ideally she'll go for the top man because that will create the most confusion."

"Or the top woman."

"Granted, maybe there's a top woman, not a man." Fletcher rubbed a hand over his face. "Let's put the gender politics aside and work on the assumption that when I say man or guy, I'm using the term in a gender-neutral way. Which, incidentally, is exactly what I was doing."

"Okay. You've made your point."

"Now, we know from the FBI files that there are five organizations or gangs that own four casinos apiece. They'd be the obvious targets. I don't think she'll go for any of them. First off, all the various gangs will know every bit as much as the FBI do about the escalation. That means there will be increased security in those places. Both with Thomson sending undercover agents in to provide a presence, and the natural measures taken by the gangs to make sure they're not next. This makes them far tougher targets than they originally were. Now the Mantis may revel in this challenge, or she may see it as a welcome distraction that allows her to strike elsewhere."

"You're making sense so far." Quadrado rolled a hand in Fletcher's direction. "Go on."

"As I see it, the Mantis has two options if she chooses not to attack a four-casino gang. She can either step back down to a three, or miss a step and go up to a five. Possibly even two steps and go for a six."

"Going for a five or six would really screw things up. There's enough chaos as it is."

"Agreed. However, while we don't know the Mantis's ultimate goal, we can assume that whatever it is, its achievement lies in the chaos she's creating. Whether it's a power grab by some of the larger gangs or an outsider just upsetting the status quo so they can muscle in themselves, the process will be the same. Hit the targets you want to claim. Possibly hit a couple of others as red herrings so there's no retribution delivered to you, and then set up yourself. It could be the Mantis has already achieved her aims, but the casinos of Las Vegas are a rich prize and I don't think someone who has gone to these lengths will stop at just claiming a few."

"You're still not saying what you think the next target will be."

Fletcher eased his muscles into a few stretches to alleviate the stiffness creeping into them. Quadrado's last words held an unspoken question, and it was one whose answer he'd been wrestling with.

"I think she'll target a level five and that she'll go for the flagship casino of that five."

"Why do you think that?"

It was typical of Quadrado to want to hear not just his answer, but also his thought processes as he worked this kind of thing out. He had no problem with sharing this with her. "I've looked at the psychology of it. A skip forward in the chain will wreak the most havoc and that seems to be the initial goal. The gangs are turning on each other and doing part of her job for her. She'll want that to continue. By targeting a flagship, she'll also be testing herself.

They'll have their measures in place and will be ready for her. In her place I'd see that as a challenge, and I'd want to rise to that challenge."

"Really? You think she'll want to take even bigger risks than she's taken already?"

"Without a doubt. You won't understand this if you've never been in a proper firefight, but there's one hell of a rush that comes with surviving a dangerous mission and executing a plan exactly to order. You feel ten feet tall and invincible, yet there's also a desire to puke as your body reacts at how close you've been to being killed. It's not easy to explain, but as well as the money, the chasing after that feeling is why a lot of ex-soldiers find work as mercenaries. It's addictive and only those who are truly strong can kick the habit and have a normal civilian life."

"And you? Are you addicted to that rush?"

"No. But I'll never deny enjoying the feeling of not being killed." Fletcher pointed at the papers Quadrado had been arranging. "What does that lot say about the other casinos? About fours and fives?"

Quadrado sourced the list of casinos that was cross-referenced against the gangs who owned them. "There are two fives. One owned by a Mexican outfit, the other by a family from Boston. The Mexicans are the gang that was attacked."

"She'll target the Boston family then."

"You seem very sure."

"Think about it. If her aim is to cause mayhem or chaos, the finger of guilt has already been pointed at the Mexicans. If she targets the Mexicans at this time, she'll be effectively exonerating them. Much better to attack the other lot and let the Mexicans take the rap. She can come back to the Mexicans later. What's the flagship casino for the Boston family?"

Quadrado checked the file. "The Gold Mine."

"Right, that's where we're going to focus our initial energies. To do this, we'll need to go into the casino and be regular gamblers. That means you'll have to change."

"What do you mean change?"

Fletcher kept a smile on his face, as he knew it'd be easy for Quadrado to take offense at his words. "I mean you look like you're dressed to be a fed. You need to change into off-duty clothes. Release the ratchet on your ponytail and maybe put on a dab of lipstick or mascara. The guards at the casino are going to be on high alert. We need to blend in so we don't arouse their suspicions."

"Screw you, Fletcher. There's nothing wrong with how I look."

"I never said there was. It's just the wrong look for tonight. If you didn't bring any civilian clothes, there's a twenty-four-hour market across the street. You can probably pick something up there."

The slamming of the door was Quadrado's way of answering.

CHAPTER FIVE

Quadrado pulled at the side of her dress and cursed Fletcher and his logical mind. Rather than waste time trying outfits on, she'd grabbed a couple of dresses, a pair of jeans and three tops from a rail at the front of the store. None fit as well as she'd hoped.

Fletcher was already in the Gold Mine casino. He'd entered five minutes ahead of her, saying he'd be near the roulette tables to start with. She changed forty dollars into chips and prepared to experience a Las Vegas casino for the first time.

Las Vegas wasn't somewhere that had ever been high on her list of places she wanted to visit. There was a certain pull created by the glitz and the glamour, but there was no mistaking that every aspect of the Gold Mine was geared towards emptying her pockets into their coffers. From the workers dressed as miners, to the mine theme that ran throughout the entire building, all the trappings were nothing more than a fleeting distraction to the rows of slots and the various gaming tables.

A half-remembered school lesson where the teacher had stressed the people who made the most money from America's gold rush were those who sold picks, shovels, other mining equipment and food to the prospectors came to Quadrado's mind.

It might be after midnight, but the casino was in full swing. The gaming tables were crowded and there were knots of people everywhere. Chatter and clatter filled the air as people whooped with joy at a win and cursed a loss. Slots disgorged wins with rattles and sirens or recorded voices. All around there was an energy in the air that ebbed and flowed with the fortunes of those feeding the Gold Mine with dollars, greenbacks and dead presidents. The air hung with the noxious smells of greed and body odor, although there were wafts of something forest-like she attributed to hidden air fresheners.

Although she'd only been in the casino a short time, Quadrado had spotted plenty liveried security guards and several who were undercover. It was the eyes that gave them away. They weren't looking around in awe, frustration or celebration. They were looking with suspicion, trying to spot unusual behavior, furtiveness and any issues that might require a subtle intervention. There would always be some people who would see what they consider a chink in the liveried guards' behavior and try to exploit it. The undercover guys were there to stop them. More liveried guards would have the same effect, but she supposed too many of those would give the casino a less friendly feel, and therefore some guards were in plain clothes, to make sure the Gold Mine maximized its potential for parting suckers from their money.

The ceiling was festooned with security cameras as backup to the human presence. Each positioned directly above a gaming table or line of slots.

She could see Fletcher had situated himself at a roulette table and was laughing and joking with those around him. There was a beer in his hand and a smile on his face. For a regretful second she couldn't help but wonder if he was treating this mission as a jaunt and living it up in Sin City.

As soon as the thought entered her head, she dismissed it. Fletcher wasn't the kind of man who said one thing and did another. He was old school; his word was his bond and his bond was unbreakable. To think such things of him was an insult to his integrity and every other aspect of his character. Besides, she had seen the look in his eyes when Soter had mentioned the murder of young Frankie. They'd held pure disgust and a fury that was chilling in its intensity.

A space opened up at a blackjack table, so she filled it. Not because she wanted to gamble, more that she wanted to blend in, and if you don't want to stand out in a Vegas casino, you gamble. Being a beginner at entering a game, Quadrado didn't know the etiquette of entering a blackjack table mid-play was to ask if any existing player objected. Superstition played a part for some gamblers and there are always those who count cards.

The dealer was experienced enough to ask the question and, when there were no objections, flashed a smile Quadrado's way.

A woman on Quadrado's right had the pinched nervous look of someone who'd already gone past their limit and was trying to recoup unintended losses. The man on her left spilled bourbon breath and bonhomie her way with equal measure. The pile of chips in front of him substantial.

With a practiced flourish the dealer dealt the cards from the shoe, flipping them face up to each player. Quadrado looked down at her card.

A ten. A good start.

By the time the dealer worked his way round to her, she'd observed enough of the other gamblers' behavior to know what to do.

Her second card was an eight. Good but not brilliant. There were more cards likely to bust her than there were to run her to the magic twenty-one, so she gave her hand a sideways motion and waited until the dealer played his hand. A queen and a three.

There were plenty cards that might increase his odds of winning. He turned another card for himself. A nine. He was bust.

A red, five-dollar chip to match, Quadrado's stake was passed her way and the game moved on.

By the time the game had gone twice more round the table, Quadrado had both won and lost another five dollars. She was five up and that was more than enough for her. The woman on her right had vanished with a hearty sigh and withering scowl at the dealer as if it was his fault she'd lost.

The guy who'd been beside the woman was another matter, as once the woman had left, he'd shuffled round to her side. He'd slugged bourbon like it was the nectar of the gods and bet five hundred dollars a time. His good-natured bumps of her arm weren't a problem, but since she'd positioned herself at the table, he'd attributed his good fortune to her good looks in a way that was meant to be flattering but came across as creepy.

As she made to leave, his arm snaked around her back until his hand rested on her hip. This wasn't a problem until his fingers wound through the loose material of her dress and tucked themselves into the hem of her underpants.

"Come on, baby, what do you say we go celebrate my luck and your beauty?"

CHAPTER SIX

Fletcher backed away from the roulette table, his two-dollar stake left on a dozen bet on the third twelve box. When he'd spotted Quadrado take up a station at the blackjack tables, he'd made sure to keep an eye on her.

To date he'd identified nine undercover guards and a pit boss who roamed with the sleek efficiency of a shark circling its next meal. The pit boss would exchange rapid glances with his staff and keep moving, his trajectory seemingly random yet never anything other than a graceful glide around and between the customers. Once in a while he'd be stopped to answer a question, and on one occasion pose for a selfie with a couple of brightly dressed women old enough to be his grandmothers, but other than these moments, he never stopped in one place for a second longer than was needed.

Fletcher didn't like the way a guy had his arm around Quadrado, and he was damn sure that she wouldn't either. By the same token, she wouldn't thank him for a white knight-style rescue. She might not be the tallest person in the room, but she was big enough to fight her own battles.

Another consideration was that it was their plan to stay disconnected from each other. Rather than make any kind of scene, Fletcher contented himself with sauntering over until he was a dozen paces away. He saw there were security guards coming their way, too, and the pit boss was approaching the lecherous moron from his blind side. A moron was the only way Fletcher could

think of the guy, as only a moron would try to attract a partner
in such a heavy-handed fashion in a place as public as a casino.

The guards, the pit boss and Fletcher were all a dollar short and
a day late. Quadrado could take care of herself. Her hand grasped
the moron's pinkie and pulled it the wrong way until he released
his hold on her. Once she could turn to face him, she launched
the contents of a glass in his face and followed up with a slap that
carried plenty of venom and a sound as intense as a whip crack.

The moron stood with a look of stupefaction and wobbled as
he wandered away. Two guards went to intercept him, but a signal
from the pit boss halted them. Instead of having his security guys
deal with it, he stepped in close and spoke in the guy's ear.

That told Fletcher just how good the pit boss was at his job.
And how low the man's moral standards were.

Before they'd got here, Quadrado had asked how much to
bet. He'd suggested that as a novice she might want to stick with
wagers no more than five or ten bucks a time. It was what he was
also doing. No fan of gambling, he enjoyed the camaraderie of
an occasional poker night with a few buddies, where there was
a five-dollar limit on raises so nobody got burned, but the last
place he'd choose to take a vacation would be a casino. Las Vegas
might have more than casinos to offer its visitors, but the glitz
and glamour held no appeal to him. Fletcher's idea of a vacation
involved adventure sports, like white-water rafting, or historical
monuments that both entranced and educated him.

He watched with interest and no small amount of cynicism as
the pit boss did his thing. Quadrado was a novice placing small
bets. The drunk moron was being allowed to go unpunished with
almost no interference from the pit boss. That meant he spent big.
Instead of chucking him out on his ass, as he should have done, the
pit boss had delivered what was no doubt a warning. Big spenders
would always trump lone novices placing small bets. By rights, the
moron should have been tossed out at the very least. If Fletcher had

his way, the moron would be sore for long enough for a lesson to be learned. That kind of predatory behavior needed to be stopped before it went too far. Before a more helpless victim was chosen.

Fletcher kept pace behind Quadrado's would-be suitor as he lurched off. There was an outside chance the guy got away with such behavior because he was known here, and that in turn led to the possibility that he was known because he was connected. Therefore he bore watching.

As did the pit boss. His face had given nothing away at any point when he was dealing with the moron, only smooth professionalism. What bothered Fletcher about the pit boss more than anything else, was the fact he'd not had the moron ejected. His loyalties lay only with the casino, and the fact a sexual predator had been allowed to remain in the Gold Mine spoke of the pit boss's, and also the casino's, lack of ethics and morals.

A quick check around him showed Fletcher that none of the guards were paying him any attention, so he set off at a slow amble after the moron.

Two minutes later the moron barged open the door of the men's room. Fletcher picked up his pace. A men's room was a good place to deliver a spot of retribution. In a place this size, it was unlikely he'd get any decent alone time to properly deal with the moron, but he'd be free from cameras and security measures long enough to make the moron regret his wandering hands.

CHAPTER SEVEN

When he went into the men's room, Fletcher found himself confronted with an issue he wasn't expecting. There were perhaps twenty people in the men's room, including an attendant who was busy wiping down sinks.

The moron stood at a urinal. One hand on the wall in front of him and the other directing his flow. It was a typical stance for men in a men's room, and one that left them vulnerable to attacks from their six. The moron was ripe for a push on the back of his head that would shatter his nose against the wall. Or maybe a kidney blow that would drop him to his knees. The options for attack were endless, although Fletcher discounted some as too brutal for the moron's crime.

The problem with the attack was there would be no way to execute it without other patrons or the attendant being aware of it. A walkie-talkie on the attendant's hip warned Fletcher an alarm could be raised in a hurry. That didn't worry him, as if guards were called, he'd simply be ejected from the casino.

Unless the moron was something else. If he was connected to the casino in any way, as proven possible by the pit boss's mild reaction to his behavior with Quadrado, being caught hurting him would provoke a reaction from the people who owned and run the casino.

To instigate a reaction is a proactive action. It's a decision based on the expected reaction and whether that will further the aims of the instigator.

Detective work like tracking an assassin is predominantly reactive.

Battle situations call for proactive measures.

Fletcher was a soldier not a detective.

With a course of action in his mind, Fletcher fished in his pocket and took hold of a couple of casino chips. "Sorry for the mess, buddy." He put the chips on the sink beside the attendant and walked towards the moron.

With the attendant now aware something was going to go down, Fletcher was making sure he'd get a reaction.

The moron was still in place. He'd finished splashing into the urinal and had two hands at his groin as he pulled up his zipper. It was the perfect moment. Fletcher waited until he was two paces from him, then stepped forward, fast. His right hand open and arrowing towards the back of the moron's head with the weight of his body behind it and the power of his work-honed muscles powering it forward.

Fletcher's hand collided with the base of the moron's neck, jerking him forward, his head tilting back until the bones of his vertebrae stopped further movement.

At the moment of impact with Fletcher's hand, there was a two-foot gap between the moron's face and the wall above the urinal. Two feet isn't far. With the power Fletcher was putting into his movement, there wasn't time for the moron to stiffen his body in resistance, to lock his bracing hand against the wall.

The human nose is soft. Made up of cartilage, tissue and skin, it never fares well when brought into contact with hard objects. It fares even worse when it's propelled at speed into them.

Fletcher made sure he put enough force into his move so that the moron's nose was spread across his ruddy cheeks. Enough power to make sure the guy's forehead and chin also crashed into the unyielding surface. Enough power to stun, yet not so much as to leave him with permanent brain damage. It was one thing to teach the moron a lesson, another to inflict life-changing injuries.

The moron went weak at the knees. His hands extending, trying to find something to grip to support himself. He was too late. He crashed to the ground and slumped forward into the urinal.

Fletcher turned and left him where he was. The attendant would deal with him in a moment; there was little chance of him drowning unless the urinal flushed itself.

The attendant had backed away from the sinks he'd been cleaning and was speaking into his walkie-talkie. No doubt whistling up some security guys.

He didn't try to stop Fletcher, and Fletcher didn't make any attempt to engage with the man. It was time to get outside into the main body of the casino to see how the security guys dealt with him.

CHAPTER EIGHT

Upon exiting the men's room, Fletcher took several rapid strides until he was on an aisle formed by rows of slot machines. There were people at most of them. Rather than mark his guilt by hurrying any further, he slowed so he could observe people. Namely the security guards he was sure would be coming his way.

In an environment as heavily guarded as a casino, a security guard would never be far away, but as the altercation had taken place in the men's room, the levels of security were decreased.

Fletcher found a good vantage point and watched as five security guards marched towards the men's room. They weren't running, which told its own story. Had the moron been some kind of colleague, even a regular who always lost big, they'd have moved with more haste. They weren't running, so the moron couldn't be important to them. Their pace was enough to indicate something was amiss, but not so great as to alarm the general spending public.

By the time they got in, made a quick assessment of the moron and got a description of him from the attendant, a minute or two would have passed. More than enough time for Fletcher to escape the casino.

But Fletcher did not escape. Instead he sauntered away from the slots and back towards the roulette tables. He found a place where he was maybe forty yards from the men's room and took up a position that let him blend far enough into the other gamblers to make it hard for the security men, yet still open enough for him to observe them and for them to find him.

The key to this hastily concocted plan was to not do anything that made the security guards realize he was checking out their abilities and response times.

He caught a glimpse of Quadrado's back as she wandered off to another of the roulette tables. She hadn't locked eyes with him in any way, nor had she given him a signal of any kind.

The guy opposite Fletcher was of average height, but his neck alone seemed to make up a quarter of his height. He was dressed in the style of a pimp from a 1980s B-movie and he was animated, but in a good way. He'd lean back and forward, and side to side, making expansive gestures as the croupier did her stuff.

All in all, the giraffe pimp made for a distracting sight. There's a lot to be said for hiding in plain sight. People who skulk and cower in a public place stand out and are never that hard to find. Those who go about their business in a normal way are harder to catch, but those on the periphery of a standout character are the hardest of all to spot.

Fletcher knew that despite their best efforts, the eyes of the security guards would be instinctively drawn to the flamboyance of the giraffe pimp and his good-natured expansiveness.

Two of the security guards escorted the moron across the casino floor. They were at his elbow, but maintained a certain respectful distance. Maybe it was because the guy was a moron. Maybe it was the damp stain on his shirt from where he'd slumped into the urinal, and maybe it was because they were decent guys who had seen his behavior with Quadrado and didn't want to get any closer to him than they had to.

The other three security guards split up and fanned out as they made their way across the casino floor. Again there was no great urgency about their movements, but neither did they waste time.

Across the table the giraffe pimp picked up the woman beside him and swung her round as they celebrated a win. The movement turned the head of the two guards Fletcher could see.

Neither made any noticeable gesture of recognition. There were no second looks his way. No words mouthed into a wrist or collar mic. It was as Fletcher planned. The giraffe pimp's larger-than-life persona shielded him from observation.

As the guards resumed their search for him, Fletcher laid a small bet and kept a discreet eye on them. Other than not spotting him, and he blamed his chosen location for that rather than a lack of skill on their behalf, they appeared to be good at what they did. The guards moved across the room in unison, their eyes scanning that bit quicker than before, but not so fast they'd miss him if he was hiding out somewhere.

The guards were maybe twenty yards or so away when Fletcher felt a tap on his shoulder.

"Excuse me, sir. May we have a word?"

Fletcher looked behind him and saw the pit boss and four burly security guards. None had weapons drawn, so he was confident he could take them down if need be, but that wasn't his plan.

CHAPTER NINE

Quadrado didn't need a forty-page manual to work out what was going on. The guy who'd grabbed her had been led bleeding from the men's room a couple of minutes after Fletcher had followed him in.

After whatever he'd done in there, Fletcher had returned to the casino floor acting as if nothing had happened. While she didn't need Fletcher to fight her battles, she wasn't sorry to learn the lecherous guy had suffered at his hands. The way security guards had scuttled to the men's room told her Fletcher would have known any action he took against the man would be noticed; therefore he was acting on some plan or other.

As he'd made no move to leave the casino, she guessed he'd decided to test the security measures and the response times of the guards. The question was, what did he want her to do?

Was he creating a distraction so she could slip in somewhere? Or was he expecting her to step forward and bail him out?

If there was one thing she knew about Fletcher, it was that he never got himself into something he couldn't get out of.

With a ring of security guards around him, Fletcher was being escorted to the rear of the room. It was where the bar was along with access routes to the kitchen areas.

They bypassed all of these areas and kept going until there was a single door. At first glance it looked like it was part of the mine decoration, but a closer look showed a disguised keypad and fingerprint scanner.

There were seven guards round Fletcher, as well as the guy who seemed to be in charge of the part of the casino where the blackjack tables were. He was well and truly outnumbered. The guards all carried nightsticks, although she was pleased to see none carried pistols, or if they were carrying, their guns were concealed. As good as he was, Fletcher wouldn't be able to fight so many opponents alone.

Fletcher was pushed through the door, and three of the security guards turned away while the remaining four and the boss all filed into the room after him. Better odds for Fletcher, but he was still heavily outnumbered, and against four men wielding batons, he'd have little chance.

Quadrado didn't need to think about her next move. She made no attempt to go near that door and instead set a course for a different part of the casino. She wanted to explore the areas where staff would travel from the kitchens to the private quarters of the casino's owners. To this end, she sauntered casually past the kitchen's swing doors and with its location planted in her mind, set a course to find the point where servers would deliver food to the guest bedrooms.

A second set of swing doors, one in, one out, opened onto a short hallway that connected the casino floor to the public elevators. There were no Staff Only signs on any other doors. No storage closets tucked away for housekeeping supplies. A pair of double doors was at the end of the hallway, but as she wandered that way she saw one open and a pair of men dressed in maintenance uniforms bring out a trolley with a slot machine on it. With the door open she could see a workshop of sorts, where a number of slots were in various stages of repair.

She went back to the elevators, planning to go up a floor or two to check out what options were on the buttons, in case there was a special floor that was solely for the owners, as was the case with the Aurier guy who'd been killed in his penthouse.

No dice. There was a slot for a key card to summon the elevator. She could try bluffing her way to a new key card from reception, but that would bring her to someone's attention. Better she wait things out and follow someone into the elevator and then use the stairs to return to the casino floor.

The second elevator pinged to a halt, and its doors opened to disgorge a family of three. The child looked upset, the woman furious and the man contrite, the side of his face still bearing a bright red handprint. Had he lost too much money at the tables, been caught in one of Las Vegas's many strip clubs or had he maybe received an offer from one of the numerous hookers offering their services? The reason for their argument was their business, and Quadrado dismissed them from her mind as she went into the elevator.

There were eight buttons on the elevator. One for each of the floors. The owner's room could be on any of the floors, secreted behind any of the doors that the regular guests couldn't get past.

However it was, she didn't have time to search the whole hotel looking for a room or door that may or may not be there.

She'd learned a little, most of it negative confirmation, but that was better than not learning anything. It was time to go back to the main casino to see if there was any sign of Fletcher.

CHAPTER TEN

Fletcher kept his eyes on the pit boss, as he was the power in the room. He would issue the order to attack. He would control the narrative.

The room they were in was little more than a holding cell. It had one chair and two doors. The one they'd entered via, and a second one at the back. As he'd been ushered in, a sweep of light came under the rear door as a vehicle moved outside.

Upon seeing the layout of the room, Fletcher's first instinct was to prepare for trouble. The lack of carpet didn't bode well, but there were no bloodstains on the concrete floor, so that was one positive. All the same, he figured this room was the place wrongdoers received their punishment before being ejected out the back of the casino.

The pit boss indicated Fletcher ought to sit.

"No thanks. I'm getting something of a bad vibe here."

One of the guards flanking Fletcher reached for him. "Sit down, you scumbag."

The guard held Fletcher's shoulder and was half pulling him, half rotating him. Fletcher rolled with the pressure on his shoulder, slipped his right hand onto the guard's left and used the guard's arm and his own momentum to dump him into the chair.

"If it's all the same, I'll stand." He took a step back from the guard. "I could have hurt you. It would have been easy for me to straighten your arm and then crash my elbow through yours. I could have rammed you into one of your buddies. Could have tossed you over my hip onto the hard floor. If you'd called me a worse name than scumbag, I might have been inclined to help myself to one of your weapons. You're sitting in that chair because I decided not to hurt you. If you lay another hand on me, I'll reverse that decision."

It was risky, baring his teeth in this way, but Fletcher was aware they already knew enough about him to have marked him as dangerous. Better to show he didn't fear them in a way that got nobody hurt, than to escalate the situation.

A slow clap from the pit boss told Fletcher he had the most important person, if not on his side, at least appreciative of his talents.

"Drop it, Andy." There was an order in his tone and a hint of a European accent. Fletcher couldn't place which country, but if pushed he'd guess at somewhere like Germany. "Sir, my name is long and unpronounceable. Folks call me Len. I'd be obliged if you'd be so kind as to let me know your name."

"It's Grant Fletcher." There was no need to make a name up. Len wouldn't know who he was; therefore, there was no point lying to him. "Why have you brought me here? It looks like you intend to give me a beating. Or at least try to."

A scuff from behind him told him that Andy had risen from the seat. "Oh, we'll do better than try." Fletcher turned ready for action.

"That's enough, Andy. Please resume your duties on the casino floor. We'll let you know if we need you or anyone else." Len waited unto the door behind Andy was closed and the tension in the room had dropped off a little. Fletcher didn't miss the unspoken threat. Andy and others may be recalled if Len decided that he wanted things to get physical. "Mr. Fletcher, you seem to have some skills. When you were speaking to Andy, you showed a lot of confidence. Yet you also showed restraint. That speaks of military training to me. Would I be right?"

"You would."

"Thank you, I served myself. Would I also be right in saying that you got Fletch, rather than Fletcher?"

"You're right again, but that was then and this is now."

Fletcher gave a shrug, which Len nodded at. If he was ex-forces, he'd understand. When a group of young men and women are put together in the hard environment of military training, they become close in a way that non-military people can't always understand. Part of this closeness is displayed by the various monikers and nicknames that are bestowed on each other. He'd been Fletch pretty much from the day he signed up until the day he was cashiered out. The nickname had been left behind in the Royal Marines, and while one or two civilian buddies had tried to resurrect it, he'd asked them not to. The only person he'd exempted from this rule was his wife, Rachel.

"So, Mr. Fletcher, would you be so kind as to tell me why you attacked Mr. Montgomery?"

To Fletcher's ear, it sounded like Len had learned English from a succession of period dramas about the British upper classes.

"I saw him getting a handful of a woman's dress. She had to throw a drink in his face before he let go. That's not acceptable behavior." Fletcher wanted to point out Len knew all of this, but for the moment he didn't want to give too much away.

"I agree it's not acceptable behavior, but I wouldn't say smashing someone's face into a wall is acceptable either. Would you?"

Fletcher was caught on a rock by this question. If he said yes, he was condoning violence and that meant things could get ugly for him. To say no would be to condemn his own actions. He needed an answer that was neither a yes nor a no.

It was time to go on the offensive. "Personally, I don't believe behavior such as his should go unpunished. I saw you approach. Watched as you spoke in the guy's ear. What was it you said? A friendly warning? A reminder that whoever owns this casino wouldn't appreciate such conduct? At the very least the guy should have been tossed out. You didn't do that, so I took matters into my own hands and taught him a lesson." Len's face gave nothing away, so Fletcher pressed on. "Is that your usual policy with people who manhandle women? I'd guess not, so either that guy is someone who drops a lot of money in here, or he's important to you for other reasons. Either way, you let him off scot-free. Think of what I did as a deterrent to him behaving that way again. He'll not bother any other women tonight. Maybe he'll learn a permanent lesson, or maybe he'll need a refresher course. Time will tell on that one."

"It would appear that you are an intelligent man, Mr. Fletcher." Len did a weird curl of his top lip that made his mouth look as if it was shrugging. "Perhaps someone of your intelligence ought to be wise enough to mind their own business. What happened was unfortunate for the woman, but you escalated it. It was our problem to deal with. Not yours. Mr. Montgomery is threatening to sue the casino for negligent security measures thanks to you."

"I'd be happy to persuade him otherwise for you." Fletcher meant it. "However, I'm sure that your first line of defense would be the recordings from the security cameras. They'd show how he was out of order, and therefore it'd be hard to convince any judge of your culpability in not protecting him." A new thought came to Fletcher. "Although, you wouldn't come out of it very well, would you? If it did go to court, you would be asked why he was allowed to remain in the Gold Mine casino after sexually assaulting a woman. I'm sure that would take some explaining under oath."

"Thank you for your offer, Mr. Fletcher. I have some colleagues who are *quite* persuasive enough to convince Mr. Montgomery the folly of suing the casino. This will never get to court. Tell me if you will, why did you really step into this? Are you some kind of morality vigilante? Do you know the woman involved? Were you trying to hook up with her yourself and Mr. Montgomery's actions ruined things for you? Let's be frank here. The woman was pretty, very pretty. But this is Las Vegas, there's a hell of a lot of very pretty women here. A lot of very beautiful ones too. So I ask you again, do you know the woman he grabbed?"

"I don't know her. She's just some stranger who got the wrong kind of unlucky in your casino. I didn't deal with Montgomery for her; she could handle herself. I dealt with him for the next woman he gets stupid ideas about. Actions have consequences, and since you chickened out of dealing with him, I delivered the consequences you should have. On a side note, what do you think would have happened if the woman had called the cops and they found out that you'd let Montgomery remain in the casino? What do you think will happen if she goes onto social media and tells her story, mentioning how you didn't toss her attacker's ass onto the street? That won't be a good look for the casino, will it?"

A bead of sweat had sprouted on Len's temple. "Do be careful, Mr. Fletcher, it almost sounds like you're threatening us, and we don't approve of people who threaten us."

"Now it sounds like you're threatening me. There's four of you in here. If you want to rumble, let's rumble, but I can tell you now, regardless of who wins the rumble, you and your boys are going to get hurt. That's not a threat, it's a fact, so take it any way you damn well like."

Fletcher kept his eyes on Len and his ears alert for the sound of movement behind him.

Len's top lip gave another shrug. "I think that we ought to conclude this meeting, Mr. Fletcher. There will be no, as you call it, 'rumbling.' But, perhaps it might be in everyone's best interests if you did your gambling at one of the other casinos in town."

Len stepped to the door and reached for the keypad.

"Suits me." It didn't, but Fletcher wasn't going to give Len the satisfaction of seeing he wanted to remain at the Gold Mine.

Two minutes later, Fletcher had left the casino and was walking along the Strip. There had been no sign of Quadrado, so he ducked into the first place he could and went straight to the bathrooms. Once in a cubicle, he fished his cell from his pocket and sent a message to Quadrado, telling her where he was. He needed to talk to her, as there were a few things he'd spotted during his time in the casino.

CHAPTER ELEVEN

Fletcher opened the door of his hotel room to find an exhausted Quadrado. He'd gotten a reply to his message almost at once. She'd seen him leave the room and walk straight out of the casino. As he'd walked with a singular focus, she'd continued gambling for a few minutes and had then left in a different direction.

"What happened in that room? And why did you have to beat up on that guy? All it did was bring you to their attention."

"I beat up on him because he deserved it for what he did to you. His blood was up and after seeing how he was with you, I could see him doing the same, or worse, with another woman. That won't be happening now. And walking around the casino floor was getting us nowhere. They only let us see what they want us to see. For a better idea of what goes on behind the scenes, we'll need to look at the blueprints and the schematics. I dare say with a team of people trained in surveillance we could gather quite a bit of information in a week or two. We don't have that time though. The Mantis appears to be striking every other day, which means she's due to strike again tomorrow."

Quadrado flashed him a glare. "I know all that, and agree about not learning much. That still doesn't explain why you chose to draw their attention to you. Or are you just so macho, you have to beat up on any guy who wrongs a woman?"

"I've already explained how hitting him was crime prevention, and I'm sorry if that's a problem for you." Fletcher washed a hand over his face. "Look, it's the middle of the night, so can we draw a line under it? As for drawing their attention to me, that moron gave me a window of opportunity."

"You didn't have to smash that window though, did you?" Quadrado strode across the room and flung the door to the minibar open. A minute later she was splashing gin into a glass. "Jesus Christ, Fletcher, does it not bother you that you're here to kill someone? To kill a woman? I tell you, the more I think about it, the more I'm realizing that Soter is using you as his private assassin. You're the same as the Mantis and I'm your damned handler."

Fletcher didn't reply to Quadrado's statement beyond putting a rueful expression on his face. He'd known as soon as the deal was offered to him that he'd effectively be a contract killer working for Soter. He'd long ago made the decision to salve his conscience by telling himself the targets he'd be given would no longer deserve to live.

"Well, are you going to answer me?" The glass in Quadrado's hand was raised to her lips and she took a healthy slug. "I thought better of you than to agree to kill a woman, even one who's a killer herself. In a lot of ways you're little better than that guy at the casino."

Fletcher stomped to the minibar and retrieved a beer. "Do you believe in women's rights? I'm guessing you do. Women can join the army, the Marines and the police. Like the men who join, there's good and bad and plain average among them. But they're there doing their bit. Now when it comes to a battle situation and I'm shooting at the enemy, it doesn't matter to me whether the person beside me is male or female or nonbinary, gay or bi; it matters whether they can shoot straight when the enemy is shooting at us. Now, let's address your question about me shooting a woman. First off, I was brought up to respect women. I'm nothing like the moron in the casino, and if you ever insinuate such a thing again, the whole deal is off and I'll face what's coming to me. You got that?"

"Yeah, sorry, I was just—"

"Second." Fletcher didn't want to listen to her apology. He knew it was Quadrado's frustration talking more than a real belief. "It would be hypocritical of me to fight alongside a female comrade and not be prepared to fight a female enemy. Third, it would surely be sexist if I treated a female enemy any different to how I would treat a male one. Fourth, yes, I'm somewhat conflicted by my upbringing and points two and three, but we're not talking about an innocent woman here. We're talking about a stone-cold killer who, in Las Vegas alone, has infiltrated three separate places and left a trail of bodies behind her. One of whom, I'm surprised to have to remind you, was an eight-year-old kid with Down syndrome. The Mantis has deprived others of their lives, and you can rest assured, if she's caught by one of the gangs she's attacking, they won't hesitate in killing her. At least if I do it, she'll get a quick death. If that's not good enough for you, tough. Ask yourself something, would you kill her yourself if you knew doing so would save the lives of others? The Bible might say 'thou shalt not kill,' but it also says: 'an eye for an eye.' Think about that if it helps."

Fletcher popped the top off his beer and put the bottle to his lips. Bringing the Bible into the conversation was his trump card. Quadrado was a practicing Catholic and wore a crucifix around her neck for her faith rather than as a decoration. Truth be told, despite everything he'd said to Quadrado, he wasn't as comfortable with the idea of killing a woman as he was making out. The manners instilled into him by his parents had gone deep, and he still practiced old-fashioned behaviors like holding doors open and rising from his seat when a woman entered a room.

"Damn you, Fletcher. Why do you always have to be so logical about things?" Quadrado chinked her glass against his bottle to steal the offense from her words. "What happened in that room, then?"

"It's not so much what happened in there as what happened to get me there. Within ninety seconds of me leaving the men's room, they'd found and surrounded me. They must have used the CCTV cameras to track or find me. That's properly efficient, as the first thirty seconds would be what it took them to get there and get the story from the attendant. The next thirty to devise a plan and divert their security men to look for me, and the last thirty to find and ambush me. Three of the ones who went into the men's room acted as a diversion by making it obvious they were looking for me. It all speaks of protocols and practice to me."

"They're bound to have their fair share of trouble. Surely you've factored that in?"

"Of course I have. I just didn't expect them to be so good. The whole place is as tight as can be. The pit boss, a guy called Len, is very smart and not afraid to lay down a threat. He's very well spoken, smart and ex-forces. I can see him being so much more than a pit boss."

"Isn't he the one who dealt with the guy who grabbed me?"

"Sure is. I made a point of positioning myself in his area when I came out of the men's room, as I wanted to ask him why he didn't toss that guy out after he grabbed you."

"And what did he say to that?" Quadrado drained her glass and pulled a lock of hair off her face.

"He didn't give an answer. Although, he did know the guy's name. That tells me the moron who assaulted you is a regular there, and I reckon he must be someone who regularly loses big in here because if he was a random small-stakes punter, his butt would have hit the street rapid style."

"He was betting big enough before he grabbed me. I watched as he came out of the men's room. The guards with him took him to the door and left him there. When he wandered off towards a cab, I turned my attention back to you."

"Seems like he is known but not liked. Which is fair enough considering what a moron he is. Did you learn anything?" Fletcher sat back and took a sip of his beer.

"Much the same as you did. There's no easy and obvious way to find the owner's quarters, and, I have to say, my thinking is that they'll be secreted away somewhere."

"I thought as much. It looks like a tough target, but remember what Forbes said about the guy who'd installed the electronic security getting tortured then killed with the Mantis's signature head and eye shots? Plus the escape from the Golden Chance? The Mantis has a way of getting whatever information she needs. We need to get that same information, so we can predict how she might strike and then put measures in place to stop her."

Quadrado looked at her watch. "You make it sound simple. Are you forgetting she's due to strike again in about twenty hours or so?"

Fletcher didn't get to answer Quadrado, as her cell started to ring.

At this time of night it wasn't likely to be good news. The expression on Quadrado's face as she listened to what the caller said made him think the Mantis had moved her schedule forward.

When the call was over, Quadrado's jaw was tight, and there was a quiver of frustrated anger in her voice when she spoke. "That was Forbes. A team of hoods from one of the gangs whose bosses had been killed have just gotten into a gunfight with the gang they blame for the attack on them. They were defeated, but not before three of their men and five civilians were shot dead. How many more will die before this is over?"

"As few as possible."

CHAPTER TWELVE

Quadrado went back to the minibar and got herself a soda. The gin had seemed like a good idea at the time, but she didn't want any more alcohol. She needed to keep her head clear and be alert to the nuances of the case. "We should get over there. See what we can learn."

"No, we shouldn't. What's happened tonight is a tragedy for the innocents involved, but it's not our job to mop up the gang fights. We're here to catch and kill the Mantis, not to get involved with the repercussions. The local cops and the FBI can sort that lot out. Not us."

As much as Quadrado knew that Fletcher was right, the FBI agent in her wanted to go and do what she could to arrest people for the latest killings. She knew it was a knee-jerk of the conscience, a natural reaction to want to achieve something tangible rather than chase shadowy figures with no discernible results. All the same, she wanted to be out there, doing something proactive.

"Oh, c'mon, surely we can help."

"You probably could, but there's little I could do. I need you with me and your focus on what we're doing, not on what's happening elsewhere. And another thing, we're exhausted and we need to be thinking with clarity, instead of sleep-deprived brains."

"Are you saying I'm not focused, not up to the job?" The words were out before Quadrado could stop them. The caustic tone enough to make her feel shame.

Credit where it was due. Fletcher didn't rise to the accusation or the derision. "I'm not saying that at all. I'm saying we need to channel our focus onto what's important to our mission, rather than what's important to us as people."

"Surely we can go for an hour or two. Maybe there's a clue to be found."

"If there is it will have been found by the time we get there. Let's drop it, yeah? We're not going. Not me. Not you."

Quadrado clunked her soda onto the desk before she launched the can at Fletcher. "Who the hell do you think you are? It's not your place to decide where I do or don't go."

"You're right it's not." Fletcher gave one of those infuriating shrugs he was so good at. "But as I've already said, I need you here to help me. If not tonight, I'm going to need you tomorrow. I want you at your best, not like some half-shut knife. That shoot-up tonight is a tragedy, but it's a reaction to previous events. It's not even the latest hit by the Mantis, but a sideshow. Getting involved in that is a distraction that would be us reacting to something unconnected to our mission. We need to be proactive and get a jump ahead of the Mantis so we can predict where she'll be. We've had a long day today. Tomorrow is going to be another long one. We need to not be distracted and that's what you're allowing to happen to yourself." Another shrug. "I'm not telling you *what* to do. I'm telling you what I *need* you to do. If you want to pull rank on me and flash your badge, go right ahead. It won't make the slightest bit of difference to me, as we both know that as far as our partnership is concerned, I'm the one in charge. Soter didn't recruit you. He used you to recruit me."

"Oh, screw you."

Fletcher's tone had never risen, but his logic was bludgeoning her like the flow of a rain-swollen river.

"You're angry because you're frustrated. Channel that anger and frustration in the right way. Don't focus it on me just because I'm telling you what you don't want to hear. You're more than smart enough to have worked all this out for yourself. That's another reason you're angry. You know I'm right and that we should stay out of it. Your training and instinct is to run towards trouble to solve it, to make a difference, and that's commendable. Highly so, but your best chance of making that difference is to retain the focus I need you to have, so we can identify and find this Mantis woman."

"You and your damn need to always be right." Quadrado flapped a hand his way. "What do we do now then?"

"We rest and let our subconscious minds do their thing while we sleep. With luck, one of us will have an epiphany in the middle of the night."

Quadrado left Fletcher's room and returned to her own. With her phone plugged in next to the bed, she went to the bathroom and picked up her toothbrush; its electric motor and the running faucet were enough to drown out the ping indicating an incoming email.

As Quadrado laid her head on the pillow, she had no idea that bosses of another casino were being slaughtered.

CHAPTER THIRTEEN

Fletcher stifled the yawn—four hours' sleep wasn't enough after such a long day—and took a pull on his takeout coffee. They were in the foyer of the hotel attached to the Utopia casino.

Sited near the famous Caesars Palace, Utopia had a place on the Las Vegas Strip, but it was overshadowed by its far better known neighbor. Caesars Palace attracted far more attention than Utopia. Even at this time of the morning, people were taking selfies with the casino as a backdrop. As grand as it was, Caesars Palace held no interest for Fletcher. One of his first questions for Special Agent Forbes had been the identity of all the owners of the well-known casinos. While organized crime syndicates may own the lesser casinos, all the big household names were owned by consortiums that had no known links to organized crime.

Inside Utopia, there were four gang members dead along with their boss, Eyeball Horton, and Horton's wife. Horton had reputedly earned his unusual nickname from the part of the body he liked to attack when dealing out retribution. Construction nails, hot pokers and acid-filled syringes were just some of the things he was rumored to have insert into the eyeballs of his victims.

His death would make the world a better place, but the fact he'd died at the hands of the Mantis was a curveball that threw their theorizing off-kilter. Utopia was the only casino on the books of Horton's gang, and as such, was at the opposite end of the spectrum from Fletcher's predictions.

Quadrado was at his shoulder as he followed the trail of the various cops and FBI agents to the part of the hotel occupied by Horton and his family. None of Horton's children had been harmed, which was a mercy, but by the same token, it was the first time a spouse had been killed by the Mantis.

Nothing about the selection of Horton as a target made sense to Fletcher, but he supposed that would be the Mantis's aim.

The place was crawling with cops of all descriptions and ranks. Goons, who Fletcher supposed were part of Horton's gang, milled around, denying there had even been a murder.

Thomson was standing in front of a well-dressed man who was a lot calmer than Thomson appeared to be. The man's suit was sharp for so early in the morning, and his demeanor was that of polite denial. It stood to reason he was someone important, either within the casino hierarchy or the FBI's.

Fletcher got close enough to listen in on the conversation.

"Look here, Adebayo, we know there were six murders here last night. We strongly suspect it's the same person who's been killing people at the other casinos. Now you can either stop jerking me around, or you can prepare for us locking the whole building down until we have spoken to every last person on the premises and conducted a thorough search of every inch of this building. Only after all that is done—and I warn you now that I'm short on manpower so it'll take a few days—will I allow your casino and hotel to reopen."

"You'll need grounds to do that. A warrant."

"We have three 911 calls recorded about murders in this location, so don't you worry, one of my men is speaking to a judge right this minute."

Adebayo's eyes flicked over Thomson's shoulder to where Fletcher was standing. "You're crossing a line here, Special Agent Thomson. There's members of the public behind you and I don't appreciate being threatened."

To Fletcher, Adebayo's words were a stalling tactic. He'd be buying time to think. Thomson would have the power to back up his threat, so Adebayo would have to choose a course of action.

"It's not a threat. It's how things are. So what's it going to be? You can either give us the access we want, or delay us the hour or two it'll take us to get the warrant. You need to choose, Adebayo, you can go the easy route, or the hard one."

Adebayo stepped aside.

As Fletcher made to follow Thomson, he found his path blocked by Adebayo. "Sir, the police are handling things now. I would suggest you return to the main casino. If you are a resident, I would ask that you use the other elevators or stairs."

Quadrado's badge appeared in her hand as if she was a conjuror. "He's with us."

"If it's Eyeball you're hoping to find, you're going to be out of luck. He's on vacation."

The claim Eyeball was on vacation had to be a crock. The reports they had indicated he was dead, that he was the real target. Adebayo's claim meant he'd disposed of the body in some way. Why he'd do that was a mystery, but a mystery that could wait for a later time.

CHAPTER FOURTEEN

Fletcher cast his eyes over the room for what seemed like the thousandth time in as many seconds and shook his head. A number of thuggish-looking guys whom Fletcher suspected belonged to Horton's gang were being questioned by FBI agents. Thomson was directing things with curt orders and expressive gestures.

From what he'd gathered by listening in to various conversations, they were all sticking to the same story. There had been no murders and Eyeball Horton was on vacation. The story Horton had taken a Winnebago on an unplanned tour of New Mexico, with some of his men for protection, was laughable.

Quadrado appeared at his elbow. "What are your thoughts?"

"This whole thing stinks like rotting fish. It sounds me to me like one of two things have happened. Either Adebayo is covering up the murders to stabilize things for the gang, or he's planning to make a power grab now that Horton and his wife are out of the way."

"I spoke to Forbes. Adebayo is the natural successor, so I'd say it's more likely to be the second one."

"That makes the most sense to me. It wouldn't surprise me if later today a Winnebago is found with all the alleged victims in it. If I'm right, I'd also guess that it'll be burned out."

Fletcher saw understanding in Quadrado's eyes. If the burned-out Winnebago was found with the remains of all the bodies inside, Horton's gang could not have been victims of the Mantis. And burning the Winnebago would destroy evidence. The outcome was that it would raise their standing with the other gangs.

CCTV cameras around the casino and Automatic Number Plate Recognition on the highways might trip up this lie, but for the time being, every man working for Adebayo was sticking to the same story.

"So what next?"

Fletcher glanced down at Quadrado. There were bags under her eyes, although her brown irises were filled with determination.

"We get proactive. These goons are all on the same page as each other. We need to kick one of them beyond the margin."

"How are you planning to do that?"

"The less you know, the happier you'll be. Although I'll need your help to get one of them."

"Fletcher."

The warning in Quadrado's tone wasn't so much missed by Fletcher as ignored. "It'll be fine. I'm going to find a vacant room. I'll message you when I have. What you have to do is use your badge to get control of one of those goons and bring him to me. I'll ask him some questions, and trust me on this, he *will* answer them."

It took Fletcher five minutes to find a room. He'd gone to the far end of the hallway and spotted a storeroom for cleaning products and replacement items such as light bulbs and shower heads and hoses. It also had a small staff area with lockers, a mini kitchen and a table with eight chairs around it. A search around the room saw him discover a packet of zip ties.

This would be more than suitable. There was a chance one of the housekeeping team would return for something, but if that happened, the worst result was that they'd get the cops, and that in turn would be resolved by Quadrado's badge.

He sent a message to Quadrado and loitered outside the door until he saw her coming his way. The guy she had in front of her walked with a swagger. His head was up and there was a shit-eating grin on his lower face.

When the guy was four paces away and he saw Fletcher's arm pointing him into the room, a puzzled expression replaced the cocksure one.

He hesitated at the door.

A single kidney punch from Fletcher dropped him to his knees.

As the man gasped in pain, Fletcher hauled him into the room and dumped him in a chair he'd prepared near the door and zip-tied him to it. He'd already torn a section of sheet to use as a gag and once that was applied, he was confident he was in total control of the situation. Torturing someone was never his first option, and with so many cops and FBI agents around, he couldn't risk having the guy screaming in agony. To get his answers, he'd have to scare the man into talking rather than anything else.

"Quadrado, can you stand outside and make sure we're not disturbed?" Fletcher moved so he was standing three feet from the now-captive goon. "As for you, you're going to answer some of my questions. To start with, nods or headshakes will do. All you need to understand is that you're going to answer my questions. It's entirely up to you if you make me hurt you first. Do you understand?"

A nod.

"Are you going to answer my questions?"

A headshake and a defiant stare were the goon's answer. He'd chosen to call Fletcher's bluff.

CHAPTER FIFTEEN

The man's refusal to talk was no great surprise to Fletcher, but it was a complication he could do without.

To get the information he wanted, he was going to have to either hurt the guy, or at the very least, make the guy so afraid of what he was going to do to him that he'd talk without being harmed.

Torture is a crude method of getting information from someone. When those being tortured feel a certain level of pain, they'll say whatever they can to make the torturer stop. Or, they'll see the whole torture thing as a matter of pride, a competition between the torturer and the victim. A low-level goon like the one in front of him would be sure to have witnessed some horrific things by his bosses, or at least heard about them. To this end, he'd be afraid of crossing his boss. Hence, presumably, this goon's resistance.

So the first step was to make the guy properly fear him. The more he could terrify him, the better the chance he wouldn't actually have to hurt him. The victim may suffer the most but—unless the person inflicting the torture is a sadistic psychopath—the act of torturing someone always came with a cost, and Fletcher didn't want to put himself into emotional debt if he could avoid it.

"Okay then, Loser." Fletcher waved a hand at the goon. "I'm calling you Loser because that's what you are, a loser. Only a loser would take the stance you're taking. You could tell me what I want to know and walk out of here without as much as a hangnail. Instead you've as good as invited me to hurt you."

Loser's face gave nothing away. Fletcher didn't expect it would. Loser would be steeling himself for the pain that was about to come. He'd expect punches to be thrown. He'd probably be confident he could take that kind of beating without weakening. In his shoes, Fletcher would have the same confidence.

Now it was up to Fletcher to break that confidence, to shatter it so Loser's resistance could be broken. Fear is a powerful motivator, so that's what Fletcher planned to use.

"There are a lot of ways I can hurt you." Fletcher pulled a gallon container of bleach from a shelf and held it in front of Loser. "I've heard about Eyeball Horton's reputation. Maybe I should tape your eye open, take the top off this, rest it against your pupil and wait until you're ready to talk."

Loser's face didn't move, but there was no mistaking the bob of his Adam's apple as he gave a manful swallow.

Fletcher put down the container of bleach and used one hand to lift Loser's chin. The other hand he placed on Loser's throat, digging the tip of one finger into his neck. "The finger you can feel is pressing on your carotid artery. If I maintain this pressure for anywhere between thirty seconds and two minutes, you'll pass out from a lack of blood to the brain. After the first minute, some of your brain cells will die." Fletcher drew his hand back. "I could hold that pressure on after you've blacked out. Three minutes will leave you with brain damage. If I choose to hold my finger in place for five to ten minutes, you'll end up in a coma, from there you'll have permanent brain damage and you may even die. How does that sound to you? Say you do survive and come out of that coma, how do you fancy having someone wipe your ass for the rest of what will be a miserable life?"

Loser's eyes now held a trace of uncertainty, and there was a prickle of sweat running down each of his temples.

"Maybe I'll kneecap you. I'm sure you'll have heard about kneecapping. It was very popular with the Irish Republican

Army back in the days of the Troubles. Basically, they'd shoot out someone's kneecaps with a low-velocity gun. Their victims would never walk properly again." Fletcher pulled out the pistol he'd requested the FBI equip him with and screwed a sound suppressor onto it. "Traditionally, they'd shoot from the back of the knee, and on occasion from the front. It'd be agonizing for the poor victim." Fletcher placed the tip of the pistol's barrel on Loser's kneecap and lined the barrel up so it was pointing straight down Loser's leg. "Now if I pull the trigger from this angle, the bullet will take out your kneecap, or the patella as it's known, and then keep on going until it's shattered the top of your fibula or tibia. Maybe there'll be a large enough piece of bone shrapnel to damage them both. Certainly the flesh just below your knee will be torn to shreds by pieces of bone impacted by the bullet. You might be lucky; a surgeon might just be able to save your leg. However, if I do kneecap you and you still don't tell me what I want to know, my next step would be to grab your foot and twist your leg until you're overcome with a desire to become Mr. Talkative."

The trickles of sweat on Loser's temples were now rivulets, and he'd taken to making manful swallows every second breath. The uncertainty in his eyes was now full-blown terror. He was exactly where Fletcher wanted him.

Fletcher lifted the gun away from Loser's knee and used it as a pointer. "I'm going to give you a choice. Look down for the kneecapping, look left for the bleach and look right for the brain damage. If you look up, I'll take that as a sign you want to talk to me. Take too long to answer and I'll do all three. So, what's your decision?"

Loser glared at Fletcher for a moment then lifted his head until it was as far back as it could go. It was all Fletcher could do to not breathe out a sigh of relief at not having to carry out any of his threats.

Fletcher pressed on right away before Loser could recover any misplaced bravado. "Start talking: where is Eyeball Horton really at?"

"He's dead. Whoever tipped you off was right. Eyeball, his wife and four other guys all got whacked by someone last night. Adebayo got us to put them all into Eyeball's Winnebago. It's being driven out to New Mexico. It'll be left burned out with the bodies laid around the different areas of the Winnebago."

"Who killed them?"

"Adebayo thinks it was that Mantis bitch, and I agree. I saw their bodies; they all had the same two shots the Mantis's other hits had."

"You'll hear things I never will. According to the word on the street, who's paying the Mantis for these hits?"

"I've heard a few people blamed, but J.B. Ronson is the latest favorite." A smear of distaste spread itself on Loser's face. "He's got the backing of the Mafia and has been trying to buy out some of the smaller guys like us for a few years now."

"What about the fight the other night where all the innocents were killed? Why aren't they targeting Ronson?"

"I dunno. Power grabs. Hostile takeovers. His name wasn't really mentioned then. Take your pick."

"Is there any proof of their involvement?"

"It's only the small guys who are getting hit. What more proof do you need?"

Fletcher pulled his knife and cut the zip ties securing Loser to the seat. He was done with Loser. The man's answers had dislodged his own thoughts. J.B. Ronson's flagship casino was the Gold Mine, the place he'd been staking out with Quadrado last night.

CHAPTER SIXTEEN

Quadrado's eyes held a thousand questions as they escorted Loser back to the room where all the other goons were being questioned by the local FBI agents. She had the good sense not to ask any of them, a fact Fletcher was pleased about as he had his own agenda.

Once they were relieved of Loser, he brought her up to speed. Loser's testimony was pretty much what they'd surmised had happened, but Fletcher had doubts about the whole hit on Eyeball Horton and his crew.

"Listen up a minute, things aren't running true for me. I don't get the whole cover-up by Adebayo. Nor do I see why the Mantis has changed her pattern from every second day to one hit per day. There's a chance she's making sure she's unpredictable, but I still don't see why she's hit Utopia when there are far juicier targets. I think Adebayo is the person who killed Eyeball and the others. He's pretty much taken over already, and that makes far more sense to me than the Mantis being the killer here."

"You could well be right. How can we prove it though? You can bet the house on Adebayo not confessing."

Fletcher smiled at Quadrado's use of a gambling term. "I'd say that if you can intercept that Winnebago before it gets burned out, bullet analysis will help. Maybe there'll be something on the security tapes that'll help, but I'd guess Adebayo has already had them wiped or at least overwritten."

"I need to go and tell all this to Thomson. Hopefully, he'll take his head out of his butt long enough to listen."

"You go do that, I have something I want to run down anyway."

Fletcher walked into the Gold Mine with one single objective in his mind. Speak to J.B. Ronson. It wouldn't be an easy thing to achieve. He was a nobody to Ronson. A freelancer connected to the FBI. He'd be viewed with as much suspicion as a massive wooden horse gifted from an enemy.

All the same, Fletcher had to verify what Loser had told him. No way would Ronson admit any guilt, but that was only part of the reason for the meeting. For all Loser and the lower-level gangs blamed the bigger syndicates, they had no evidence. If Ronson was as connected as Loser said, then maybe he'd be able to shed a little light on things. Fletcher didn't expect a mailing address for the Mantis, but there was no telling what Ronson might share.

Even though it was still mid-morning, the casino seemed as busy as the night before. Fletcher guessed those gambling at this time of the morning would be the smaller stakes type. Addicted enough to the thrill to bring them out this early in the day, but not so affluent as to run with the high rollers who visited in the evening and the night.

His first thought was to look for Len, but as there was no sign of him, he opted to try another avenue. He clocked someone he suspected to be one of the undercover guards. A big guy with a bald head and an Iron Maiden T-shirt atop a pair of beige cargo shorts. The man wandered aimlessly, his eyes restless, but never once did he make an attempt to play a slot, or join in at one of the tables.

A woman drunk enough to have been here all night was creating a scene of many slurs as she insulted the three security guards who were escorting her out of the casino. The bald man's hovering presence trailing after the other guards confirmed his status.

Fletcher waited until Bald-and-Not-Very-Undercover was near him and then walked directly up to him.

"Let's cut to the chase. I know you work here." Fletcher pointed to an alcove table near the bar that was empty. "Can we talk there for a moment?"

"You got a moment, buddy, not a minute. Use it wisely."

Fletcher took three steps across the room until he was standing by the alcove's table. Bald-and-Not-Very-Undercover did the same.

"I want to speak to J.B. Ronson. Face to face. No bullshit, no wild goose chases and no threats. I'm connected to the FBI, but I have no jurisdiction. I mean him no harm, and as a show of good faith, I'm going to turn around. If you lift my jacket you'll find a gun. On the outside of my right leg, tucked into my boot, you'll find a knife. I repeat, as a show of good faith, I'm telling you about the weapons I'm carrying and inviting you to relieve me of them. Feel free to pat me for other weapons. You'll find a suppressor for the pistol in the left pocket of my jacket."

"What do you want to talk to Mr. Ronson about?"

"That'd be his business, not yours. I want to talk to him face to face. Tell whoever you report to that if he wants to have some guys with guns trained on me, I have no objections if it'll make him feel easier about meeting me."

Fletcher knew it was a gamble to enter the lion's den this way, but he couldn't see another way of verifying what Loser had told him regarding the Mantis's paymasters.

Rough hands removed the gun and knife, then patted him down for other weapons. "Wait here." Bald-and-Not-Very-Undercover wandered off and put his cell to his ear.

It didn't take long for him to get an answer. When he came back there was a look of wary suspicion about him, and when he gestured Fletcher's way, there was a grim expression on his face.

He directed Fletcher towards a doorway, and as he passed Bald-and-Not-Very-Undercover, Fletcher felt the press of a gun at the base of his spine.

CHAPTER SEVENTEEN

Quadrado took a brisk walk around the areas of Utopia she suspected Fletcher might be. He wasn't getting something to eat, nor was he scoping out the casino floor or loitering near where all the FBI agents and cops were gathered.

Fletcher had said he wanted to run something down and that's what he'd be doing. The problem was, he'd been his typical enigmatic self about it. Rather than share a half-baked theory, he kept his own counsel until he could support whatever point he had with a well-reasoned argument.

That in itself wouldn't be so bad, except he had a tendency to go renegade when he was running down clues. He'd do things she, as an FBI agent, couldn't condone. An example in point was the way he'd gotten information from the goon earlier. How he'd persuaded him to talk wasn't known, but she would bet the threat of extreme violence featured.

She'd never agreed with the way Fletcher went off to do his own thing. They'd been put together as partners, ill-fitted admittedly, but they were still supposed to work together.

A ping from her pocket had her reaching for her cell. The ping was a distinctive one she'd set for emails from Soter.

Quadrado found a space against a wall where she could read her message without worrying about anyone looking over her shoulder and opened the email.

HEARING ABOUT MORE DEATHS ISN'T WHY I SENT YOU
AND FLETCHER THERE. MANTIS MUST BE TERMINATED
ASAP

SOTER

The email just added to the pressure they were under. Since
they'd arrived in Las Vegas another fourteen people had lost their
lives. Five of them innocent civilians. She put in a call to Fletcher
that went unanswered, so she backed it up with a message relaying
the contents of the email and asking him to let her know where
the hell he was and what he was up to.

She wasn't expecting a fast response. He'd reply in his own
good time and probably not before he needed something from her.

Quadrado put the phone into a different pocket. There was
something in the pocket, it rustled like paper and when she drew
it out, she found a typed note.

I HAVE NO BEEF WITH YOU OR THE EX-ROYAL
MARINE, BUT IF YOU DON'T LEAVE TOWN, I
WILL KILL YOU.

The note was signed with a drawing of a mantis. A sure-fire
calling card.

Quadrado's first instinct was to whirl around looking for the
person who'd put the note into her pocket. Even as her body twisted
she knew it was a waste of time. There was no telling when the note
had been secreted into her jacket, in a reverse pickpocket move. As
a matter of course she'd report it to Forbes and Thomson. They'd
analyze the note and get someone to watch Quadrado's every move
in the casino, in case they could pinpoint whoever had delivered
the note. She didn't think they'd get anywhere. Her suspicion was

the note had been inserted into her pocket on the street, away from the cameras that covered every inch of the casino floor.

For all Quadrado was an FBI agent, for all she carried a gun and knew how to use it, she couldn't help being unnerved by the idea that the Mantis knew about them and could get so close.

Another worry was that—knowing the Mantis was onto them—Thomson might be asshole enough to use her and Fletcher as tethered goats.

CHAPTER EIGHTEEN

Bald-and-Not-Very-Undercover directed Fletcher through a series of corridors. When there was a keypad to get through a door, he made Fletcher face the wall with his head turned away.

Fletcher bore this as a small price to pay for getting what he wanted: an audience with Ronson. It also showed that, while the man holding a gun at his back might not be very good when it came to working undercover, he was no slouch at controlling a prisoner. Fletcher could have reversed their fortunes and reclaimed his gun, but that wouldn't have gotten him what he wanted.

A pair of hoods loitered outside a door. When they saw them coming they stopped Fletcher and performed another search. This one far more thorough than the first. When satisfied, they stood aside and opened the door for them to enter.

All three hoods followed Fletcher into the room. Once the door closed behind them, they fanned out behind Fletcher as he stood in front of the desk.

The room was decorated in a shade of paint that was far enough off-white to be approaching mushroom. There was waist-high paneling in the same wood as the desk. Fletcher's best guess was walnut. Glass shelves were decorated with ornaments that were halfway to being objets d'art.

On the desk were the usual suspects. Telephone, computer monitor and various files plus a photo frame. All in all the room presented itself as the kind of comfortable space occupied by a powerful executive. All that was missing was the powerful executive.

A door behind the desk swung open with no more than a whisper where it brushed the thick carpet. The man who came through the door was in his sixties, stooped but otherwise as fit as Fletcher. There wasn't a spare ounce on him, and he moved with the grace of an athlete.

"I'm JB. Now what the hell do you want?"

The brusque tone was supposed to intimidate Fletcher. Instead it rankled him. As soon as he'd seen the stooped man, he'd known right away he wasn't the person he'd come to see. Fletcher had been searching for tactful ways to bring this up when the man's tone had made him give up on tact.

"I'd like to speak to the real J.B. Ronson. You're not him."

"You got some cheek on you." The man tapped his chest. "I'm JB. Ain't that right, boys?"

All three hoods replied at once. "Yes, you are, sir."

"See," a reptilian look came over the stooped man's face, "if you think you're coming in here and calling me a liar, buster, you don't know what kind of man I am."

"I know exactly what kind of man you are. Your name is Darrel Zelter. You're J.B. Ronson's right hand. You used to be his enforcer back in the day, but you not only had the smarts to leave that work to others, you have enough smarts to have never been charged with anything more serious than a parking ticket, despite the cops and FBI having a file on you that's three inches thick." The last part was made up; Fletcher didn't have a clue how thick the file was, he just knew a few scant details and was trying to boost Zelter's ego. "J.B. Ronson is five inches taller than you, he's heavier set and he has a scar on his left cheek that's a memento from his days as a bareknuckle fighter."

"You got a nerve coming in here like this, buster."

Fletcher gave a shrug. "Maybe, but I am trying to get to the bottom of the Mantis killings. To do that I need to speak to J.B. Ronson." He flicked a hand in the general direction of Bald-and-

Not-Very-Undercover. "When I approached your man, I did so in good faith. I told him where all my weapons were located and allowed him to take them from me. I have complied with the instructions given to me by your men as they brought me here."

"You want to talk to us about the Mantis? You wearing a wire?"

"No. Want me to prove it?"

"Damn straight I do."

Fletcher rolled his eyes and stripped to his briefs so Zelter could see he wasn't wearing a wire or any other kind of recording device.

"Satisfied?" Fletcher tried to stay in control of the narrative, but he could see the four gangsters examining the various scars decorating his body. One of them stepped in front of Fletcher. His fingers reaching towards the locket that hung around Fletcher's neck. "What's this? Some tough guy you are, wearing a pussy piece of jewelry like this."

The locket was Fletcher's most prized possession. It held pictures of his wife and daughter. Its bumping against his chest as he went about his day was a source of constant comfort.

"I'm tough enough to wear it. Don't you worry about that. I don't care how many guns your buddies are pointing at me. If you touch my locket, I'll beat you to death." Fletcher backed up his threat with a hard stare. When the guy stepped away, he flicked his eyes to Zelter.

"Now may I speak with J.B. Ronson? I'm practically naked, unarmed and willing to comply with you. If it makes you feel any safer, have one of your men put a gun at my back again as you take me to Ronson."

The door behind Zelter whispered open again. J.B. Ronson walked in with the confident air of someone who wields immense power.

"Sit down, son." A click of his fingers at Bald-and-Not-Very-Undercover. "You heard the man, he wants a gun against him. Let's see how he likes one at the back of his head."

CHAPTER NINETEEN

Fletcher knew he had to get some semblance of control, but with a personality like Ronson who oozed power, it would be an uphill battle.

"Thank you for seeing me, Mr. Ronson. I appreciate it."

Ronson cast a pair of dead eyes his way. "It irks me that you have disrupted my day. There I was enjoying the company of my accountant and my lawyer, and I hear of a strange man who wants to talk to me about things I cannot possibly know about." His voice hardened. "Mr. Ronson was the name my gym teacher called me, and I'll thank you not to bring back memories of the first person I wanted to kill. You will call me JB, or lose a finger."

"I apologize for disrupting your day, JB. That was not my intention. You will, I'm sure, appreciate the matter with the Mantis is one which requires urgent action, and therefore I couldn't spend the time going through formal channels. Nobody from the FBI is aware I'm here. I tossed my FBI cell in a trash can before I got here. I'm out on a limb here. I'm not a cop, not a fed, I'm a specialist contractor. Freelance, usually, but I do work for the government from time to time."

"You're either a very brave man, a fool or a liar to come here and tell me what you just told me. I wonder which of the three it is."

"I'm neither a fool nor a liar. I'm not going to insult your intelligence by pretending that I don't think you won't have heard about what happened at Utopia, or the shootout that claimed six lives. I spoke with a guy at Utopia, and the general school of thought is that you're the one paying the Mantis. I really don't think that's the case, so as a courtesy to you, I'm here to give you fair warning of what others are saying. My job is to catch the Mantis and stop her. I was in your casino last night, scoping the place out because I thought you were likely to be one of the Mantis's next targets. If I can figure out how she'll attack you, I can catch her."

Fletcher knew he was on dangerous ground laying things out the way he had, but he didn't believe Loser's theory about Ronson being the Mantis's paymaster. The question now was, what would Ronson make of what he'd just told him?

"So you figured you'd come give me a warning, did you?" Ronson leaned back in his chair. "That seems very charitable of you. It puzzles me as to why you'd be so charitable. Why you'd put yourself at risk to do such a thing."

"I have three reasons. Number one is that I don't want any more innocent people to die. If the other casino owners think you are behind the Mantis, I'm sure they'll want to extract some kind of revenge. If you are behind her, I'm sure you'll be expecting a backlash of some kind. There's been two instances of that happening so far and civilians have been caught in the crossfire both times. That's something I want to prevent from happening again if at all possible. If, as I suspect, you're not behind her, I'm sure you will have ways of putting the word out to the other casino owners that you are not responsible, and that you will look upon any accusations unfavorably." Fletcher chose his words with care and made a point not to say gangs or any of the other words that might be deemed an accusation of illegality.

"I find the loss of civilian life equally regrettable and unnecessary." Ronson steepled his fingers. "Your other reasons?"

"If you're not behind the Mantis, then you're at risk from her. You'll know who her targets have been and you'll have worked out that she's escalating. She's only a step or two away from taking on someone of your status. Unless you know something I don't, you'll have learned that there's been no trace of her. No sightings, no clues as to how she knew so much about access routes and so on. She's good, damn good, and if you're not worried about her, you're nowhere near as smart I've been led to believe."

"If I were you, I should pick my words with more caution." Fletcher was pleased to see that he'd rankled Ronson with his comments. It was a dangerous ploy, but it would get his message across, as it'd make Ronson think. "You're forgetting the attack on Utopia. They are small, as inconsequential as a gnat. That hardly seems like escalation to me."

"That was an inside job. Adebayo used the Mantis as a fall guy. He saw an opportunity for a power grab and took it. Far be it from me to cast aspersions on your colleagues, but the same could happen to you. I'm here because if I'm to stop the Mantis, I'm probably going to need an ally. You seem like someone it'd be advantageous to know. To have as an ally."

Ronson leaned forward and planted his elbows on the desk. The action enough to remind Fletcher of a cat getting ready to pounce. "And what would I get from allying with you?"

"Your life. If I'm right, your assistance may be enough to help me stop the Mantis before she targets you and your colleagues."

"I rather think that my own men—men whose loyalty I would never question by suspecting them of plotting to depose or replace me—are more than capable of protecting me from any threat this girl may pose."

"I'm sure your men are very capable. However, the Mantis is deadly, to say the least. Your men might well repel her, but how many of them will she take out before she's stopped? You said you wouldn't question the loyalty of your men. Surely you want to return that loyalty by not putting them at unnecessary risk?"

A fraction of a smile flickered across Ronson's mouth. "You'd make a damn fine lawyer. Say I felt disposed to become the ally you seek. What would you want from me?"

"Information. If you know stuff the cops don't, I'd like to know it too. Anything that can help me will be gratefully received, and then it'll be a case of me doing my stuff and removing the threat to you and your colleagues."

"You seem very sure of yourself. What exactly is your role in all of this? How do I know that you aren't the Mantis and that the legend of her being a girl is nothing more than misdirection?"

"I'm a fixer. I investigate problems then make them go away. As for me being the Mantis, if I were, you and your men would be dead by now."

"That's a big statement to make."

Fletcher held Ronson's stare. "As I said earlier, JB, I'm not a liar."

"I appreciate your candor. I have nothing to tell you beyond what will be on record with the cops and the FBI. That does not mean I'm not listening for new information." A card was produced from a pocket and tossed Fletcher's way. "Get yourself a burner phone and call this number twice a day. If I have anything I feel will be useful to you, I will share it. In return you will make no mention of my involvement in your quest. Should my name be mentioned in the wrong ear, I would be displeased and the consequences for you would be... most unfortunate. I will bid you good day now."

Fletcher had been threatened many times, but never had he been threatened in such a polite way. He didn't doubt the threat's seriousness though. JB was a dangerous man and it would never do to forget that.

As Fletcher walked to the back of the room to collect his clothes, Bald-and-Not-Very-Undercover put the gun to Fletcher's back again. It was off to one side, the right, as Bald-and-Not-Very-Undercover was right-handed.

It was time Fletcher made a point of his own.

He whirled to his left, raising his arm so his tucked elbow passed over the hand Bald-and-Not-Very-Undercover was holding the pistol with. The first point of such a move is to remove the threat of the weapon. Fletcher did this by bringing his left arm up and clamping the gun arm tight to his body in a way that prevented Bald-and-Not-Very-Undercover from turning the gun on him.

With the gun out of action, he switched from defense to attack and delivered a palm strike to Bald-and-Not-Very-Undercover's chin that dropped him in a heap.

Rather than risk any retaliation by Ronson's men who were reaching for their weapons, Fletcher raised his hands and continued walking over to his clothes. He could retrieve the gun when he was dressed.

"What reason do you have for doing that?" Ronson's tone was colder than an arctic wind.

Fletcher turned to face the gangster. "I'm not without talent when it comes to hurting people. I think it's important you and your men know that in case you decide to sell me down the river in some way. Your man should come round within a few minutes. I could have broken his jaw. I chose not to. I could have grabbed for the gun. I chose not to. You showed your cards when you laid your threat on me. I've just shown you mine."

CHAPTER TWENTY

Fletcher paced back and forth until he heard a knock on the door. He let Quadrado into his room and took in her appearance. She was in her smart FBI duds, but there was a wildness about her expression.

"What's happened?"

"The Mantis put a calling card into my pocket." Quadrado pulled her cell out and showed him a picture of the card and the message it carried. "It's with Thomson for analysis. Not for a second do I think we'll get anything from it, but we have to try."

It took no more than a second to read the message. Working out the implications would take longer.

"Who else knows about it?"

"Thomson briefed his team. I've given them a list of places where I've been, and they're checking to see if any footage shows the card being put in my pocket. Again, I don't think we'll get anywhere with it."

Fletcher pulled a face and felt the tightness of his jaw. "I hate to say it, but I think you're right. What are your thoughts?"

"Most of all, I'm pissed. I'm an FBI agent, how dare she threaten me like that? For all you're a killer, you're actually a force for good. How dare she threaten you?"

Quadrado's tone was rising as she gave vent to her feelings. Fletcher suspected she'd kept them bottled up and professional around Thomson, as she'd know any kind of outburst from her would hand him the excuse he needed to get rid of them.

"Yeah, it kind of pisses me off, too. You said most of all, what else do you think?"

The way Quadrado didn't answer told Fletcher all he needed to know. She was scared. Worried that someone bold and capable enough to pull off the assassinations the Mantis had, as well as slipping the card into her pocket, was more than good enough to make good on her threats. She'd be pitting her professional instincts against the human desire to stay alive. For him it was a no-brainer. If the Mantis wanted to play those kinds of cat-and-mouse games, he'd step into her litter box and take her on. What Quadrado did was up to her.

"What was Thomson's take? Does he want to use us as bait or is he trying to use this as a reason to send us home?"

"A bit of both. He offered me the chance to pull out, and said that if I chose to stay, he wanted to put a tail on me. He said it was for my, well, our protection, but we both know it's because he'll want to use us to draw the Mantis to us."

"It's not a bad idea, but with someone as good as she is, she'll be expecting that response and will take measures to counter it."

Quadrado raised an eyebrow at him. "I figured you'd say that. In her position, how would you attack a tethered goat?"

"From a long way away. A sniper rifle would be my first choice. Two shots fired from a quarter mile away or so and it's good night, Vienna. Possibly a car bomb, but they're not always reliable and they're likely to take out innocents as well, although she doesn't seem to have an issue with that."

"You're so reassuring, aren't you?"

"If you want your hand held, go call your mother. If you want to face reality, keep talking to me."

"I can handle your realism. But don't think that I like it."

"I don't either. I take it you're not going to accept Thomson's offer of going home?"

"What do you think?" There was defiance in her face, but her eyes told him she was using every scrap of courage she had to face this down.

"Not for one second would I doubt you'd stay. You're scared. That's normal. I'd think you were an idiot if you weren't. But you're gutsy enough to stay and not let her scare you off. That's more than good enough for me." Fletcher rose from his seat and started packing up his possessions. "I'm thinking we should move to a motel on the edge of town. Somewhere a little down-at-heel, but not so rough it rents rooms by the hour. We should also max out our cards, so we can use only cash to stay off the grid, get two or three burner phones, change our appearances and hire a car. Until we show up at a casino again, we ought to be safe enough, as she won't know when you found the card, or whether we're obeying her instruction. But we do need to drop off the grid as soon as possible."

"Agreed. I'll go and pack."

"Before you do, we have something else to consider. How did she know about us and our mission? How did she know what we looked like? To my mind there's only three people who could tell her these things: Soter, Thomson and Forbes. Therefore one of them has to be the person who let the Mantis, or her paymaster, know about us."

Fletcher could see the fight between Quadrado's professionalism and fear escalate into a pitched battle. Before long it would become a fight to the death.

"Thomson's a big enough douchebag to do that. But, you don't get to be the head of an FBI office without being thoroughly vetted. Forbes seems to be his right hand, and while I don't trust Thomson's judgment, I trust my own. My money is on Soter."

"Mine too, although I do think that in his position, Thomson will be ripe for being blackmailed by the gangs who run Las Vegas. We shouldn't discount him, as it may come back to bite us."

"I get why Thomson or Forbes might be manipulated into working with the Mantis, but Soter setting her on us doesn't make sense to me?"

"Either he wants us to fail and die, or he has some ulterior motive in mind." Fletcher stuffed some clothes into his bag. "If it's the first, there are easier ways and he's no call to kill us, when he could simply hand me over to the cops in Georgia for what went down there, and have you put on desk duty for eternity. If it is him, I reckon he's had Thomson plant the card on you to gee us up. His chosen moniker—Soter—is that of a protective god. People are dying and he'll want to see that stop. Therefore he's turning the screw on us."

"I hope it's him playing games."

"Hang on." Fletcher needed a moment to get his thoughts lined up. "What if Soter is the Mantis's paymaster? Could he have hired her with the intention of having her eliminate a few of the casino bosses? And now she's gone beyond her remit, and that's why he's brought us in?"

"You mean he's using her like he's using you? That there's more than just us on his books?" Quadrado's brow furrowed as she thought through all the different implications. "Then why bring us in, only to pit her against us? That doesn't make sense to me."

"Nor me, but it's possible he doesn't know she's aware of us. Technically, you're my handler, right? It'd be fair to assume that if the Mantis is working for Soter, she'll have a handler of some kind as well. Maybe the handler got wind of us and their loyalty is aligned with the Mantis, rather than Soter. I know yours is with me."

Fletcher's shoulder received a friendly punch. "Thanks, that might just be the nicest thing you've ever said to me."

"Don't get used to it. We still have to contend with the Mantis and the possibility Soter has set up his two teams against each other to see who's best. And that means we'll have to be at the top of our game."

Quadrado waved her hand at the boxes as she moved on from the topic of Soter betraying them. "What about these files? We can't take them all with us, unless you're planning to keep the FBI car."

"No chance. We ditch everything that might have a bug or tracker. On the subject of tracking devices, before we leave here it'd be best if you run your tracker app over your stuff before packing. I've done mine and it's all clean. As for the files, you can get them on your laptop. I know it's going to be harder to assess them, but at least you can still get what we want."

"Fair enough. I'll contact the office and have someone come pick them up."

"No. I'll put them all in the trunk of the FBI car so the maid doesn't find them."

As he was doing the packing, Fletcher's mind was working out everything they had to do to drop out and hide from the Mantis. Also, at the back of his brain, his subconscious was already figuring out their next move in terms of nullifying the Mantis. There was an obvious step. There was another gang that owned four casinos that was on his list of potential targets, topped only by the Gold Mine. Once they'd relocated to a motel on the edge of town, he knew the next steps they would have to take.

CHAPTER TWENTY-ONE

Fletcher tossed his bag onto the bed of one of the motel rooms he'd booked and tried not to compare it to the plush hotel rooms booked for them by the FBI. This was a functional space for the down-at-heel. Quadrado's nose had crinkled when he'd suggested the motel, but when she'd seen for herself that it was at least clean, if tired and dated, she'd parked her objections.

They'd both taken as much as they could from their cards at the same ATM. After that it was a case of ducking and diving through backstreets until they were sure their countersurveillance measures were as good as they could make them.

"What are you thinking our next move should be? I figure we ought to do what we can to change our appearance and then go back to the Gold Mine."

"We've tried there. They're braced and are on side with me. If the Mantis has it planned as a target, that may well be where she picked us up. I say we move down the list. The next set of casinos is owned by a Cam Drewitt. The flagship one is called Auric, although he doesn't live on site: he has a house in a private, gated community."

"Doesn't he have a reputation for extreme brutality? Isn't he the guy with the enforcer who supposedly—?'

"Yes and yes. Don't worry, I'm not planning on having any contact with Drewitt or his enforcer. I'm just scoping them out for now." The lie fell easily from Fletcher's lips. It wasn't that he was a good or habitual liar, more that he knew Quadrado was already afraid of the Mantis. He didn't want her to lose focus by worrying about Drewitt's enforcer with his reputed assortment of drills and power saws.

"So what are your plans?"

"Drewitt lives in a gated community. The security will likely be good but not brilliant. If I was the Mantis, I'd want to make my move at his house rather than the casino, where there are more members of the public and more armed guards."

"I thought you favored crowds. Liked being able to blend in and lose yourself in a crowd."

"I do. It's just that if I was in the Mantis's role, I'd prefer to attack the house. That way almost everyone I meet can be considered a hostile. The split second it takes to separate hostiles from civilians can be vital when the bullets are flying."

"She doesn't care about killing civilians, so your thinking is off."

"It's not. If she's killing non-hostiles she has no need to kill, then she'll be wasting ammo and time. That's an unnecessary risk that only a fool would take, and we're agreed she's not a fool."

"Trust you to think like that. I say it's the casino we should be watching, as that's where most of her hits have taken place."

"Then we'll split up. I'll take the house, you take the casino." He pointed at Quadrado's laptop. "Fire that thing up, will you?"

"What do you want?"

"A Google Maps view of Drewitt's place."

While Quadrado fiddled with the laptop, Fletcher unpacked some of the purchases he'd made at a nearby 7-Eleven.

Drewitt's house was ringed by a large wall. The house was central in the plot, and there was little to no obvious cover between the walls and the house. It may be that the image was a few years old and some bushes or shrubs had now been planted, but Fletcher doubted that would be the case. Someone in Drewitt's profession would take precautions to not make things easy for someone who wanted to attack them. The images on the screen weren't clear enough to show any electronic security measures, but Fletcher knew they would be there. He pushed the laptop back to Quadrado and picked up the clippers he'd bought.

First he shaved all the hair off his head. Then he used the clippers to remove the beard he grew every winter. When he laid the clippers down, the only hair left on his head were his eyebrows and a mustache whose ends he twiddled until they formed a handlebar design.

Fletcher caught the smirk on Quadrado's face as she assessed his new look. Her amusement wasn't going to last.

"You're next." He pointed at the stool he'd positioned in the middle of the floor.

"No way. You're not shaving my head. Not happening."

"Yes, it is. Sit down." Fletcher put the guard onto the clippers and slid it so it'd leave an inch of hair on her. "I'll leave you an inch. There's some hair dye you can use to color what's left."

"No way, Fletcher. I used to wear it super-short when I was younger, but it's taken me years to grow my hair."

"And that's why cutting it will work. You have nice hair, and anyone who's seen you won't expect that you'll change it so radically. Think about it this way: not being recognizable will add a layer of security to us. A layer of safety, if you will."

Quadrado's mouth pinched and her words were a lot gentler than her tone. "What color is the dye?"

The fact she asked the question meant she was softening towards his idea.

"Red."

"What shade of red? Please tell me you got a nice burgundy."

"Nope. Fire truck red. Coupled with the fact your face will change shape by not being in a ponytail, nobody would believe people trying to hide would change their appearance to eye-catching. Hence my flamboyant mustache and your look-at-me hairstyle. If it makes you feel any better, I've got a ginger dye for my mustache."

"You and your damn logic." Quadrado sat herself on the stool, one hand extended towards Fletcher. "I'll do it myself. And FYI, no, it doesn't make me feel any better."

CHAPTER TWENTY-TWO

Quadrado walked into the Auric casino feeling as if all eyes were on her. In her mind, the scarlet hair she'd teased into blunt spikes was a beacon that summoned everyone's gaze. If that wasn't bad enough, Fletcher had insisted that her new style should be boho. The loose-flowing clothes she now wore felt alien against her skin when compared to her usual attire of tight pants and fitted blouses.

Like every other casino and hotel, the Auric had its own theme, and as its name suggested, gold was that theme. The servers wore gold, the paintwork was gold and there were enough gold-themed accessories to make Quadrado wonder if her eyes would end up strained.

To Quadrado there was something false about Las Vegas. It dangled temptation of all forms in front of people, and few visitors appeared to be able to resist its siren song. The glitz and glamour were a front for a rapacious beast that somehow managed to chew up and spit out its victims. What's more, it managed this in a way that sent them home thinking they'd had a good time.

As with the Gold Mine, there were people gathered round tables, standing in front of the slots and generally milling around taking in the sights. Facial expressions told of the gamblers' fortunes. A woman passed her with the wide smile of a winner. Across the room, a man stared into his glass as if the reason for his losing streak could be found in its depths. There were smells of cooked meat and burned dreams, yet around her the majority of people wore smiles wide enough to dimple their cheeks.

All of these sights were assessed for threat in rapid succession. Yes, it might be late afternoon, yes, she might be in a crowded place, but the overriding feeling she'd had since parting ways with Fletcher had been one of fear. Everywhere she looked seemed to be full of places the Mantis could spring from.

She and Fletcher had worked up their own profile of who the Mantis might be. They'd put her between thirty and forty-five; young enough to be able to move quickly and with agility, yet also old enough to have undergone extensive training and to have garnered enough experience to plan her missions with the meticulous attention to detail that had been evident in her hits. When it came to her physique, Fletcher had been insistent that she'd be of average height and her body would have the toned muscle of a long-distance runner. They both agreed she'd be pretty enough to use feminine wiles when necessary, yet not so beautiful as to draw attention to herself. In short, the Mantis would be an average woman who could blend into a crowd.

Fletcher's assessment of her skills was that she'd be at ease on her missions. There would be no nerves about her, and until it was time to strike, she'd behave just like everyone else.

It was all these things which jangled Quadrado's nerves. The woman pulling a cell from her purse could have been producing a gun, just like the woman scratching her lower back could have been drawing a weapon from a waistband. She knew she was jumping at shadows, imagining the worst when witnessing the mundane. That the chances of the Mantis breaking cover in a public place that was littered with security cameras was miniscule. Most of all, she knew she had to get a grip of herself and trust in the changed appearance.

As she walked around the casino, she dropped the odd coin into one of the slots, and while she pretended to play, she went through the checklist she'd drawn up with Fletcher. By the time she'd done two circuits, she'd identified the guards' positions, the access routes to the non-public areas of the casino and a dozen other points they'd discussed.

With the inside scoped out, it was time to move onto the next part of her surveillance. The outside. Fletcher had been insistent they look for points where the Mantis might breach the casino's ring of security.

The Auric was sandwiched between a designer clothes store and a Mercedes dealership, central on a block at the north end of Las Vegas's infamous Strip, so she didn't worry too much about the frontage. It all led into the main body of the casino, so it needed no assessing. Likewise, the two sides of the casino were abutted onto the store and dealership, so there was no way for the Mantis to gain access.

Even so, she took a walk in each place, in case the businesses were owned by Drewitt and there was a way he could get big winners straight from the casino floor to a place where they could spend their money on his overpriced goods.

Neither the dealership nor the store had a door leading to the casino, so she made her way round the back. This wasn't anything like as attractive as the Strip at the front of the casino. It was a more utilitarian area with services such as auto repair shops and hardware stores.

An alleyway provided access to the rear of all the buildings, so after a surreptitious look around her, Quadrado set off down it. There were trashcans, a delivery truck and the kind of detritus found at the rear of any business.

The delivery truck rumbled off, its driver forcing her to step aside, as he wasn't for slowing. From her position she could see there were access points for goods in to all the businesses. As the largest, the Auric took up the most space: as well as a loading hatch, there were a pair of doors.

Quadrado walked towards the doors. The loading hatch had a metal roller door and would undoubtedly lead to a busy area;

therefore it didn't matter. The doors would be for staff coming and going. They'd also provide points where the Mantis could potentially get into the casino.

Fletcher would want to know more about the doors. She did too. Both were metal clad, in metal frames. Each had a handle, but there was a keypad beside them; therefore the handle was nothing more than something to hold.

As she got to within eight feet, one of the doors opened and four men came out. All four had the same hard look and an identical tattoo below their chin.

"Who are you and what are you doing here?" The first out of the door was the speaker. A tall man with flinty eyes and a voice that was husky enough to tow a sled across the Arctic on its own.

"Sorry, I just got my ass lost." Quadrado tailored her language to her new look, but kept her tone bright and breezy, as if she was an innocent airhead unaware of the threat presented by the four men.

"It's a dead end. You don't get lost in a dead end. What are you doing here?"

"I told you, I got my ass lost." She set off to walk past them. "No harm, no foul."

"I don't think so, lady."

CHAPTER TWENTY-THREE

The guard at the gate of Canyon Village had the air of an ex-cop. There was arrogance in his body language, and Fletcher was sure the guard would recognize that he was driving a rental car and thus condemn him for having the audacity to not meet the automotive standards set by the residents. That didn't matter. He'd done his research and learned the mayor lived in Canyon Village.

The cheap suit Fletcher now wore, along with his changed look, gave him a different vibe from his usual, but it wasn't enough to have the guard welcoming him.

"Can I help you, sir?"

The honorific suggested politeness, but the question was asked in a tone that spoke of pre-formed ideas.

"Hi, I'm here to see Mayor Crane. Name's Grant Fletcher."

"I'm sorry, sir. I haven't been given your name."

"That's not a problem. I'm sure that if you call the mayor's house, they'll tell you it's okay."

Fletcher had gotten Quadrado to include a request to drop their names into the mayor's orbit when she'd first contacted Thomson. He didn't know if the request had been actioned, but its purpose was supposed to be something of a universal key to open doors for them. Or in this case, a gate.

"Mayor Crane left an hour ago."

"Then Mrs. Crane will vouch for me." Fletcher made sure there was a gentle smile in his tone, as if he was completely at ease with the delay. The truth was he wasn't sure if the mayor would know of him, let alone the mayor's wife.

The guard went back to his booth, a slight limp evident every time he put weight on his left leg.

Fletcher watched as the guard picked up a phone. Two minutes later the gates eased open and he was waved through.

Cam Drewitt lived halfway along one of the main boulevards. His house a faux Georgian effort that made up for in size what it lacked in originality. As Fletcher drove past the house, he saw nothing except a huge wall, and a pair of paneled gates that looked strong enough to withstand all but the most serious assaults.

There were no trees showing above the wall, but he did spot a post at the corners of the property. The posts were laden with CCTV cameras and what he suspected were sensors that would pick up an intruder scaling the wall. Short of pole-vaulting high over the wall, there was no way of crossing that wouldn't set off alarms. And that was before you took into account the CCTV cameras.

There were no separate entrances for delivery drivers and staff, just the one main gate. It had a keypad at one side and a screen that could be used to show the face of someone in the house, or perhaps it was a biometric scanner. Fletcher would have stopped for a closer look, but there were two cameras overlooking the road side of the gate, so he kept his distance.

What he did to give himself a chance to examine the gate was double back and park on the opposite side of the boulevard. With his cell at his ear to give the cover of taking a call, he examined the gate and wall as much as he could.

For all the boulevard was tree lined, the trees were all stunted poplars that didn't begin to reach the boundary wall's height, let alone have branches overhanging it that could provide an access route for the Mantis. It could be that she might trick her way into the house, but after recent events, the one thing Fletcher was certain of was that anyone who might be a target would be extra cautious and less susceptible to being fooled.

He was sure the Mantis would follow the same logic, and to the best of their knowledge, she hadn't used trickery yet.

With the front of the house a bust in terms of being easy to attack, Fletcher started the car and set off to check out the rear of the property.

CHAPTER TWENTY-FOUR

Quadrado eyed the two men blocking her way with suspicion. So far, they were intimidating but not threatening. They stood a way off from her, but their hands were loitering at a place where they could move for a weapon with the slightest provocation.

There were also the two behind her to worry about. She heard no footsteps indicating they were closing in on her, but that didn't mean they hadn't drawn their weapons and aimed death at her back.

The tall one in front of her seemed to be the top guy, as he was the one who was doing all the talking.

"What are you doing back here? You been with a john?"

"Huh?" It took a moment for Quadrado to get the meaning of his question. "God no. I'm not a hooker. I told you, I took a wrong turn and got my ass lost. Now if you'll haul *your* ass out of my way, I'll get on with my day and leave you to do the same."

It was as she finished speaking that Quadrado wished she'd come up with a better lie for being at the back of the casino like this. The thug had unwittingly handed her a plausible excuse and she'd batted it away before thinking. A far stronger reason would have been to say she was looking for a dog that had run off, but she hadn't thought of that.

"You're going nowhere, lady." A click of his fingers and one of the men behind her put what she was sure was a pistol to the base of her skull. "You don't come down here and skulk about. We been watching you." He pointed upwards towards the casino, and when Quadrado's eyes followed the direction he was indicating, she saw a camera. "You ain't here 'cause you're lost. You're here 'cause you're looking for something. Something to do with the casino. Now do you want to tell me what you're looking for?"

Quadrado knew the only way she could get out of this was to drop all pretense. "I'm an FBI Special Agent. If you let me get my ID from my purse, I can let you see my badge."

"No dice." A hand extended towards her. "Give me the purse."

There was silence as he took the bag, although that changed when he opened it. "Well, lookee here, she's got a gun." He gave it a quick inspection. "A Glock 17. That's a serious gun to be carrying around, lady."

The Glock got tucked into his waistband.

"It's standard FBI issue. Look in the zippered pouch, that's where my badge is."

He produced the wallet that held the badge and opened it, his eyes narrowing as he scanned it.

"See?" He showed it to the thug at his side. "Looks like the real thing, don't it?"

"Of course it's the real thing. I *am* an FBI agent. I'm working the Mantis case. I'm here looking for possible areas where she may breach your security, because my partner and I believe your boss, Cam Drewitt, is a potential target."

"Bullshit. You're here because you're the Mantis and you're scoping us out. Do you really think we believe your bull? The ID is fake. You having an FBI issue gun is a nice touch, but you're selling pigshit and I'm not buying it."

Quadrado's own Glock was now pointed at her head. The other thug in front of her had also pulled his weapon and aimed it her way.

"Okay, lady. You're coming with us. We need some real answers from you, and trust me, we will get the truth from you."

Until she could get a chance to escape or convince them that she wasn't the Mantis, Quadrado knew that it would be in her interests to cooperate. All the same, she couldn't help but imagine their enforcer being the one who'd question her.

CHAPTER TWENTY-FIVE

Fletcher counted the houses until he figured he was opposite the rear of Cam Drewitt's. Drewitt's rear neighbors' houses were just like his. High walls, security measures and little that suggested a warm welcome.

To him the idea of living behind walls like these was wrong. However nice you made your home, its setting would always have the feel of a prison. For Fletcher, part of the pleasure in living in the area he did was the connections made with neighbors. The chats during chance encounters, the favors exchanged, the invitations to dinner or a backyard barbecue. They were what made you feel like you belonged, not high walls and enough security measures to rival Fort Knox.

Where he lived, people looked out for each other. When Rachel died, his neighbors had descended with enough meals to keep him and Wendy fed for a month.

The owners of these houses wouldn't have any of that, and they were poorer for it. Fletcher guessed they probably thought they'd made it when they bought one of these properties. To him being cocooned away in a house like this would be a form of ostracism. Yes, the fancy houses would be plush and filled with the latest gadgets and have garages full of flash cars, but so far as Fletcher was concerned, these fripperies were nothing more than a placebo for empty souls.

He turned around and took another pass, hoping to see something he might have missed. He didn't. The walls were the same, as were the gates and the rooftops he could see. To attack Drewitt's house from the rear would just mean two lots of security to get past.

It was possible one of the residents could be coerced into having their property used as an access route, but it wouldn't be Fletcher's first choice of strategy.

All the same, as he steered the car back towards the gates at the entrance to Canyon Village, Fletcher was making a mental note to have Quadrado or the FBI team find out who all of Drewitt's neighbors were. Perhaps there would be one who might be in collusion with the Mantis.

CHAPTER TWENTY-SIX

There was no answer when Fletcher knocked on the door of Quadrado's room at the motel. He hadn't gotten an answer when he'd called her. Nor when he'd messaged her. It wasn't like her, and while he knew it was unlikely that she'd run into a problem, they'd agreed that if one of them called or messaged, the other would at least acknowledge the attempt to contact if they couldn't answer or form a proper reply.

Rather than hang around waiting, Fletcher sent another message, saying he was going to the Auric. They could then meet up somewhere nearby.

Fletcher hailed a cab and tried to imagine a way he could potentially attack Drewitt at his house as a lone agent, were he the Mantis. He knew the ruthless assassin was capable of locating the right person to disable security measures, but that was only one part of the issue. While security cameras could be put on a loop showing a previous time's footage, independently arranged measures like motion detectors might not be connected to the same system as the cameras. He'd be the first to point out that he wasn't an expert when it came to such things, but he couldn't see a reason why a motion detector or pressure pad would need to be connected to a server. To his mind, they'd connect to an alarm and nothing more. It was possible that whoever installed the system had aligned everything for remote testing, but a canny operator would recognize it as a potential security breach. Not connecting them also added the bonus of a site visit for maintenance or repairs, which would also mean a callout fee.

Even if all the electronic measures were taken out of the equation, there was still the challenge of getting into the house undetected. Cam Drewitt would have enemies in Las Vegas and, as such, he'd take precautions with his safety. The evidence of that was on the posts at the corners of his walls. Fletcher expected that the doors to his house would be solid affairs with dead bolts on the inside that would prevent easy entry. They'd certainly prevent a silent one. The windows would likely be bullet-resistant glass and therefore impervious to any clandestine attempts to cut them. As a lone assassin, the Mantis would need the element of surprise on her side. She'd want to be inside long before a gun was aimed her way, let alone a trigger pulled. To breach a building that is being defended by an unknown number of people requires a team, not a solo operative, no matter how good they may be.

The more he considered it, the less Fletcher liked the house as a place where the odds of a successful strike against Drewitt were in the Mantis's favor. That left the casino or another of his businesses. Another location might make the hit easier, but to date, the Mantis had made statements with her kills. A sniped shot would be safer for her. A drive-by, less safe, but still less dangerous than her chosen methods. She hadn't done either of those things. She'd entered her target's domain and executed them and anyone who stood in her way.

For his money, if Cam Drewitt was on the Mantis's list of targets, he reckoned the casino had to be better than the house as a location for the hit. If Quadrado responded to his messages before he got there, so be it, he'd only have wasted a small amount of time, and as he wasn't driving, he was using the time to process all the information he'd learned.

There was, of course, the slim possibility Quadrado was still pissed at him for cutting off so much of her hair. Or that she was teaching him a lesson for his sudden absence earlier in the day. He doubted it though. Quadrado was feisty, brave and smart, but she wasn't petty, and nor was she someone who played games. If she was pissed at him, she'd speak up and tell him rather than show him through her actions.

As he walked through the Auric's foyer, Fletcher's eyes were hunting for the scarlet shade that was now Quadrado's hair color. Now he was looking for it though, he realized he'd never noticed how many people dyed their hair that particular hue.

Three times he circled the casino floor. His eyes both searching for Quadrado and checking out the casino's security measures. He found plenty, but not so many that he didn't feel the Mantis could breach them. As for Quadrado, he found not a single sign of her.

As he'd told her to check out the casino's exterior, he planned to do the same. He didn't want to think so, as it was a betrayal to her, but he couldn't help but wonder if the reason he couldn't find Quadrado was because she'd bailed on him. She'd been shaken up by the card the Mantis had put in her pocket, and if there had been another incident, it wasn't so unthinkable that she'd lost her nerve.

What he didn't dare think about was that the Mantis had followed up on her threat.

CHAPTER TWENTY-SEVEN

There were throngs of people on the street as Fletcher made his way back out of the casino. He figured they would be the early evening crowd, happy to spend a few hours gambling, but not such hardened players they planned to spend the whole night chasing their luck. Many of them were gawping at the eclectic styles of architecture employed by the hotels and casinos, heading to one of the many shows or simply enjoying the various displays put on by the dancing fountains.

The multitude of people wandering about made navigating a path while observing all around him tougher than it ought to be, but he managed. With the casino mid-block, his main concern was finding the rear access.

Fletcher found the alley that led to the back of the casino. It was as he'd imagined it would be. Secure on all points, and as he walked towards the end of the alley, he counted two security cameras surveying the alley itself and another two pointed at the doors along the rear of the building.

A row of industrial-sized trash cans was on one side of the alley and when he'd passed them he stopped. Quadrado wasn't here. Though, even if she were here, there would be no sign of her. For all the area wasn't well maintained, it was monitored and he knew no good would come of poking around looking for clues when there were cameras covering the area.

Fletcher turned to leave as one of the doors opened. Four quick paces got him behind a trash can. He peeked out enough to see who was exiting the casino.

It wasn't Quadrado. Not even close. The four people who came out could never be classed as having Mexican heritage like she did, nor indeed as female.

In fact, each of them wore their masculinity as if it were a badge of honor. They postured and preened as they fanned out and started walking down the alley. The leader had his hand inside his jacket, and Fletcher knew from the way his arm was positioned the man was holding a gun.

"Dude, we know you're hiding behind a trash can, so why don't you save us all a lot of trouble and come on out?"

Fletcher had his gun in his hand ready for use if needed. He was confident he could ease himself far enough out from behind the trash can to get at least three shots off before any of the men had time to draw their weapons and return his fire.

That was the nuclear option though. He didn't know what this set of henchmen wanted. They wouldn't know who he was, so there was a strong likelihood they were just here to run him off. If that was their aim, there was no reason to kill them. With four opponents, there could be no half measures. He'd be shooting to kill.

Therein lay another issue. The trash cans were on the right-hand side of the alleyway, and there wasn't space enough for him to round them. This meant he'd either have to shoot the henchmen with his weaker left hand, or step far enough away from the trash can to be able to use his good right hand.

He could try to intimidate them with a drawn pistol, but with four to watch at once, it would be an uneasy standoff, and if just one of them was shielded by another, they'd have the opportunity to draw their weapon unseen.

Fletcher wasn't sure enough of his reasoning to start shooting, so he took the barrel of his gun between thumb and pinkie and extended his arm out from behind the trash can.

"I know you have a gun in your hand. As a sign of good faith, I'm showing you I have a gun and that I'm not holding it in a way that I can use it."

While he wasn't sure enough to start shooting, he was sure he wanted to find out why these guys were so quick to come out, if not brandishing weapons, then at least holding them in a semi-discreet fashion. His first guess was that they were reacting to even the mildest possibility of a threat with greater alacrity and force due to their fear of the Mantis. This made him wonder if they, or their boss, knew something he didn't, and that made him curious. He was also wondering if Quadrado had befallen a similar fate as himself.

Whichever way up he stood it in his mind, Fletcher always came back to the same point: letting these henchmen take him in for a spot of questioning seemed like an opportunity for him to learn as well. All he had to make sure of was that he was always in a position where escape would be possible.

CHAPTER TWENTY-EIGHT

Fletcher allowed himself to be led by one of the four henchmen while the other three followed behind. He had no idea how many guns were aimed at his back. For the time being that didn't matter at all. He had no desire to get physical yet. There was still too much to learn.

The henchmen were in the same position as him and therefore he didn't expect to come to any great harm just yet. There might be a few punches thrown his way, but he could take that. After the life experiences he'd had both in and out of the Royal Marines, he'd grown used to feeling beat-up. It wasn't something he welcomed, but nor did he fear it.

The henchmen were efficient and practiced with their movements. Each knew their role and, as such, they barely had to speak to each other as they guided Fletcher into the building.

"I'm telling you guys, you've no need to do this. I was round back of the casino because I heard there were some hookers there."

"It's Vegas, you don't need to come creeping round here to get yourself a hooker. And what makes you think we'd allow that kinda thing outside our casino?"

For all the henchman referred to the Auric as "our" casino, Fletcher knew he was nothing more than a low-level grunt employed to keep order and little more.

Fletcher had to find a way to get past the henchman and speak to either Drewitt himself or one of his top men. That way he'd have a chance of learning something, and he'd also have the chance to broker a form of peace as he had with J.B. Ronson.

The unpainted walls told Fletcher the area they were in was not one the public had access to. When the leading henchman stopped outside a door and used his thumb on the biometric lock, Fletcher tensed his muscles and rose onto the balls of his feet, ready to react if things turned ugly.

A hard shove propelled him forward until he was in the room. Quadrado was in the room. Her hands were tied around a five-inch steel post that ran from floor to ceiling. She had a cut above her eye, and it trickled blood down her cheek. Her lip was split, and there was a redness to the skin on her face that spoke of multiple slaps.

It was all Fletcher could do to not whirl round and fell each of the four men he'd allowed to take him captive.

"In you go. Arms round the post." Another shove forward. "Come on, we haven't got all day. You and this nosy bitch can keep each other company."

Fletcher did as he was bid and put his arms around the post. As he did so, he eased his hands into fists he clenched as tight as he could. The difference it made to the thickness of his wrists wouldn't be much, but it would be something and that was enough for him. When he'd been pushed into the room, he'd noticed that Quadrado's wrists were secured with traditional hemp rope. The leading henchman made a good job of tying his hands together. There was so little play as to be negligible, and the coarse fibers were already digging into his tensed muscles.

A blow to the back of the head thrust Fletcher forward until his face collided with the steel pole. It was the same move he'd used on the moron who'd grabbed Quadrado in the Gold Mine. Fletcher reeled a little, but fought the dizziness the blow had induced and turned to face the four henchman.

"There was no need for that."

"Oh, boo-hoo. You can expect a lot worse than that if you don't cooperate."

CHAPTER TWENTY-NINE

A fist buried itself in Fletcher's kidney. The blow hard enough to have him staggering round the pole until he was facing the opposite way.

"Jesus, man. There was no need for that. I'm cooperating with you." Fletcher raised his head to look at the lead henchman. "You got no need to beat up on me. I'll tell you what you want to know."

"I know you will." Another punch, this time to the other kidney. "So who are you and why were you really round the back of the casino?"

Fletcher made a point of keeping his eyes away from Quadrado's as he launched into a lie. "I told you. I was looking for some company. I lost a packet at the tables and needed comforting. Couldn't afford none of the usual hookers I see, but there was this guy who told me that some cheap hookers could be found behind the Auric." Fletcher nodded Quadrado's way. "Looks like you got one here."

Quadrado launched herself forward at him. Her right leg trying to kick him round the post. "You goddamn douchebag. I ain't no hooker. I'm a waitress in a diner. You better hope I don't get my ass free before you, mister, because I'll kick your sorry butt all the way from Vegas back to wherever the hell you're from."

The attack from Quadrado was welcome. He'd noticed there was defiance in her eyes, and he'd gambled that she'd pick up on his calling her a hooker and react against him. The altered speech patterns to fit with her new look were a touch he approved of, as was the attempt to attack him. For all it looked like she was trying to hurt him, he knew she was positioning herself so the pole limited her movements and therefore her attempts to attack him weren't anywhere near as violent as they looked.

"Ease up. It was an honest mistake."

"You pair are full of bull." The lead henchman slapped each of their faces. "I saw the way she looked at you when you came in. She knows you. There was recognition in her eyes. Wasn't there long, but it was there. So, which one of you is going to tell us why you were both scoping out the back of the Auric? And why, lady, are you changing your story? First you claimed you were FBI and now you're saying you're a goddamn waitress. Which is it?"

"Scoping out? Jeez, I was looking for some action. I've told you. Next thing I know is you're pointing a gun at me and then beating on me. On top of that, you've tied me to the same post as a crazy woman. I never met her before and you're saying she recognized me. Damnit, man, you've misread it. Think about it from her position. She's been captured and tied to a post. When she saw me coming in, she either mistook me for your boss, or someone who's come to save her. As for her saying she's FBI, haven't you heard of women getting a fake badge to protect themselves from sex attacks?"

The lead henchman snapped off a punch that twisted Fletcher's head to one side and split his lip. "Nice try. I'll tell you what I think, shall I? I think she's the Mantis, and you're her backup. She came armed. So did you. You're playing the innocent, but I reckon you're a lot tougher than you look. So, you wanna tell me what's going on, or do I have to get persuasive with you?"

"Yeah, get persuasive on his ass. Damn creep thought I was a hooker."

A fist was raised until it was an inch from Quadrado's nose. "Either tell us the truth, or zip it, as I may decide to get persuasive with you instead."

"Screw you."

For all the bravery of her words, there was no mistaking the flutter of fear in Quadrado's voice.

"Who or what is this Mantis you're accusing her of being, anyway?"

"What, you haven't seen the news?"

"Of course not. Who comes to Vegas to watch the news?"

The henchman pulled a face. "The Mantis is a woman who's killing casino bosses. And other folks who get in her way. She can get in just about anywhere, and she disappears after her hits. I reckon that we caught her right in our own back yard. It's going to be winner winner, chicken dinner for us tonight."

"Look, believe me, will ya?" Fletcher tried to put an imploring tone into his voice. "I don't know anything about no Mantis nor about no casino bosses getting killed. I'm a construction worker from Ohio, who blew his cash and was looking for a little female company before flying home. How's about giving a dude a break, buddy?"

A violent shove from the henchman slammed Fletcher's nose against the pole. Cartilage will never win against steel. Fletcher's nose broke with a crack and streamed blood down his face.

"I'm starting to lose my patience with you." A pistol was put to Quadrado's temple. "If one of you hasn't started telling the truth by the time I get to three, she dies."

There was no way Fletcher was going to gamble with Quadrado's life. He'd played enough poker to know when to fold and when to bluff. "I'll talk. But not to you. I'll tell your boss, Cam Drewitt, the absolute truth, but not you."

"One."

"I said I'll talk to the organ grinder. Now be a good monkey and go get him."

"Two."

"If it turns out you have caught the Mantis, do you really want to tell Drewitt you killed her before he got to question her?"

The pistol was removed from Quadrado's temple and thumped into Fletcher's. Things went woozy for him as his knees buckled.

CHAPTER THIRTY

Quadrado would have breathed a sigh of relief at the pistol being removed from her temple had it not been used to incapacitate Fletcher. As he slumped, his weight was pulling her to the floor. Rather than try and hold him up, she did what she could to ease him down gently.

The henchman who'd been questioning them scowled at them and the room in general as he leaned over Fletcher's prone body. "You picked the wrong man to insult. Mr. Drewitt has trusted us to guard the rear of his biggest casino, and he's warned us to watch out for the Mantis."

It was then Quadrado realized how Fletcher's last sentence had saved her life. She also caught how the henchman had given his boss a title. That showed a built-in respect for the man who paid his wages. Respect for the boss was a common thing among gang hierarchies, but it usually slipped when the boss wasn't around. There'd be a chance fear also played its part; Fletcher's unspoken warning of Drewitt's reaction, should his men kill the Mantis without giving him a chance to get involved, played on the henchman's fear of repercussions.

"Mmmmmaaaaahhh." Fletcher's eyes opened, and he tried to focus on her. His eyes looked as if he'd spent twelve solid hours slamming tequilas, but his head was lifted from where it had slumped against the post. His ruined nose still leaked blood, and there was a significant bruise already forming on his temple.

Where their legs were intertwined, Quadrado gave a gentle press to offer him some support. He responded with a wink of his left eye, the one the henchman couldn't see.

Fletcher's suggestion of her being a hooker was a masterstroke, as it gave her a chance to show pretend animosity for him. She decided to back that up while they waited for Drewitt to arrive. "The sooner your boss gets here the better. I can't wait to get away from here, away from this douchebag who thinks I'm a hooker. You've got this all wrong."

Quadrado caught the warning in Fletcher's expression. He had a plan of some description and whatever it was, it was clear it no longer involved them pretending they didn't know each other.

Fletcher was rumbling his body about, as if trying to stand. So far as Quadrado could tell, he'd never regain his feet if he didn't pull his arms back to the pole and use its help. For some reason his arms were straight out and against her side as his shoulder pressed against the pole.

"Unnggghhh." Another failed attempt to rise to his feet saw Fletcher slide back onto his butt to the amusement of the henchmen. It was this unusual lack of what Quadrado was beginning to think of as Fletcherlogic that made Quadrado fear the pistol slamming into his temple had done permanent damage, which was affecting both his motor skills and thought processes.

The henchman turned his focus on her. His gaze as friendly as a crocodile's smile. "My men and I think you're the Mantis. What you got to say about that?"

"She's no such thing." Fletcher turned his head and looked up at the henchman. "She's Special Agent Zoey Quadrado of the FBI. Check her purse, you'll find her ID."

"And who might you be?"

"Grant Fletcher, but seeing as how you took my wallet when you brought me in, I dare say you'll know that already."

"Finally, some truth. Are you saying she's really FBI, or are you yanking our chain?"

Quadrado flashed the henchman a hard look. "I *am* an FBI Special Agent. I tried telling you that from the start, but you weren't too keen on listening to a truth that you didn't want to hear."

"Pah. You're shining me on. That's all a cover. You're really the Mantis, and I'm not going to fall for your bull."

Fletcher's elbow pressed against Quadrado's side as he turned to address the henchman. "Maybe if you call the FBI office on Lake Mead Boulevard, and put her on, she can prove she is who we say she is? After all, if she is a fed and you kill her, that's not likely to end well for you, is it?"

"That still doesn't explain who you are though, does it? I've got your name, but you ain't carrying a badge. Nor are you claiming to be a fed. So who the hell are you?"

Quadrado could see uncertainty in the henchman's body language as he stared down at Fletcher. It was this and the idea that he might again strike at Fletcher that made her make a quick decision. She hadn't failed to notice the slur in Fletcher's voice when he spoke, and she wasn't happy about the idea of him receiving another blow to the head.

"He's a specialist fixer. He and I are sent to problem areas to find unusual solutions. The Mantis is such a problem. Fletcher gets the dangerous jobs because, and he won't like this but it's true and you've got the gun, so far as the FBI is concerned he's expendable."

"Then why did you both lie to us?"

"Because we're an undercover unit. Be honest, do I look like an FBI agent? We are who we say we are. You've got the truth from us. Now it's time to let us go before you bring a whole world of trouble on yourself."

"I need proof. You've lied to me once already, no way am I trusting you now."

Quadrado nodded at Fletcher. "Then do what he suggested: call the FBI office and put the phone on speaker. The number's in my cell."

The henchman pulled a face and reached into his pocket and pulled out Quadrado's cell.

He laid the cell out of reach of Quadrado, but the speaker function meant everyone in the room could hear the person who answered.

"Las Vegas Federal Bureau of Investigation, how may I help you?"

"It's Special Agent Quadrado. Can you put me through to Special Agent in Charge Thomson, please?"

"He's in a meeting and isn't to be disturbed. I can have him call you back."

Quadrado added a layer of iced steel to her tone. "Not good enough. Either you get him on the line in the next twenty seconds or both you and he will be clearing your desks tomorrow."

"One moment, please."

It didn't sit well with Quadrado to threaten an innocent with a job loss, but with Thomson being such an asshole, she hadn't dared only threaten his job, in case the woman who answered seized an opportunity to get rid of someone who was bound to be a pain in her butt.

"Damnit, Quadrado, where the hell do you get off interrupting my day like this? I'll have you know I was on a conference call to the director himself, and he wasn't happy about me having to put him on hold. So help me, I'll have your shield if you pull another stunt like this."

"Screw you, Thomson, your threats are as empty as the Grand Canyon."

"Fletcher? I might have known you'd be there. Does one of you want to get to the point of this call? I do have the director on hold, after all."

"The point of the call is to prove a point. That's done, so you can go back to the director now."

Fletcher lifted an eyebrow at the henchman as he cut the call. "See? We're on the level."

"No, you're just well prepared and have a backup team. I'm going to go and check the number online. Then I'll call them myself to verify you're not shining me on."

Quadrado flashed the henchman a look. "See when you come back, it might be an idea to bring your boss with you. No offense, but I suspect this decision is well above your pay grade."

CHAPTER THIRTY-ONE

Geoffrey Elliot leaned back in his chair, his eyes on the ceiling and his thoughts in Las Vegas. As director of the FBI, it was up to him to manage a behemoth of an organization, and that meant dealing with people like Eric Thomson. The man was a solid investigator who'd been over-promoted by Elliott's predecessor. He was more than competent at running an investigation, but his people skills were lacking.

Even with all his talent for pursuing bad guys, Thomson had come up short in the hunt for the Mantis. That's why Elliott had called in Fletcher and Quadrado. The fact Quadrado had bulldozed a call he'd been having with Thomson had brought a smile to his lips, although he'd had to think on his feet when a grumbling Thomson came back on the line. Thomson, like Fletcher and Quadrado, had no idea he was the person who'd sent Fletcher and Quadrado to Las Vegas.

Only the directors of other agencies such as the CIA, DEA and ATF knew about the black-ops team that comprised Fletcher and Quadrado. He'd personally pushed for them, and with the backing of the other agency directors, he'd siphoned some money from his budget to fund them.

What had removed the smile from his lips was Thomson's retelling of the conversation he'd had with Quadrado. From what Elliott could gather by reading between the lines, Quadrado had called to prove a point. There had been no need for her to prove anything to Thomson, which meant she'd been proving something to someone at her end of the phone. Fletcher was one option, but he doubted he was involved in any direct way. If Fletcher wanted to prove a point to Thomson, he'd do it with his fists or enough logic to make a computer crash.

Elliott guessed Quadrado was proving she was an FBI agent. If that was true, she was in some kind of trouble. Calling Thomson and getting him to verify it was a smart move he hoped would pay off.

Again Elliott doubted Fletcher was a part of what she was doing. He was too capable to get himself into a position he couldn't get himself out of. In turn, this knowledge merely increased his concern for Quadrado's well-being.

Elliott was smart enough to recognize he had two options. He could either stay out of things and leave Fletcher and Quadrado to it, as he'd always done. Or, he could raise an alarm and have Thomson find Quadrado.

Both options had pros and cons. Leaving them to it might endanger Quadrado, and while he'd never shirk a difficult decision, it wasn't his goal to risk lives needlessly. On the other hand, perhaps Fletcher and Quadrado were playing an angle he couldn't see, and any action he took would not only blow their theories apart. It might put them in greater danger.

He sent an email to Quadrado, asking for an immediate update, and turned his attention to his computer. If he heard from Quadrado in the next couple of hours, he'd know she was okay. If not, he'd have to rethink his decision on not intervening.

CHAPTER THIRTY-TWO

The door to the storage room burst open and the henchman strode in. Somehow his face was both pale with shock and flushed with anger.

Fletcher didn't know for certain what had upset the man, but he guessed that upon checking the number and getting through to the FBI, he was furious with himself for making the mistake of not believing them. The paleness could be inspired by fear. If he'd told his bosses about the two people he'd captured and they'd learned one was an FBI agent, he may fear he was in line for a reprimand.

Whatever was bugging him, he was livid and he strode over to Fletcher, gun drawn and raised as he closed the gap.

Fletcher could see the henchman's eyes. They were fogged by red mist as the pistol was aimed at Fletcher and the knuckle of his trigger finger began to bend.

There was nothing Fletcher could do to protect himself save aim a kick at the henchman's leg.

For all the man had lost his senses, he still had the wisdom to stay out of reach. Fletcher's boot missed by two inches, which in the circumstances might as well have been two miles.

"Jesus, Ned. What the hell are you playing at?"

One of the other henchmen barged Ned to one side as he pulled the trigger. The bullet flying close enough to Fletcher's shoulder for him to feel it disturb the air.

"They're dead. Mr. Drewitt, his wife. The Twins are dead as well. Every one of them has been shot in the left eye and the heart. That's the Mantis's work."

Fletcher recalled Drewitt's advisors were twins. As much as he wanted to think about what it meant for the Mantis to have struck far earlier in the day than usual, his immediate focus had to be on surviving the next minute. He tried again to get to his feet and into what had now become his usual shoulder-against-the-pole method of standing. When Ned had been out of the room he'd made four more attempts as the henchmen laughed at him.

Let them laugh. He'd feigned worse injury than he'd received from the blow to the temple. He'd seen Quadrado register concern at the slur he'd put in his voice. She had nothing to worry about: he had a plan, and every time he'd tried to rise to his feet, it had caused a distraction from his real purpose—getting his hands free.

The ropes binding him were too tight for him to slip his hands free, but his trick with the tensed wrists had given the bindings a tiny degree of slackness. Since the rope had gone around his wrists, he'd taken great care not to pull at the rope in an attempt to wriggle free. Such moves only worked in the movies and never with large powerful hands like his. Instead, he focused his energies on manipulating the ropes into a position where he could pick at the knot. It wasn't easy, but he'd managed to do enough to loosen the first part. If he could just buy enough time to finish what he'd started, he'd get his hands free and then he'd have a chance.

Fletcher would be the first to admit that four on one, with the four all armed, wasn't ideal, but if this was to be his last day on earth, he wanted to be on his feet and fighting when he was killed, not tied up like an errant dog.

"Hey, Ned." Fletcher turned his head to where the henchman was holding Ned back from coming at him again. "Surely you can't still think Quadrado is the Mantis. She's been here the whole time since you caught her. Your buddies will vouch that she never left the room. You went to call the FBI office yourself, so surely you must know we're who we say we are."

Ned managed to get round the other henchman long enough to kick out at Fletcher. His foot slamming into Fletcher's side and reigniting the pain from the kidney punches he'd taken earlier.

"I never got to make the call, did I? They were all in the office, dead. Blood and brains everywhere and now it's all turned to shit. It's your fault. You're here as a distraction so she could get in. No way are you walking out of here. Not after what you've been a part of."

Fletcher made another attempt to rise as Ned wrestled with the henchman who was holding him. One of the others who'd been guarding them joined the grappling, his hands closing around the gun.

Not knowing the third man's intent, Fletcher resumed work on the knots, only to feel a warmth at his side as Quadrado positioned herself so she could help while all four henchmen were all distracted. Her fingers were dexterous and able to reach the parts of the knot where he couldn't get any purchase.

Fletcher felt the ropes loosen then start to slip away as Quadrado freed him. He was rolling away from the pole as Ned pulled the trigger again, shooting his own buddy in the foot.

CHAPTER THIRTY-THREE

The howl from the man whose foot had been shot filled the room, but Fletcher didn't let it distract him. He had fractions of a second to pounce before the henchmen realized he was free and turned their entire focus his way.

Ned was wrapped up with the guy who'd joined the grappling; the fourth was at the back of the room and he was drawing a weapon as Fletcher scrambled to his feet. The fourth man was too far away for him to get anywhere near, so he launched himself towards Ned. He had two reasons for doing this: the first was to use him as cover; the second was that Ned was the nearest source of a weapon. The shot man was backing away, hopping on one foot as he cursed Ned and the world in general.

A hard shove sent the hopping man toppling to the ground. For a second or two, Fletcher wouldn't have to worry about him. Ned was trying to bring his pistol round to shoot Fletcher while one of the men who'd been grappling with him was drawing his own weapon.

Ned was the closest to getting a shot off, so he'd have to be dealt with first. At least that was Fletcher's theory until a bullet whipped past his ear. Ned's reaction to the shot from the fourth man gave him the chance he needed. A backhanded upward sweep of his left hand deflected Ned's pistol out of harm's way. There was no room for thoughts of mercy, no reason to believe he'd receive any from the henchmen, so Fletcher didn't hesitate. His right hand drove up in a palm strike that connected with Ned's chin and lifted him off his feet and dropped him in an unconscious heap.

Rather than waste time trying to retrieve Ned's weapon, Fletcher turned his focus on the man who'd been at Ned's side. His gun was now drawn and was coming Fletcher's way.

This time Fletcher knocked the guy's arm with a forehand sweep that drove the gun downwards. As the guy spun with the change in his equilibrium, Fletcher helped him on his way by looping an arm over his shoulder and around his throat.

A bullet grazed Fletcher's shoulder as the fourth man snapped off a shot. It was a minor wound, but he knew it'd sting like slapped sunburn later. Fletcher now had the henchman in front of him as a shield to prevent the fourth man getting a clear shot. The henchman's sweat filled Fletcher's nose as he hauled the guy onto his toes and made sure no part of his body was exposed to shots from the fourth man.

This was the critical point. If the henchmen were anything like professional, Fletcher and Quadrado were screwed. All they'd have to do to was aim one of their guns at Quadrado, and Fletcher would have no choice but to surrender to them.

The fourth man extended his gun, his intention to shoot Fletcher clear and obvious. As he took slow steps forward, the man Fletcher had in a headlock was raising his pistol to shoot at Fletcher's head over his shoulder.

Fletcher's empty right hand closed over the pistol and twisted it from the henchman's grip before he could pull the trigger, the man's index finger snapping as he wrenched the gun free.

Now he had a weapon, Fletcher could even the odds.

The fourth man panicked and pulled his trigger three times in quick succession. Each bullet slammed into the henchman Fletcher was holding. Fletcher didn't know if the guy was dead or not, but all strength went from his body, turning him into a dead weight, pulling Fletcher downwards.

Fletcher resisted the gravity-induced pull long enough to put two bullets into the fourth man's chest.

He slumped to the floor, allowing Fletcher to rest easier. There was still the guy who'd been shot in the foot to deal with. He was scrabbling on the floor, trying to get his weapon out from under him.

Fletcher trained his pistol on the guy. "Don't bother, buddy. It's over. Nice and slow, put your hands where I can see them."

The guy froze, his body language screaming indecision. Fletcher could see it from his point. He'd expect Fletcher to kill him. Yet he knew he was at a disadvantage and any attempt he made to fight back would put him at far greater risk than complying would. There would also be his future to think of. If he did get out of this alive and Fletcher got away, there would no doubt be fear of punishment from whoever would fill Cam Drewitt's role in the organization.

"I said put your hands where I can see them." Fletcher made sure his tone was hard, but he leavened it with his next sentence. "I don't want to shoot you. You saved my life. Put your hands where I can see them and let me check you for weapons and we're cool. Do you understand me?"

The guy nodded. A series of rapid head jerks that flopped his hair back and forth.

It took Fletcher two minutes to frisk the other three henchman and relieve them of their weapons and then free Quadrado. Two were dead, one was unconscious and one was emitting low moans at the pain in his foot. He'd know he was going to face prison time. That he'd have to take what was coming to him, or live in fear if he ratted the gang out to reduce his sentence.

All of Fletcher's and Quadrado's belongings had been tossed into a corner, so they retrieved them and put all the henchmen's weapons into Quadrado's bag as she called in the incident. No doubt Thomson would have some colorful thoughts about this whole mess.

CHAPTER THIRTY-FOUR

Special Agent in Charge Thomson was angrier than anyone Quadrado had ever seen. He was barking orders at his team like a guard dog that's just been alerted to an intruder. Agents were scurrying all over the areas where there were fatalities and casualties. The CSI technicians were busy setting up their equipment and placing markers to identify pieces of evidence.

To the untrained eye it would look like chaos, but Quadrado could see the efficiency of the various professionals as they went about their jobs.

Thomson's eyes swiveled their way and bulged. Somehow his face turned a darker shade of puce without him stroking out. "You pair." A finger jabbed their way as a vein in his forehead pulsed. "You're responsible for this mess. All the people who have died here today, their blood is on your hands."

"I beg your pardon?" Quadrado wasn't going to let Thomson get away with such a crass statement. "You're blaming us for this, are you? You were on the case long before us. But it was our theories that put us at the scene of the crime. Where the hell were you and your men?"

Thomson marched over to them. His face a beacon of blood vessels that were threatening to burst. "We were following procedure. Unlike a silly girl and her trained ape, we were doing our jobs in the proper way. There's no blood on my hands, and my conscience is clear. If you hadn't been here, at least two of the dead would still be alive. Dammit, girl, you pair might well be the Mantis for all I know."

"Don't be so ridiculous. If you want us gone, kick it back up the chain of command. We'll see who they decide to keep and who they tell to stay home. Spoiler alert, it'll be us that stays on the case. I bet you complained about us to the director when you spoke to him. Did he tell you to run us out of town? That he'd speak to the man who sent us and get us pulled? I'm guessing not because it's you that's threatening it, and you don't have the pull to make that happen. As for calling me a silly girl, that just shows what a buffoon you really are. It's the twenty-first century, you Neanderthal."

From the corner of her eye, Quadrado noticed movement at her side. She went to step in front of Fletcher, lest he take a swing at Thomson. God knows the man deserved it. She was tempted herself. She knew that as a rule Fletcher had a remarkable amount of self-control, but his moral compass was on a different heading than hers, and it often pointed to violence.

"You don't know jack and that's your problem. I'd advise you don't make it ours." The words from Fletcher were spoken as he turned away and set off walking towards the hallway that led out.

"Hey, I'm talking to you."

"No, you're not. You're making a cretin of yourself, and I'm done listening."

"Come back here, Fletcher. That's an order."

Fletcher kept walking, and Quadrado followed him. Screw Thomson, he was nothing more than a man out of his depth, floundering to keep his head above the water.

Thomson tried again. "Hey, asshole. Who the hell do you think you are, walking away when I'm talking to you?"

"I'm someone who respects their colleagues." Fletcher stopped and turned to face Thomson. His expression harder than a quadratic equation, and his tone icy cold. "I'm someone who doesn't address a hard-working agent who's just escaped a potentially fatal situation as a silly girl. I'm someone who works with people rather than lording it over them. I'm someone who can park their anger and focus on the real issue. I'm also someone who doesn't have to listen to you. I'm someone who knows better than to raise a hand to you in a room full of Feebies. You want to keep shouting at me and Special Agent Quadrado, that's up to you, but from now on I'm going to be in a place where none of your men will be around to witness me recalibrating your sensibilities." Fletcher gestured down the hallway. "Want to come this way and shout some more?"

"Screw you, Fletcher. You can't threaten me."

"And yet, I just have." Fletcher waved a hand, indicating all the agents and technicians in the room. "All of these good people will be witnesses if I recalibrate your sensibilities, but you have to ask yourself, how many of them will be hoping and praying they get to watch that recalibration? How many of them have you chewed out for no good reason? How many have you belittled? Insulted?" Fletcher pulled a fifty from his wallet and held it up. "I'll bet you this that if I did recalibrate your sensibilities, they'd all put money in to pay for my defense lawyer."

Thomson stood there trying to find a comeback from Fletcher's verbal assassination. When he couldn't find one, he settled for pulling his phone out and tapping it as if he was making a threat.

CHAPTER THIRTY-FIVE

Fletcher kept walking along the hallway until he found a room that had neither FBI agents nor technicians in it. The room itself was an office space, and if the piles of delivery notes were anything to judge by, it was where the casino's bookkeeper worked. He took a chair and waited until Quadrado did the same.

"What do you think?"

"I think Thomson is a complete idiot. I swear, Fletcher, part of me was hoping you'd hit him."

"That wasn't what I meant. No way would I give him the satisfaction of making me lose my cool. I actually meant what are your thoughts regarding the Mantis and this hit?"

Quadrado scratched at her ear and pulled a face that furrowed her brow. "I'm not sure what to think. Either she's been watching the place and, like that Ned guy suggested, used us getting captured as a distraction, or she was planning the hit anyway and it's just a massive coincidence that she struck when we were being held captive. What I don't want to think about is the idea that she was watching either one of us and took her opportunity there and then."

Fletcher was pleased Quadrado reached the same conclusions he had. He hadn't wanted to put the thought into her mind that the Mantis was watching them, as she was already nervous enough as it was.

"Yeah, I was thinking that way too. The timing is off as well. The other hits took place in the middle of the night. This one was early evening. Why?"

"Would it coincide with a shift change? Is she getting access by posing as a server or bartender?"

"It's possible, but it's the first thing Thomson and his men will look at. As will the gangs who've been targeted. We've heard nothing to suggest that's been the case previously, so it's unconfirmed." Fletcher leaned back in the chair and lifted his feet onto the desk. The more relaxed he was, the better his brain could function. "We should also consider external factors that are out of the Mantis's control. Maybe it was something to do with Drewitt's routine. Perhaps he was someone who didn't stick to a routine other than when he was in his office here. I've seen Drewitt's house, and I wouldn't class it as an easy target for anything short of a tank. If I had to assault it, I'd want a dozen men and I'd expect heavy casualties. Therefore the hit on Drewitt would have to take place here. Yes, there would be more people, but that's never worried the Mantis before."

"Say you're right, how does the Mantis find out his routine?"

"Good old-fashioned surveillance. Basically watch and follow each target until you learn the weaknesses in their routine that can be exploited."

Quadrado's fingers drummed on her leg. "The hits are every other day. Two days isn't long enough to get a proper idea of someone's regular movement. She must have surveilled her targets long before she started killing them."

"Agreed. Now, in terms of gaining access, I reckon she was running her final checks in preparation for the kill when she learned of a commotion. That commotion would be first you and then me getting captured. She wouldn't know what it was, but she'd know it would give her an opportunity she could exploit. Now, look at things this way: Drewitt's henchmen were distracted by us. One of the Mantis's victims was found near the door we were brought through. That tells me the henchmen dealing with us were replaced by someone else. Ned obviously didn't scour the whole building counting up the death toll. He must have just gone from where we were to Drewitt's office and then back. Somehow the Mantis managed to get in with a gun, take the replacement guard out, get to the office, kill another henchman, and then the Twins and both the Drewitts. She then made her way back out the way she'd entered. She might well have been planning the hit for later in the day, but when she saw what happened to us, she sized the opportunity we presented."

"So Thomson was right: it was our fault. We do have their blood on our hands."

"No way do we have any blood on our hands. The Mantis was coming for them anyway. Our part in it just brought it forward. If she'd been planning to come anyway, all the guys who brought us in would have died. Two of them are still alive, though, so celebrate that instead of beating yourself up about the ones who died." Quadrado's face told its own story about her thoughts on their culpability. Fletcher had said his piece, so there was no point carrying on that part of the discussion. "Right, can you do two things for me? One, get Thomson here: we need to bring him up to speed; and two, get a copy of the security tapes sent to your laptop."

Quadrado whirled away to do his bidding.

Two minutes later, Thomson opened the door with a pair of burly agents at his heel. They were alert enough to be witnesses and big enough to be bodyguards. At least that's what Fletcher expected Thomson wanted him to think. He thought of them as a couple of palm strikes, a headbutt and a knee to the groin.

"What do you want, Fletcher?"

"Look, we're never gonna be buddies but, like it or not, we're on the same case. So, in the spirit of cooperation, I want to share our thoughts with you."

"Go on?" Thomson eyed him with the suspicion a gazelle reserves for an approaching lion.

Fletcher ran him through what they'd worked out. Explained how he would have done it if he were the Mantis. By the time he'd finished, there was less suspicion but still plenty of animosity from the FBI man.

"Why are you telling me this? If you're looking for a pat on the back, you're not going to get one."

"I told you, it's the spirit of cooperation. You're in charge of the Las Vegas office, so you must have some skills. Personally I don't care whether it's you or us who catches and stops the Mantis. I just think she needs to be stopped as soon as possible." Fletcher stood and made for the door, the movement enough to alert the two bruisers Thomson had brought with him. "We've a couple of ideas we want to follow up on. If we think of anything that needs to be shared with you, we'll share it. Quadrado will check the FBI databases for updates on what your men learn about today's hit. I'm going to trust that you'll update the files in a timely fashion and not play any games like delaying the inputting of information to deprive us of a lead."

"Damn you, Fletcher. Don't you dare accuse me of doing anything that might hinder an investigation."

"Like I said, I'm going to trust you."

With his point made, Fletcher left and went in search of Quadrado.

CHAPTER THIRTY-SIX

Fletcher went to the bathroom and brushed his teeth to rid himself of the taste of the chili dog he'd picked up from a street vendor. He'd only managed two bites before dumping it in a trash can. Quadrado had been wise enough to not eat from the questionable vendor, but he'd expended a fair amount of energy during the brief fight with the henchmen and felt the need to replace it with some food.

Quadrado fired up her laptop and logged into the security tapes. They watched as first Quadrado was captured and then Fletcher. The urge to fast forward was strong, but Fletcher wasn't one for taking shortcuts with such a critical piece of evidence.

A drinks company made a delivery five minutes after Fletcher was taken. It reversed up to the loading bay, and from an internal camera they could see a pallet jack remove two pallets stacked with bottled beers and cases of spirits.

Even as he watched the footage, Fletcher's eyes never left the cameras that were on the alleyway. Nothing happened anywhere that he could see.

Ten boring minutes after the truck left, a delivery van appeared. Not FedEx or UPS, a smaller, local firm. The driver got out; they were wearing a liveried uniform, and a baseball cap was jammed over unruly blond hair. There was no way to tell if the driver was male or female, and this jangled Fletcher's instincts. Before he could speak, Quadrado paused the footage and opened up a browser window.

A google search of the name on the side of the van brought up nothing. No mentions of the firm in any of the results. No social media posts, no website, nothing.

"Run the phone number, see what you get."

As Quadrado typed the number into her laptop, Fletcher fed it into his cell and listened to the ringing tone until an answer machine kicked in. When he heard the recorded voice say Spring Valley Medical Center was closed, he cut the call. On Quadrado's screen was a series of search results for the medical center.

"The name on the van is false. That firm doesn't exist. I'm going to run the license plate. How much do you want to bet that's false too?"

"A dime."

"A dime? Wow, you're a big spender."

"I only bet what I can afford to lose."

"Here we go." Quadrado's fingers danced over the laptop's keypad. "That license plate is registered to a '67 Chevy Impala from Missouri."

"That's a nice car."

"I'll take your word for it. This is looking very promising." Quadrado's voice quivered with excitement as she went back to the footage. Fletcher understood why; finally, they had a solid lead to follow.

Fletcher found his fingers restless as he watched the delivery driver retrieve a small package via the van's side door and set off towards the door they'd been taken through.

They had to switch to a different camera to follow the driver as they knocked on the door. The whole time the driver was in the alleyway, their head was down and there was no way of identifying their gender. There were no feminine curves, but nor was there a muscular build. Fletcher was reminded of his attempt to profile the Mantis. He'd guessed she'd have the body of a distance runner, and that's exactly what the delivery driver had. If it was the Mantis, the androgynous look was a clever move. Guards would be more vigilant about unknown females, but by dressing in a way that made her look male, the Mantis was giving herself an advantage.

The door opened and the package was offered to a man.

"Wait. Pause it there and zoom in on his face." Fletcher didn't waste words on manners, and he knew Quadrado well enough to know she'd not mind, that she understood how things were.

Quadrado filled the screen with the man's face. "It's the guy we found dead near the door, isn't it?"

"Yeah. Can you advance it frame by frame?"

After a little fiddling to get the right option, the screen jerked forward frame by frame. The man seemed to be standing still at first, but after perhaps a minute of the stilted footage, Fletcher was able to discern that he was staggering backwards, his face a mix of shock and confusion and pain.

Fifteen seconds later a bullet hole appeared in the middle of his forehead and he slumped to the ground, although in real time it would have been around one second.

"Okay, so we've got her. That's the Mantis dressed up as a male delivery driver. Let's catch this bitch."

"I'm with you there. Let's see when she comes back out though. And here's a thought, maybe the legend of the Mantis is a false one. Maybe the Mantis is actually a man and the legend of them being female is a smokescreen to allow them to slip under the radar. You've seen the footage, that driver could be a man or a woman."

Quadrado didn't answer. There was no need for her to, and they resumed watching the footage until the driver returned. Rather than come from within the building, the driver walked down the alleyway, jumped into the van and drove away.

Fletcher wasn't sure about the way the driver came back for the van. It made logical sense not to leave it behind, but there was all kinds of risk in returning from a different direction to collect it. If it'd been him, he'd have returned to the van the way he'd arrived.

That way he'd be able to deal with any reception committee that had formed. To enter the alleyway and travel as far down as the Mantis had was fraught with danger. This made him think the Mantis had either had to revise her plans, or had planned this route all along.

He considered what he knew for certain. They'd seen the Mantis shoot her way in. They'd been in a room with Drewitt's henchmen while the Mantis did her stuff. There had been no great commotion when they'd exited the room. He'd been prepared for more henchmen. There weren't any though. Those who survived would have seen the writing on the wall and got out while they could. The Mantis's path back to the van would have been free and clear, yet she hadn't used it. That told him she'd never planned to come that way; it had always been her intention to return for the van from the outside of the alleyway.

He thought about how he'd plan that. His first thought was that he'd have left the van far away and walked down the alleyway. The Mantis hadn't done that. Instead she'd purposely left a possible treasure trove of evidence in a place where it might not be easy to retrieve. This along with the work that had been put into mocking up the van spoke of a lot of preparation. Again he thought about how he'd plan for a potentially hostile situation awaiting him in the alleyway. The answer was simple: he'd want a spotter there. Someone to watch for activity, both obvious and furtive.

"Run that footage again for me, please. Specifically, focus on the camera that shows the best view out of the alleyway."

As the footage came onto the screen, Fletcher got Quadrado to zoom in a little so the footage they were watching showed little of the alleyway and lots of what was beyond it.

At this level of zoom, the picture was grainy at best; all the same, they could see passing vehicles and could make out the shapes of people on the street. A vehicle appearing and parking was what Fletcher was hoping for. It would be how he'd plan it.

That didn't happen. All they got was a clear view of pedestrians going about their day, and the odd vehicle driving past.

"Hold on." Fletcher pointed at the screen and craned forward for a closer look. "That person there, it looks like a woman. They seem to keep walking back and forth. Can you zoom in and track them?"

Quadrado reached for the laptop. "I'll do my best. I'm not an expert at this."

For ten minutes they watched as the shape of the woman moved back and forth. From time to time it looked as if she was glancing down the alley. Her hand was in front of her as if she was holding her cell. It was a common look these days. Fletcher recognized the stance as one of Wendy's favorites.

At one point the woman paused and looked straight down the alleyway. Quadrado had it paused and was zooming further in before Fletcher could even make the request.

"Aha. Just remembered this." Quadrado directed the laptop's cursor to a settings tab and navigated her way to a part Fletcher had yet to see her use. She pressed a symbol and the clarity of the screen's image became twice as good. "That's as good as I can get it."

"That's good enough for now."

Fletcher took in the screen's contents. There was a clearer view of the woman. He could make out she was wearing a form-fitting dress and a huge pair of sunglasses that covered most of her face. To his suspicious and cynical mind it was a variation of his and Quadrado's attempts to make themselves look different.

"I can't see how she's involved." Quadrado's fingernail pointed at the woman's knees and then her feet. "That dress is way too tight. And she's wearing heels. I wore a similar dress to a friend's wedding along with a pair of heels and all I could do was totter back and forth. No way could I take a decent stride, let alone break into a run if I thought I'd been spotted. She'll be the same."

Quadrado's logic made sense to Fletcher apart from one fact. The dress went from mid-calf right up to the woman's neck, but it was sleeveless and she wore no jacket. That might not raise a red flag to most people, but this was winter. He checked his cell for today's weather.

"Look at this." He held the phone for Quadrado to see. The average daily temperature was listed as being around forty-four degrees Fahrenheit, not too far above freezing. "It was overcast today. She'd have been frozen wandering about dressed like that for the best part of a half hour."

"You clearly don't know much about women and what we'll suffer in the name of fashion, do you? Personally I'd sooner wear her dress in these temperatures than the heels she's got on. You're on the wrong track with her. I reckon she's a call girl, waiting to be collected by her pimp."

CHAPTER THIRTY-SEVEN

As much as she disagreed with Fletcher's insistence the woman was the Mantis's spotter, Quadrado couldn't find a better candidate. So either Fletcher was wrong and there was no spotter, or she was. If she was wrong, she wanted to own her mistake and be the one to prove it. To do this she needed some peace. Something she wouldn't get with Fletcher either looking over her shoulder or spouting theories.

"You didn't eat much of that chili dog. Why don't you go and find a decent place that does takeout while I keep looking at the tapes?"

With Fletcher gone she returned to the footage. The first thing she did was check the notes she'd made regarding the timeline. Her capture had been the first event of note. So she began watching from that point and focused on the area where the woman was. There was no sign of her, so she kept watching the footage until she appeared.

The woman made an appearance seven minutes after the hoods had taken Quadrado captive. This was forty-two minutes before Fletcher had walked down the alleyway. Quadrado watched the footage in two-minute installments until Fletcher came into view. The woman was in every still she viewed. Not one of the stills showed her face beyond what could be seen below the sunglasses; not one gave any clue as to her identity. She was just a woman pacing back and forth, fiddling with her phone.

At the point where Fletcher was taken, the woman paid attention to the alleyway, walking with her head turned and ignoring her phone. It was out of kilter with the rest of the footage, where she'd not been paying any great mind to anything but her cell.

A minute after Fletcher disappeared into the building, the woman put the cell to her ear. Five minutes later the Mantis appeared. Eleven minutes after that, the Mantis walked back down the alleyway, climbed into the van and drove off. The woman at the end of the alleyway walked out of shot the exact moment the van started moving.

Quadrado's hands fluttered in front of her chest as she thought through the implications. It didn't matter that she was wrong and Fletcher was right. He wouldn't crow about it. He'd just move on and so would she.

What was important was they now knew the Mantis wasn't working alone. That she had help. All the same, there were many questions that needed answers. Why was the woman dressed in a way that made her memorable, and not in warmer, looser clothes? Why didn't the woman just retrieve the van? Was the Mantis really a duo, or even a team, rather than an individual? How many people could the Mantis have working with her? There were many more questions, but to Quadrado these were the ones whose answers seemed the most likely to break the case apart.

Fletcher returned with food. It was as he placed the cartons on the desk that she realized she'd never specified what she wanted. He'd got a stacked burger with fries for himself and a vegetable burrito with a side of Caesar salad for her. How he'd known to not get her a meat dish was immaterial, he didn't miss much, and she couldn't help but feel a swell of fondness for the carnivore who'd paid her enough attention to notice her dietary habits, but had retained the decency to never pass comment.

"You were right, the woman seems to be an accomplice." Quadrado pointed at the laptop as she lifted the burrito. "I checked the timelines. It's all too perfect to be coincidental."

"Okay. What does that tell us?" Fletcher grabbed a handful of fries and dunked them in a carton of barbeque sauce. "That she has a team or at the very least an accomplice. That she's trusting of that person or persons. We knew she was meticulous in her planning anyway, but when you have a team, you have to plan for everyone doing exactly what they should, and for the possibility of screw-ups. When it comes to screw-ups, the error might not be the person's fault but an external factor. Basically, the more complicated the plan, the more moving parts, the more there is for things to go wrong. If it was me, I'd want to keep things as simple as possible so there's less chance of nasty surprises."

Quadrado liked the way Fletcher's mind worked. He was coming straight to the same points she was, but looking at things from an operational point of view.

"So you think the Mantis's team is a small one? I was wondering if maybe there was a whole gang of them and it was different people, or cells within the team, who enacted each hit."

"It's possible." Fletcher pulled a face she knew was nothing to do with the bite of burger he'd just swallowed. "If you're thinking about a terrorist-style outfit with individual cells unaware of each other, it's not beyond the bounds of probability, but I just don't know. Think about combining every hit as a single operation. So many of the victims were killed by a person with the same characteristics. The autopsy reports and crime scene analysis all said basically the same thing when it came to the Mantis's height. The ballistics reports say it's the same guns on every hit. An organization might be able to recruit a group of killers with ease, but what are the odds of them all being the same height? Of them having the skills the Mantis so clearly has? Of them passing the murder weapons back and forth? These hits have all been done by a top-level professional. Believe me when I say this, I wouldn't fancy my chances of pulling off the hits the Mantis has; so, the idea someone has a private army of the country's best assassins, and they're all of a very similar height, doesn't work for me. I'd say the Mantis has no more than two or three in her team and that's including the Mantis herself."

"I guess you're right." Quadrado licked some of the sauce from the burrito off her fingers. "Answer me this, then. Why did the woman acting as a lookout or spotter dress the way she did? Surely it would have made more sense for her to be in warmer clothes that allowed her more freedom of movement."

Fletcher pointed at his mouth as he munched a mouthful of fries. Only when he'd finished and washed them down with a slurp from his drink did he speak. "Good point. I'd certainly suggest the dress was wrong in terms of allowing her to move quickly. I'd also suggest that it was a disguise of sorts. My best guess is she was playing the part of a hooker and therefore she dressed appropriately for that role. The fact she wore such a dress also tells me of their confidence. The woman for wearing it, and the Mantis for allowing it. In their place, no way would I allow you to wear something that could put you in danger."

"Oh, thanks. Big old Mr. Fletcher is going to now dress me up like his own Barbie doll." Quadrado stuck her tongue out to show she wasn't serious. She got what Fletcher was getting at. If the woman was captured, there would always be a chance that she'd rat out the Mantis. Therefore the Mantis would consider every possible aspect in terms of its threat level to both the mission and her own liberty or life.

"Now you've got it." Fletcher winked as he pushed the last of his burger into his mouth.

"There's another aspect we're not considering. Two women working together in this way is highly unusual in terms of a hit team. What's their relationship? Are they friends, accomplices, family or lovers?"

"They could be any of those. Whichever it is, they'll have to have complete trust in one another. There's no way on earth I'd take the risks the Mantis is taking without having absolute faith in the rest of my team."

"Agreed." Quadrado bundled up the takeout packaging into a neat pile. "But forgetting about the operational side, two women working together to perform hits like this is unheard of. Think about all the serial killers who've achieved fame. The only female serial killer I can think of off the top of my head is Aileen Wuornos. Women kill in a moment of passion. They defend themselves with a knife or iron when their abusive partner reaches their breaking point. It's the male killers who either work as assassins or become serial killers. They are the true sociopaths."

"There were no female serial killers until Wuornos came along, or at least none who got caught and made the headlines. The Mantis will be the same. She's a groundbreaker, a pioneer in the fight for equality for assassins. For all we know there could be a thousand female assassins out there, and they just haven't come to the attention of law enforcement yet."

Quadrado's eyes widened. "You think?"

"Not entirely, but as my daughter loves to tell me, women's stories have been neglected throughout history. Why not this area too? Maybe they're just too smart to get caught." Fletcher took a slug of soda. "Anyway, our prime concern is the how. The whole why thing about the Mantis is something for after we've stopped her. I've been thinking about why the Mantis came back for the van. It doesn't make sense to me. It would have been far easier for the woman to just walk up to the van and drive off once the Mantis was inside. The only reason I can think is they don't want us to know there's more than one of them. The Mantis's myth and reputation has us looking for one person, not a group, and that's what they'll want to continue."

"Yeah, I got the same. We need to see where the woman went. Where the van went. The main FBI team is sure to be on the same trail as us. If they're not, they'll soon catch—"

"So we either need access to the city's tapes, or whatever the FBI have found by watching them."

Quadrado didn't wait for an answer, she just put in a call to Forbes. He'd get them what they needed.

CHAPTER THIRTY-EIGHT

Geoffrey Elliott pushed back from his desk and leaned into his chair. Thomson had made a formal request that Fletcher and Quadrado be removed from the case, and Quadrado had sent through a report letting him know of their findings and what happened to them at the Auric.

Thomson had been easy enough to deal with. Elliott had simply blamed Washington and told the priggish Las Vegas head Fletcher and Quadrado were there to stay and that he'd do better if he focused on his own team instead of worrying about them.

The news Fletcher and Quadrado had found themselves in such a predicament didn't sit well. Had the Mantis entered that room, his prize black-ops team would have been among the victims. For a brief moment, he considered pulling them for their own safety. It was only a fleeting thought. Fletcher's life was risked on every mission he handed him. In fact, he'd been chosen due to the very fact that so far as Elliott was concerned, Fletcher was expendable.

Fletcher was resilient though. He'd gotten himself untied and had taken down a room of armed attackers. Another reason why he'd been sent to Vegas.

Quadrado's report detailed a lead missing from Thomson's. It had been handed over to the FBI to pursue, but it showed that, as a team, Fletcher and Quadrado had brains to back up Fletcher's brawn.

A greater concern was the pressure being put on Thomson to stop the killings. The press were having a field day, and there wasn't a news outlet that wasn't savaging him for his failure to capture or stop the Mantis. That pressure was following back up the line, and over the last couple of days, Elliot had fielded calls with the Nevada State Gaming Commission's chair, the Nevada governor and the mayor of Las Vegas.

That had been him supporting Thomson. The man wasn't a political person, so it was better he smoothed ruffled feathers and left Thomson to run his investigation. This was something he'd been doing since the start of the investigation, and while he disliked the chore, it was far better he do it than the brusque Thomson. What none of them realized as they were dumping their complaints and concerns on his desk was the fact that he was also getting heat from Washington, that he was also having his strings pulled.

The phone on his desk buzzed.

"Yes, Marie?"

"I have the White House Chief of Staff on line three, sir." Marie spoke with the measured tones of someone who could be surprised by nothing in life. She ran his admin department with a velvet glove, preferring to inspire rather than terrorize. Thomson could learn a lot from her.

Elliott knew what the Chief of Staff was calling for. Knew how the conversation would go. She'd have her own agenda and would expect him to fall in line with it.

"Thank you for calling. How may I be of service?"

"Cut the corporate bull, Geoff. What's going on in Las Vegas and why isn't this Mantis woman either dead or in prison by now?"

The opening barrage was typical of the Chief of Staff. To the public she presented herself as a warm, compassionate woman who always had an ear for the views of the populace. Behind closed doors, she was as ruthless as any man he'd met and possessed of a drive to make a difference few could emulate. She'd been granted office by a president who'd been elected on the back of common-sense policies and had reunited voters of differing affiliations with a "One Community for All Citizens" message. The Chief of Staff's mind was sharper than a diamond cutter, and Elliott pitied the attorneys who'd once faced her in court.

"I have a good man leading the investigation. He's a detective first and a politician second. I've supported him with every resource he's asked for and have made it known that he need only ask for more and it'll be granted. In addition, I have the best profilers in the country working on the case, have sent the most intuitive pathologists to Las Vegas and have removed any budgetary constraints from the investigation. In short, ma'am, I've given him a blank check and the best people the FBI has to offer."

"Yes, Thomson's your man there, isn't he? I met him at some function or other once. As I recall he came across as a self-important little prig. Tell me, Geoff, does he know you're hanging him out to dry like this? I see exactly what you're doing. You're supporting him from afar. You've given him men and resources, but you are keeping a distance from the investigation. Don't think I'm not aware of this." The line went silent for a moment, but Elliott kept his mouth shut in case he interrupted her next diatribe. "You're probably thinking about offering to go to Las Vegas yourself and then suggesting you'd have to neglect some of your other duties." That was exactly what Elliott had been thinking. "Let me spell it out for you. I want this Mantis character stopped, and stopped damn soon. You can take whatever course you want, but if it's not resolved by the end of the weekend—and I have the president's backing on this—it won't just be your man in Las Vegas who's clearing their desk. Am I understood?"

CHAPTER THIRTY-NINE

Fletcher watched the footage of the Mantis both leaving the van and returning to it several times over. He was looking at her gait, the posture she adopted and the way that her body language spoke of relaxed athleticism. His aim in rerunning the footage was to gain as much of an understanding of her as he could. He wanted to know if she favored one hand over the other. If she had a tic that might make her recognizable.

It was the sixth run-through that confirmed his suspicions. "The Mantis didn't come back for the van. Someone else did."

"What?" The surprise in Quadrado's tone was thicker than an elephant sandwich. "There's three of them? Show me why you think that."

"Watch this." Fletcher cued the Mantis arriving and set the footage running. "See how when she's just out of the van, the top of her head is level with the roof? Now look at her feet as she gets the parcel from the back, they're aligned in parallel. Think about that parcel. It's large enough to hold a bag and a change of clothes. Maybe a wig and different shoes. A pair of low heels would be my guess, as they'd alter her height after she'd changed."

"Okay. I take your point. But why do you think someone else came for the van? Why not just leave it where it was?"

"Because the van is a decoy. It's what we're meant to focus on." Fletcher jumped the footage forward until it showed the delivery driver returning and walking down the alleyway. "Now, pay close attention to the driver's feet and their height."

Quadrado said nothing until the van was moving and Fletcher had paused the footage. "When she was opening the van door, she seemed to be shorter by an inch or two. Could she have been slumping her shoulders?"

"I thought that too, thought it was maybe relief at a successful hit, but I took another look." Fletcher rewound the footage enough to rerun the point they were discussing and paused it as the Mantis was opening the van's door. "See? She's got her back straight, just as she had when she arrived."

"You're right, she does. And when she is standing still, her toes are pointed inwards. That's not a stance you adopt by accident. It's a habit that's as ingrained as how you brush your teeth. Damnit, Fletcher, she's got at least two people helping her out."

"Yep. The van will disappear off the radar somewhere. It'll be tracked until it's in a place where there are no cameras and then the driver will change the license plate, remove the decals and bring it on back. Either that or leave it burned out for the FBI to find."

Quadrado washed a hand over her face. "Let me get this straight in my head in terms of a timeline of events. The spotter arrives, then the Mantis. The Mantis goes in, kills who she needs to kill and then finds somewhere for a rapid change. She messages the spotter and the fake driver. The fake driver retrieves the van and leaves a trail for the FBI to follow, and the spotter wanders off. Meanwhile the Mantis slips into the main body of the casino and loses herself in the crowd. She's right under the noses of everyone who might be looking for her while we're chasing a trail of shadows. Damnit, Fletcher, it's simple and yet it's genius."

"You'll get no arguments from me. We've got to let Thomson and Forbes know about this. They need to also check the casino's internal security tapes, to look for any female emerging from a place they shouldn't be. I don't think they'll find anything that way, but they'll have to look."

Quadrado nodded as she reached for her cell. She had to get patched through to Thomson, as Forbes wasn't available. When he came on the line he was gruff but resigned.

"What is it this time, Quadrado?"

With the cell on speaker, Fletcher and Quadrado explained their thinking to Thomson.

"Goddamn the pair of you. I hate to say it but it sounds like you're on the money."

"Thanks." Fletcher wanted to keep Thomson on side, as he knew admitting they were right would have cost the man more than he wanted to pay.

"The decoy who drove the van away, could you tell if they were male or female?"

"Not with any certainty. They were dressed the same way the Mantis was when she arrived, and you'll have seen for yourself how androgynous the look was. If I was pushed I'd say female, but I wouldn't bet a lot of money on it as I could easily be wrong."

A pause for a deep inhale of breath. "What in the goddamned hell are we dealing with here? A team of evil Charlie's Angels? Jesus Christ, one female assassin running around is bad enough, but for her to be supported with a team of spotters and decoys just makes it worse." Another pause as Thomson gathered himself after his frustrated outburst. "I'll have agents check for signs of her accomplices at all the other hit sites."

"What about the spotter? Did you find where she went?"

"Yeah, she walked up the Strip and into the Midas Touch."

Fletcher couldn't miss the dejection in Thomson's tone. "It sounds like that isn't good news. Want to catch us up?"

"The Midas Touch is owned by the biker gang whose boss got whacked. Every time we step foot in one of their places, even if it's only chasing a suspect, they refuse to cooperate without a warrant. We tried but got stonewalled. I've got someone chasing a warrant as we speak, but we're still looking at a couple hours. She'll be long gone by the time we get anywhere near her."

"I see." Fletcher did, but where there was little Thomson could do without a warrant, there was plenty he could do. Even as Quadrado was cutting the call, he was lacing up his boots and beginning to form a plan of attack.

CHAPTER FORTY

Fletcher didn't have much of a plan as he walked into the Midas Touch casino. His basic strategy was to talk himself into a position where he could speak to either the man who'd replaced Ken Beltzer or one of his lieutenants.

On his way here he'd called J.B. Ronson, to see if the man had anything for him, but there was nothing new to be learned from him. Fletcher had told him of the hit at the Auric, but didn't mention the Mantis had a team.

The casino floor of the Midas Touch was bedecked in quasi-Greek statues, and had a distinct air of trying too hard about it. The waitresses weaving their way among the crowds were dressed in toga-style robes that left so little to the imagination they bordered on obscene. Such outfits would always attract a certain kind of customer; though why any gambler would need titillation at the tables when there were so many strip clubs in Las Vegas was beyond Fletcher. In Fletcher's opinion, dressing the female servers in such a way was both demeaning to them and insulting to their customer base.

He was maybe twenty paces inside the casino when he spotted the first security guard. He made his way to the man by a circuitous route.

"Excuse me, I've just had my wallet stolen and I'd like to know what you plan to do about it."

The security guard was a minimum of fifteen years younger, four inches taller and at least a hundred pounds heavier than Fletcher.

From the way he floundered for an answer to Fletcher's questions, it was obvious he'd been hired on the strength of his size rather than his intellectual acumen. Lots of people recoil at the idea of taking on a big, dumb fighter. Fletcher thought otherwise. Large fighters with small wits were slow to move, their weight, muscle and intellect often limiting the moves they used. Nine times out of ten they were easier to deal with than a smaller, more nimble fighter who had the brain power and the agility to counter moves and react in an offensive rather than defensive way.

"Erm. Now then. Well. I guess you'd have to speak to Mr. Gallimore about that."

"Who's he?" Fletcher made sure there was a desperate air about his body language and tone. Not aggressive, just irate. "I tell you, man, if I don't get some justice, I'll be suing this casino."

The threat was an oblique one. The guard wouldn't want to be unhelpful to someone threatening to sue, yet at the same time, he was a grunt and someone putting in a claim against the casino wouldn't affect his pocket.

"He's my supervisor." He unclipped the radio on his utility belt as if he were a Wild West gunslinger going for a quick draw. Unlucky for him, he didn't get enough of a grip of the radio and it flew from his fingers and landed at Fletcher's feet.

Fletcher handed the radio back and made a show of irritation at the guard's incompetence as the radio was lifted to the guard's mouth.

"Mr. Gallimore. Can you come down to section three, please? We have a minor situation. Over."

"I don't think having your customers robbed is what anyone would call minor."

Fletcher was still playing the role he'd assumed. The guard was full of bluster, making his job as a guard seem far more important than it was, and Fletcher hadn't missed the fact he'd released the speak button on the radio before saying "Over."

"Actually, sir." The guard was on surer footing here and straightened his back with a self-importance that wasn't merited. "We have codes for different levels of severity of any situation."

"I still don't get how you can describe theft as minor."

The guard was saved the mental gymnastics of trying to justify the codes' various levels by an older man wearing the same uniform and a weary expression. Fletcher understood the man's pain. If he had to work with the likes of the young guard, he'd tire of it in quick time.

"Thank you, I'll handle this now." He gave the guard a gentle push and turned his attention to Fletcher. "I believe you're claiming to have been robbed, sir. Can you tell me where it took place?"

"It didn't happen." Fletcher peered at the man's name badge. Vince. The young guard hadn't worn one, which, along with his manner, suggested he was new to the job. "It was a line I used because I wanted to speak to someone with a little bit of authority, rather than one of your lackeys. I need to see your security tapes for earlier today. It's connected to the murder of your old boss, Ken Beltzer. Can you help or do you need to kick it up the food chain?"

"I believe that the Mr. Beltzer you're referring to was at the Smoking Wheels casino. That's a different place altogether."

"Yeah, I know that, but I also know the same people own both, so why not cut the crap and either let me see what I need to see, or let me speak to a man who's got the balls to make a good decision."

"You're just another FBI agent who's trying to get round the rules. No way, pal. Go away and come back with a warrant. That's the only way you'll see our tapes."

"Wrong answer." Fletcher took a step back, raised his finger until it was jabbing in Vince's direction and lifted his voice until it would attract the attention of those around them. "C'mon, buddy, you have to do better than that. My wallet has been stolen from my pocket in here and you're calling me a liar." Fletcher circled an arm above his head. "The thief is probably still here. Probably stealing from your other customers right now and you're doing nothing about it."

Around him the other patrons of the casino started to feel their pockets, make sure their bags were secure and other basic precautions that they should have been doing anyway. The actions rippled outwards as word of the potential thief spread. One or two of the gamblers started heading for the exits, which played right into Fletcher's hands.

"Quit it, buster. There's no need for that."

Fletcher tapped his jacket pocket. "That's where my wallet is. I can produce it and apologize for a false alarm, or I can keep making accusations until your casino is empty. Your choice."

Over Vince's shoulder a man walked towards them. He wasn't very big, but his presence carried ten times any threat the young guard could ever exude.

"Zip it and keep it zipped. I'll ask the questions. Now you listen to me, don't think for one moment that if you start running your mouth again that you won't get yourself thrown out onto the street. And I'm not talking about the street out front if you catch my drift."

Vince's threat bounced off Fletcher unnoticed. His eyes were on the guy who was now at Vince's shoulder. Tattoos escaped his shirt collar and cuffs, and there was a languid demeanor about the man, as if he didn't care whether someone gave him a million bucks or tried to kill him.

"There a problem here, Vince?" The man's drawl was so Southern it practically dripped Cajun spices onto his chin.

"This guy wants to see our security tapes. Says it's to do with what happened over at Smoking Wheels." Vince stepped back. "He's all yours, Ter."

Ter and Fletcher eyed each other with a mixture of respect and animosity. Fletcher could tell Ter was the kind of man for whom violence was a pastime, yet there was no way he was going to let the guy dominate him.

He pointed to a quieter area of the casino floor.

"Shall we talk over there? Considering what I've got to say to you, I'm pretty sure you don't want it being overheard."

CHAPTER FORTY-ONE

"You a cop? A fed?" The questions were fired at a quick pace for a Southern drawler, but they were still easy to understand despite the thickness of Ter's accent.

"Neither. Consider me a concerned citizen who's trying to make the world a safer place."

"Then why do you want to see *our* security tapes? There ain't nothing happened here."

"Have you heard about the latest hit by the Mantis? It was over at the Auric. Cam Drewitt and several of his men are now being fitted for a toe tag." Fletcher thought it best not to mention that one of the kills was his or that another was down to friendly fire. "An accomplice of the Mantis was seen entering your casino. That's why I'm here. That's why the feds are busy getting a warrant."

Ter did his best to not show that he hadn't heard about what had happened at the Auric, but there was a fractional widening of his eyes that gave him away.

"You sound like'n you're tapped into the system. You sure you're not a fed?"

"Do I look like one?"

"No. You look like a hard-ass. Or at least someone who wants to give the impression of being a hard-ass."

"I could return the compliment, but I'm not here to argue with you. I want your cooperation, and in return I'm happy to give you mine. Your boss Beltzer is one of the Mantis's victims. Half of Las Vegas's casino bosses are after her. How high do you think your stock would rise if you were able to catch her, or help me catch her?"

Ter didn't speak and Fletcher didn't press him to. He wanted the man to reach his own conclusions. If Ter got the credit for taking down the Mantis, he would earn rapid promotion through the ranks of the former biker gang. Maybe one day he'd lead it, or be entrusted to run one of its operations. It was an appealing carrot he was dangling, and he could see Ter was tempted.

"What cooperation are you looking for from us? And what will you give back in return?"

The fact Ter made it about the casino or gang rather than just himself was telling. He was a company man, a man whose personal ambitions could be set aside for the greater good when necessary.

"You and I watch the security tapes together. When I find the person I'm looking for, I'll point them out to you. We then watch where they go, what they do and where they end up. After that we go our separate ways to look for the person." Fletcher made a point of looking at his watch. "In a couple hours tops, the feds'll be arriving, warrant in hand. If you don't take this deal now, it's going to expire on you, because the feds sure as shit won't tell you who they're looking for."

"You're taking great care not to say if'n it's a man or a woman you're looking for."

"Wouldn't you in my position?"

Ter nodded and set off walking. "You got a deal."

Unlike Fletcher's expectations, the room Ter led him to wasn't full of different screens with a team of operatives watching them. It was a private booth, eight by eight, which had a desk, a chair and a flatscreen monitor that covered most of one wall. On the monitor were eight different viewpoints.

"Is this all you got, eight cameras?"

Ter gave a throaty chuckle as he shook his head. "We got eight of these rooms. Sixty-four cameras, all overlapping. Casino floor is cut into thirty-two sections, which means that at all times, two operators have the same image on their screen. There are nine operators at work on every shift, which means there's always one spare for comfort and meal breaks."

Fletcher recognized the pride in Ter's reciting of the casino's monitoring systems and made a connection. "This is your baby, isn't it? You're the one who set up the security and now you oversee it."

"Give the man a prize." Ter clicked his fingers to get the operator's attention and jerked a thumb over his shoulder. "Go take your break. I'll take over."

Ter got himself seated and began inputting a complicated password into the computer without looking at the keyboard.

"The target entered the Midas Touch via the second door along from the Auric. The time would be ten after six today."

"Okay. That's something to go on at least. You want to tell me some more or have you got trust issues?"

Fletcher didn't as a rule have trust issues, but as he suspected that Ter would screw him over at the first chance, he was being guarded with the information he held. All the same, as soon as the woman appeared on the screen, he'd have to identify her to Ter, so there was nothing to be gained by being secretive.

"She's wearing a pale yellow dress that clings like a coat of paint, has dark hair and huge sunglasses that cover half of her face."

"Now we're getting somewhere."

Ter set the appropriate footage rolling and together they watched the comings and goings of various patrons of the casino until the woman walked in. "That her?" Ter's finger pointed unnecessarily at the screen, as there was only one woman in shot.

"It is. Now let's see where she goes."

"Sorry, buddy. This is the end of the line for you." A finger was aimed at the door as Ter rose from the chair. "Why'n you trot off now and leave this to me."

"No chance. We had a deal."

"Deal's expired. Now do the wise thing and leave."

CHAPTER FORTY-TWO

Fletcher's punch should have knocked Ter clean across the small room and into the far wall. Instead it sailed past his torso as he twisted away. When Ter curled back to his original position, his right arm was arrowing the heel of his palm towards Fletcher's chin.

By both leaning back and batting Ter's arm upwards, Fletcher was able to avoid being felled by the vicious blow. The dodge and counterstrike were more than good enough to give Fletcher an indication of how capable and fast Ter was.

Not only had he reacted with great speed to make sure Fletcher's punch missed him, the palm strike was the perfect reply. As he'd surmised earlier, Ter was a far greater threat than the self-important youngster.

A series of low kicks from Ter drove Fletcher backwards until his butt collided with the wall. In theory having your back against a wall in a fight is a good thing. It means that nobody can grab you from behind. Even so, you never want to be in contact with the wall, as you can't wind up a punch and can only throw a limited amount of weight behind it. That's why boxers never want to find themselves pinned on the ropes.

Fletcher tried a kick of his own. His old drill instructor had been explicit on the subject of kicks. Never aim higher than a knee. Kicks at the head and torso left the kicker off balance and open to having their leg caught. When that happened, you'd find yourself dumped on the ground with a very high chance your intended target's foot would very soon make a vicious contact with a part of your body.

The drill instructor had, though, advocated low-level kicks. A heavy boot making forceful contact with a shin bone could result in a break, but the drill instructor's target of choice was the patella, or kneecap. Kicked upwards or sideways, it would at the minimum dislocate and leave tendons and cartilage torn. A savage stamp on the side of a knee when the leg was straight would break bone, resulting in the target being out of commission.

It was Ter's kneecap Fletcher was aiming for. His boot connected, but only a glancing blow. Ter's counter to the move saw him whirl round and deliver a hard elbow that landed on Fletcher's cheek. Instead of an agonized howl from Ter, all Fletcher heard was his own stifled grunt.

The few exchanges they'd had so far were enough to make Fletcher re-evaluate his tactics. Single sniped attacks at Ter were a bad idea; he was too quick and was able to avoid the blows then counter with equally good moves.

Fletcher took a sidestep, and feinted an uppercut to try and draw Ter into a counter he could exploit.

Ter didn't fall for it. Instead he made two feints of his own then threw a pair of jabs followed by a scything right cross that forced Fletcher to concentrate solely on defense.

Again Fletcher feinted to try and get Ter to make a mistake. The act cost him a burst of agony from his already shattered nose and a pair of split lips.

This was a fight Fletcher was losing and he wasn't going to allow that to happen. It was time for another change of tactics. The next time Ter attacked, he charged at the man. Head down so the top of his head took the punches.

Fletcher's right arm was arrowing a sold punch at Ter's gut while his left was reaching for the man's belt. The punch found its mark and was the first blow of significance Fletcher had managed to contribute to the fight. With his left hand gripping Ter's belt, Fletcher carried on forward until he'd passed Ter. The action spinning Ter and giving Fletcher enough momentum to whip Ter round and launch him across the small room.

Ter's head collided with the wall. Hard enough to make an audible thud and introduce a glassiness to his eyes. Fletcher had never been one to look a gift horse in the mouth. The palm strike he delivered to Ter's unprotected jaw lifted the man off his feet and landed him in a tangle of unconsciousness.

A minute later Ter had been frisked and tied up with his belt.

Luckily for Fletcher the computer hadn't timed out through inactivity, so he was able to pick up the footage and set it rolling again. The woman entered the casino and made her way towards the back of the room. There was an aimlessness about her wandering, but Fletcher didn't believe she didn't know where she was going. This was all too well planned for the woman not to have checked out her route before she needed it. The aimlessness was an act intended not to draw attention.

Five times Fletcher had to swap cameras before the woman entered the restrooms. A map affixed to the wall told him which cameras covered where, so he didn't have to trawl through multiple views, but even so it wasn't as straightforward a process as he'd hoped it would be.

Fifteen minutes after she went in, Fletcher began to start thinking he'd missed her leaving. He didn't expect her to come out looking the same. He was sure the large bag on her shoulder would contain a change of clothes; he just had to make sure he didn't make a wrong assumption. By his reckoning, fifteen minutes was the greatest amount of time a woman could be in a restroom without an attendant checking they were okay. The spotter wouldn't want that. She'd want to fly under the radar, not draw attention to herself.

Before he moved onto his next review of the footage, Fletcher ran a quick look at the cameras covering any potential second exits from the restrooms. There were none.

A quick check of Ter found him to be regaining consciousness, so Fletcher gave him another palm strike to keep him still and silent. The fact he'd eventually wake up with an aching, and possibly broken, jaw was his own fault so far as Fletcher was concerned. Had Ter not reneged on their deal he wouldn't have needed to be neutralized.

Fletcher's next move was to source a pen and paper from a desk drawer then back up the footage covering the restrooms until it was fifteen minutes before the spotter entered. One by one he jotted a quick description of each woman who walked into the restrooms, scoring them out when they re-emerged. The spotter walked in, and Fletcher kept at his list until he was sure he'd identified the spotter's new persona as she exited the restroom.

She was now wearing a pair of black skinny jeans with holes at the knees, a cream blouse and a gray jacket. Her hair was blonde, but the same oversized sunglasses were used to cover her face. When Fletcher tracked her movements, she exited the casino in what was pretty much a straight line.

Fletcher rewound the footage and paused it at the best view he had of her. With that done he pulled Ter's phone from his pocket and went to open it. The screen asked for a fingerprint ID to unlock.

The cell phone wouldn't care if its owner was conscious or not, so Fletcher pressed Ter's thumb against its screen and opened the phone. With that done he took several pictures of the paused screen until he was satisfied he had as good an image as he could get. He would have used his own phone, but the cheap burners he'd bought for himself and Quadrado didn't offer that function.

With the images taken, he opened up the email app and sent the images to Forbes along with a brief message. The FBI man could get on with tracing the woman as she left the casino.

As for Fletcher, he needed a little time to think and a catch-up with Quadrado. He thought about returning to the motel, but dismissed the idea in favor of getting Quadrado to join him near where he was on the Strip. He didn't want to have to come back ten minutes after getting to the motel, if he was right and things played out the way he thought they would.

CHAPTER FORTY-THREE

Quadrado eased herself through a series of yoga positions until the Zoom call to Forbes connected. As per Fletcher's instructions, she made sure there was nothing behind her that could help the FBI pinpoint their location, and her IP address was variable which meant it could take days to trace.

Forbes's face was grim when he appeared on the screen.

"I'm after an update. Where have you gotten with the CCTV footage?"

"There's hours of it. And which footage do you mean? The stuff from inside the casino, or the backtracking of the person who drove the van away?"

"Both." Quadrado sat on the bed and rotated her feet at the ankles. "What have you got?"

"There's no telling at which point the Mantis arrived on the floor of the Auric casino. No signs of anyone being furtive or wearing shades or anything like that. We've got agents trying to backtrack the movements of everyone in the casino to see where they entered from, but with three entrances-slash-exits and guests spilling in from the hotel, it's a near-impossible task to trace everyone. Hell, if someone had a room there, they might be in the building eight hours before they reach the casino floor."

"Damn. I get where you're coming from. I guess with all the people moving in and out it'll be like looking for a needle in a haystack."

"Yeah. And we don't even know what the needle looks like. We'll get there. Of course we will, but it's not going to happen anytime soon, as there's a hell of a lot of people to check out."

"Is it possible the Mantis is a resident at the hotel? Could she be hiding in plain sight?"

"We've got people checking that out, but short of giving every last one of them the third degree, there's a lot we have to take a face value."

"I guess." Quadrado didn't push it. If the Mantis was as smart as she portrayed herself to be, she wouldn't book just herself into a room. She'd share with a girlfriend or a male partner to avoid making herself an obvious suspect. "It'd be a bold thing to do staying there after executing a hit on the boss."

"Very. It wouldn't be just us she'd have to worry about. If Drewitt's men found her first, she wouldn't have an easy death."

"What about the driver who collected the van?"

"Hah. That's very telling in itself." Quadrado had just enough time to start getting excited before Forbes crushed any hope she had of getting a decent lead. "As best we could tell it was a woman. Her face was covered with a baseball cap, and she had blonde hair the same as the person who got out of the van. We backtracked her movements to see where she came from. She emerged from a side street, walked along the Strip, cut behind the Auric and then climbed into the van."

"How's that telling?"

"I'll send you the footage so you can see for yourself. But the long and short of it is that she walks at a steady pace from the moment she appears to the moment she gets into the van. No hesitation, no loitering and no lengthening her stride."

Quadrado got it as soon as Forbes was finished speaking. "It was all timed to perfection, wasn't it?"

"To the second would be my guess."

"I won't insult you by asking if you're checking for people making the same journey in the days before so their timings are on the money."

A smile crept into Forbes's voice although it never touched his face. "We've got people on it right now."

The footage came into Quadrado's inbox, so she put it on as she talked. As the woman walked along the street, there was something about her that caught Quadrado's full attention, so she cut the call with Forbes and focused in on what she was looking at.

CHAPTER FORTY-FOUR

Fletcher waved Quadrado over as she walked into the bar. It was an out-of-the-way place, two streets back from the Strip and more suited to locals than tourists. A selection of TVs were showing various sports programs where former players rehashed what viewers had seen for themselves.

The bar was an earthy kind of place where people minded their own business and expected the same consideration in return. A couple of guys were shooting pool, and there was a jukebox which appeared to have hair metal as its only option. If they'd swap the hair metal for rockabilly, it would be Fletcher's kind of bar.

As always in a strange place, Fletcher had found a booth where he could keep his back to a wall and observe the whole room for potential threats. It was a trait he'd never gotten away from and there was only one instance where it had proven necessary, but once was all it took for an enemy to get the jump on you.

Quadrado walked across, slung her laptop bag onto the table and slid in beside Fletcher. He could see from the shine in her eyes that she had something to tell him.

"You're like a kid on Christmas morning. What have you got?"

"The footage of the replacement driver. I've seen her walking along the street towards the casino and ultimately the van." Fletcher could guess where this was going, but he knew letting Quadrado tell him would be quicker than interrupting her with questions. "Before you ask, her face is hidden and she first appears on camera from a street that isn't covered by cameras, so there's no way of tracing her original vehicle."

A server appeared, so Quadrado stopped her briefing to order herself a mocktail. Fletcher added another beer to the order. It would be his second and last for tonight, as he wanted to keep his faculties sharp.

As soon as the server walked off, Fletcher nudged Quadrado who was now setting up her laptop. "You were saying?"

"Here, look at this footage." Quadrado pointed a manicured and painted nail at the laptop's screen.

Fletcher watched as the woman dressed in the same fake delivery driver garb the Mantis had worn walked along the Strip. "I see her, but I don't see anything odd. There's no tattoos on display that might be used to identify her. You said you didn't get her face on screen and that she was on foot when she came onto the first camera. Go on, tell me what I'm looking for."

Some people might have wasted time continually looking rather than admit they couldn't see what others could. Fletcher wasn't one of those people; he wanted information and he trusted Quadrado's detecting skills more than his own. She was a trained FBI agent. His background was as a Royal Marine who'd grown up listening to his detective father and investigative journalist mother discussing their respective days. What he knew about solving crimes came from overheard conversations and the application of common sense.

Quadrado zoomed in on the footage until it was focused on the woman's feet. They were sneaker clad, and there was nothing odd about them until Quadrado set the footage running again.

Every step the woman took, the same thing happened. When her right foot hit the ground it hit heel first, the toes pointing at twelve on a clock face. By the time her toes touched down, the foot had rotated until her toes pointed at ten. With her left foot, the toes swiveled until they were aimed at two.

"Do you see?"

"I see." Fletcher thought for a moment before speaking to make sure he was on the same page as Quadrado. "She has an unusual gait. That kind of gait can be a marker unique to an individual. I'm guessing the FBI has experts in such fields and that you've sent the footage to Soter, asking him to put such an expert onto the case. You've probably also sent it to Forbes, so he can have someone check databases for a woman with such a gait." Quadrado nodded, no pride on her face. Just an acknowledgment that she'd done what he'd figured. "Good job."

Quadrado waved away the compliment with a dismissive hand. "Never mind that. Where did you go and what did you get?"

"I got the same level of nothing from the cameras you got in terms of seeing the spotter's face. I got a couple of stills." Fletcher showed her the images he'd taken on Ter's phone and sent to Forbes. "I sent these to Forbes. He'll run them through facial recognition software, but I don't reckon enough of her face is visible for it to get a definite match. She changed in the restroom, then went out onto the street. I expect she'll wander down side streets until she's off camera."

"She will. Forbes had traced her arrival to the point where she set up her surveillance and, like the second driver, she came from nowhere. I think you're right about the recognition software, but I'd be happy to be wrong."

"There is another option, and it's not even one I'm sure of. What if the original delivery driver is a stooge, just like the spotter and the second driver?"

"How does that work?"

"What if the delivery driver's role was simply to get through the initial defenses and then open a door somewhere to allow the Mantis into the private areas?"

Quadrado held her answer back until the server had placed their drinks on the table. "I don't know. That sounds complicated to me. You've been where it went down. Did you see a door the driver could have opened to let the Mantis in? To do that, the driver would have had to have killed the first guard. I think you're possibly overthinking things. You said yourself that simpler is better. The Mantis and two accomplices is simpler than three."

"I guess." Fletcher took a sip of his beer. "I suppose I'm just trying all kinds of wild theories."

"If it turns out you're right, the FBI will prove it anyway. They're going over the footage of all the cameras, looking for the Mantis's exit. They're sure to look at earlier footage to identify those already in the casino before the van arrived."

"Makes sense." Fletcher had used the same logic when pursuing the spotter, so it stood to reason the FBI would do the same. Quadrado had made a good point about the Mantis keeping things as simple as possible. It's what he would do, and for him to overcomplicate things was rare. He blamed tiredness and the overwhelming amount of information that he and Quadrado had to wade through. He knew he had to bring his thinking into a straighter line, to look for the ways he could be proactive with his processes rather than reactive.

Two women entered the bar arm in arm with a guy so drunk it looked like he needed them to hold him upright. Both wore outfits suited to a night out whereas the guy was dressed in jeans and a lumberjack shirt. The trio wobbled and cackled their way to the center of the room where they looked for an empty table.

The only tables with enough vacant seats for them all were one with two old men, who were already eyeing the women with lasciviousness, and the end of the booth where Fletcher and Quadrado sat.

The two women tottered their way over and the man lurched in the direction of the bathrooms, Fletcher thought about the irony of the situation. They were looking for three murderous women, stone-cold professionals, and were about to have their space invaded by a pair of drunken ones and the equally drunk guy they'd picked up.

CHAPTER FORTY-FIVE

"Are these seats taken, sugar?" The woman who spoke wore a blue dress and had a slur to her voice and the stench of alcohol radiating from her.

Fletcher glanced around the bar, saw there were no other seats available and realized any privacy he and Quadrado had was over. "Help yourself."

The women plonked themselves into seats. The blue dress opposite Fletcher, the other, wearing white skinny jeans and a lace top, on Fletcher's far left, right beside Quadrado.

An elbow bumped Quadrado's bicep. "You got yourself a handsome man there, sweetie. What I'd give to have a man like that in my life."

"We're not together." Fletcher could hear the amusement on Quadrado's tone.

Fletcher knew it was too much to ask that he and Quadrado would be able to continue their conversation in peace. The women were too drunk to recognize the needs of others, and he was feeling the need to rest and regroup anyway. His plan was to finish his beer and then head back to the motel. He needed to have some thinking time, and the opportunity to rest wouldn't go amiss.

A call came into Quadrado's cell, and her face showed traces of pleasure as she looked at the screen. She rose to her feet. "I need to take this."

Lace Top swung her legs out of the booth to allow Quadrado to pass, and once she'd wriggled past, made a point of sidling up to Fletcher.

"So, sugar, you're available? Or are you holding a candle for your burrito-munching friend?"

"I'm not available, and she's a friend and colleague, nothing more." Fletcher's hand rose to his chest and touched the locket that lay against his chest. Even had he been interested in the woman, the casual racism in the way Blue Dress described Quadrado would have changed his mind.

"Your friend don't know a good thing when she sees it." Blue Dress scrunched her face until she was squinting at Fletcher's hand. "You're not wearing a wedding ring. You seeing someone?"

"I'm still grieving. My wife passed."

"I'm sorry to hear that." Her expression was a long way from matching her words. "If it makes a difference, I'm only looking for some fun for tonight. Nothing serious, just two consenting adults making each other feel good."

"Leave it, Chloe. He's not interested, any fool can tell that." It was Lace Top who made the effort to rein her friend in.

"Hush your mouth, Iris." Chloe let out a long cackle. "No harm in asking."

So far as Fletcher was concerned, the drunk Chloe held no appeal for him, not for a night, a week, a lifetime. Since Rachel died, he'd never entertained the idea of finding another person to walk through life with. His sexual urges repressed as he concentrated on bringing Wendy up to be a person her mother would have been proud of.

Yet, here in this particular moment in time, this embarrassing situation, he found himself attracted to Iris. She was pretty. Not so drunk as her friend, she carried herself with better style and there was something about the way her accent fell on his ears that made it feel like a loving embrace.

He'd wondered for years if there would be a day when he felt the stirrings of attraction. It wasn't that he wanted them, more that he was too astute not to expect things would change in time.

Now they had, he was left feeling as if he was betraying Rachel. Tarnishing her memory by moving on, even if it was a fleeting attraction to a pretty stranger.

He was self-aware enough to know that now his armor had a chink in it, more would appear until he rationalized that it was time to step back into the dating pool. For now, though, it was deep water. He'd certainly not do anything about his attraction to Iris; he wasn't ready for that. It would be a slap in the face for Chloe. Most of all, though, he was in Las Vegas on a mission, not a bachelor party.

As these thoughts had been running through his head, he saw the server approach. The women had ordered drinks for themselves and they'd gotten refills for him and Quadrado. The guy they'd entered with was nowhere to be seen, but from the state he was in, it wouldn't surprise Fletcher to learn the guy had fallen asleep on the can.

When he looked for her, Quadrado was missing from the bar. The call she'd taken was a mystery to Fletcher and yet it wasn't. The cell he'd given her was a burner whose number only he had. Therefore, she'd given that number to someone else if there was an incoming call.

Fletcher took a hefty drink of his bottle of beer. He'd drink it, find Quadrado and get out of here.

Two minutes later, his beer was finished and he was ruing the pace he'd guzzled it down. He was feeling light-headed and even more tired than previously. He was also feeling drunker than he should.

Chloe bumped his arm. "Hey, sugar. You sure you don't want to come and party?"

"Why not?" Fletcher heard the slur in his voice. All of a sudden he felt the need to kick back and listen to his primal urges. Maybe having a little fun would clear his mind. He'd go party for an hour and then head back to the motel. As he lurched out of the bar with Chloe's arm around his waist, there were no thoughts of Quadrado in his head.

CHAPTER FORTY-SIX

Quadrado walked back to the main area of the bar and saw the booth was empty. Not only were Fletcher and the women missing, so was her laptop and the bag she used to carry it around.

Her first thought was that the women had decided this bar was too dull for them and that they'd drank their drinks and moved on. If Fletcher had gone to the men's room, he'd have taken her laptop to prevent it being stolen.

She waited at the bar for a good five minutes. The call from Xavier had brightened her evening. A drummer in a band, he was nothing like her previous boyfriends and that's what had attracted her to him. His laid-back lifestyle was at odds with her regimented days and routines, but somehow they were making it work.

With still no sign of Fletcher, Quadrado called his cell. He didn't answer, so she left a message and tried not to let his absence spoil the good mood speaking with Xavier had brought her.

She walked over to a table that had a view of the booth. The same people were sitting there as before. Him, mid-forties and balding. Her, older, but styled the way thirty-somethings were.

"Excuse me. But the man who was with me earlier—" Quadrado pointed at the booth. "Did you see where he went?"

The couple exchanged a troubled look. The woman dipping her head at the man. He took the cue. He swallowed long and deliberate. "I'm sorry to tell you this, but he left with those women who joined you."

The woman extended an arm and squeezed Quadrado's hand. "Sorry, but it's better you find out what he's like before he puts a ring on your finger or a baby in your belly. Pretty girl like you, you'll have your pick."

"Thanks." Quadrado wheeled round to leave then reversed the movement. "My laptop. Did he take it?"

A shake of the woman's head that was a little too vehement. "A big black bag? Nah, I think one of the girls did."

Quadrado's mind was ablaze with unsavory thoughts. She couldn't believe Fletcher had ditched her to go with the women. She knew how much he was still grieving his wife. He'd never said as much, but she was sure he wasn't dating. For him to go off like this in the middle of a case was unheard of.

Try as she might, she couldn't square the idea of him leaving her behind for a night of passion with a stranger. Not because he had any loyalty to her, more that he was too considerate a person to just take off, but most of all because he'd never shown the slightest hint of interest in sex. Not once had she caught him checking out a woman, sneaking a glance at an exposed cleavage or admiring a woman's butt as she walked away. He wasn't built that way, which meant him leaving wouldn't have been his idea. Therefore it had to have been the women's.

Neither woman had made her antenna for trouble twitch, but that didn't mean anything. If Fletcher had had any reservations about them, he'd have dealt with the situation there and then. This meant they'd both been fooled. Lulled into a sense of security by their changed appearances, and the knowledge the Mantis had already struck once that day and was unlikely to strike again.

To get a man like Fletcher to play along wouldn't have been easy. A gun or any kind of immediate threat to his well-being might work in a dark alley, but in a crowded bar, there was no way Fletcher would have been coerced into going somewhere he didn't want to go. That left two possible ways of getting him to comply:

a threat to a loved one, or a drug. It could, of course, be that he'd had one of his ideas and was checking them out as suspects, but she doubted that he'd have done that without letting her know what he was up to, or even saying goodbye.

Quadrado was confident that Fletcher had enough separation between his mission here and his home life for Wendy to be safe. That left drugs. A roofie slipped into his drink or a jab with a needle full of something similar would make him pliant, although she suspected Fletcher would recognize the effects of the drug and do something about it before there was any great threat to him.

However they'd gotten him to play ball, he was gone and she knew she'd have to find him. If the two women were the Mantis and one of her associates, Fletcher's life was in grave danger, if he was even still alive.

Quadrado strode over to the bar, pulling her badge as she approached. "I need to see any CCTV footage you have for the bar. Both inside and out."

CHAPTER FORTY-SEVEN

The world was a mess of confusion for Fletcher as he followed the women. His brain was scrambled, and he felt himself lurching around as if he'd been drinking heavily for hours. He tried to make sense of why he was so unsteady, but his mind was woollier than an alpaca farm.

"Come on, Grant. This is a great place."

The woman in the blue dress opened the door of a bar and he trailed her in. Maybe if he got a coffee instead of a beer some of his faculties would return. The coffee would also help him cope with the drowsiness he was experiencing. He didn't want to party anymore; all he wanted to do was curl up and go to sleep.

To Fletcher's eyes the bar seemed empty. He couldn't make out much in its Stygian darkness, but despite being dizzy and exhausted, he also felt like he was ten feet tall and capable of anything.

"Over here." Chloe gestured at a row of padded seats and sat down, patting the space beside her as she did so. "You can sit with me, Grant."

Somewhere at the edge of his brain, Fletcher was trying to work out how Chloe knew his name. He didn't recall telling her, but the way he was feeling, he couldn't rule it out.

"Need a coffee. Black, no sugar." If Fletcher had been able to hear himself, he'd feel nothing but shame for the lazy slur his voice had become.

"Sure thing."

Iris leaned over as if she was going to whisper something in Chloe's ear.

Fletcher's left arm was laid along the back of the seat, and he felt the presence of Iris as she approached. Before he could do anything about it, Fletcher's wrist was handcuffed to the wrought-iron railing that ran along the top of the seat.

Chloe's hands grasped his other wrist and pulled his right arm away from his body. As his befuddled brain sought out the necessary instructions to fight back, Iris whipped out a syringe and fed it into the vein in the crook of his elbow.

The needle scratched as Fletcher's muscles tensed, but Iris depressed the plunger and then stood back, removing the syringe as she went.

"What's going on?"

It was a pointless question as Fletcher didn't expect an answer. For some reason the grogginess was now leaving him, as were the other effects he'd put down to exhaustion and guzzling that last beer so quickly.

Chloe stood in front of him. "That was flumazenil in the syringe. It's what emergency rooms administer to folks who overdose on Rohypnol." A shrug, as if what she was saying was akin to a request to pass the salt. "I dropped a roofie in your beer when you weren't looking. Now you're here, I want you awake and alert so you know what's going to happen to you."

"You're the Mantis, aren't you?" He spoke to Chloe, a statement not a question. Whatever that flumazenil stuff was, it was doing a fantastic job of bringing Fletcher back to his usual self. "Why have you brought me here and not killed me the way you did the casino bosses?"

"That was business. This is personal. My client alerted me to your presence in town and the esteem in which you're held. To that end, you have become annoying and as such I'm not going to give you a clean death." Two paces behind Chloe, Iris was holding a gallon-sized gas can. "You're going to die screaming, and I want you to know that. I want to see the fear in your eyes."

Iris stepped forward and splashed as much gasoline as she could onto Fletcher and the areas of the seat around him. The coarse liquid splattered onto Fletcher's legs, and while he was trying to doge the swathes of gasoline, he was failing. He tried cowering back in the hope Iris would get within reach, but she was too smart to fall for that.

Across the room, Iris was laying a trail of gasoline around the perimeter. Empty gas cans dropped to the ground when she was done.

Fletcher's wrist rattled the handcuff. The attempt to free himself achieving nothing more than skin loss. When the gasoline running down his arm found the raw skin, it set off a stinging that Fletcher knew was nothing more than a taster of what was to come.

"You don't have to do this." Fletcher hated the fear in his voice, but he was too proud to beg. Not that he expected begging would work. The Mantis was a stone-cold killer, and all that begging would achieve would be to give her satisfaction. He'd not beg; he'd score that victory over her.

"Oh, but I do. And I'm going to enjoy it."

"They will get you for this. You made a mistake showing your faces at that bar. The cops and the FBI will track you down."

"You silly man. They won't track us down at all. We've two more targets to eliminate and then we're off on our merry way." Chloe took a grip of her brunette hair and lifted it off her head, dropping it at Fletcher's feet. Underneath the wig she had blonde hair slicked to her head. A ruffle from her fingertips brought it to life. Next she dabbed a finger into each eye and removed a colored contact lens. The lenses joined the wig on the floor, along with a pair of pads that she removed from the inside of her mouth. "You're not the only one who can change how you look." The Mantis was transformed with the removal of three simple items of disguise. Apart from the fact she was wearing the same clothes, she bore no resemblance to the woman who called herself Chloe.

"Your disguise wasn't that good. You'll still be caught."

A knife appeared in the Mantis's hand. Not a good hunting knife, not a military style weapon. An ordinary kitchen knife that had years of use about it. Fletcher clenched the fist of his one free hand and prepared to feel the sting of the knife.

The knife flew towards the bench seating and embedded itself into the padded upholstery. "You can have that. Maybe you'll take the easy way out. Maybe you'll be a tough guy and use the knife to remove your hand. Be careful though, it's not terribly sharp. You could give yourself a nasty bruise with it."

The Mantis turned away as Fletcher reached for the knife. He had half a mind to throw it after her. To stick her in the back with it. If he was going to die, he'd die easier knowing he was taking her with him. He didn't though. He'd never been adept at throwing knives. If he missed, or failed to kill her, all he was doing was giving up his one chance of survival. Even if he did kill her, the other woman would make sure that he died no more than a minute after the Mantis.

When she reached the entrance, the Mantis stopped, pulled a book of matches from her cleavage, tore one out and struck it. When she'd used it to set the other matches ablaze, she dropped the burning matchbook onto the trail of gasoline Iris had created around the room.

Within seconds there was a circle of fire. Thick black smoke filled the air as everything burned with a satanic fury.

CHAPTER FORTY-EIGHT

Quadrado looked at the bartender as if he was a Martian. His response to her query about CCTV footage had left her amazed.

"What do you mean they don't work?"

"They are mostly dummies. Put there to give the impression of surveillance. Folks who come to Vegas are so used to cameras it gives them a sense of security. Likewise, the locals we have don't mind that they don't work. They like the chance to not be on camera for a few hours. We don't get no trouble in here so it's not a problem."

It might not be a problem for the blasé bartender, but it was sure a problem for Quadrado. She needed to see the footage to find out where Fletcher was. To trace where he'd gone. A license plate of a car or a cab would do. Even a direction of travel would give her a fighting chance.

"Surely there must be one or two of the cameras that work. Surely you have a couple working for your own peace of mind. To protect the business."

The bartender pulled a face, the gesture contorting his goatee into a bird's nest. "We do. They cover the storeroom where the liquor and the safe are kept. Do you think that's where your friend might be?"

Rather than answer the asinine question, Quadrado wheeled away from the bar and walked outside.

The street was quiet. Far enough away from the Strip to have a different set of rhythms. This was the territory of locals, not those who'd party all night. At this time of day, there was nobody moving around.

A look both ways along the street offered little hope. There was a video game store, a pharmacy and a variety of other stores you'd find on any strip mall, but there were no other bars within two hundred yards. Any external cameras they had would be focused on their own parking lots and immediate frontage. There would be little chance of their cameras pointing this far along the street, or having the clarity of focus for her to identify Fletcher and the women as they left the bar.

If this was a normal case, she could get the footage from the other bars and perhaps work up a decent lead to follow. It wasn't a normal case though. It was a high-stakes mission and Fletcher had disappeared on her.

If the suspicions deep in her gut were right, and Fletcher had been captured by the Mantis, every second counted. There was only one thing for it. She pulled out her phone and sent an email to Soter. She gave him Fletcher's new cell number and requested he trace it at once.

Quadrado knew she was taking a gamble by involving Soter in this way, but she knew it was her best chance of getting fast answers. How Soter would view the fact Fletcher may have been captured by his target was a concern, but at this moment all worries about possible reprimands were small beer. The only thing she cared about was finding Fletcher before it was too late.

She paced back and forth along the street as she waited for a response from Soter. The same query could have gone to Forbes, but she knew that would have been a slower route. She'd have had to explain everything, and while involving Soter might have greater long-term consequences, it would also guarantee faster results.

"Come on, come on, come on." The words tumbled from her lips as she marched along the sidewalk, cell grasped between white-knuckled fingers. She needed Soter to respond in his usual timely fashion. There was no way of knowing if he'd picked up her email or not. No way of telling if the cell's number was being tracked right now, or if the message was languishing unread in Soter's inbox as he dined with his wife, drank whiskey or whatever he did during the evening.

The ping of an email being received made her jump. She opened the app and looked at the message. As always with Soter it was brief and to the point.

DISAPPOINTED WITH THIS DEVELOPMENT. LOCATION OF
CELL IS ANGELS, ON MERRITT AVE.

Quadrado flashed her badge at a passing cab and jumped in when it stopped for her. "Angels on Merritt Avenue. There's an extra two hundred bucks for you if you step on it."

CHAPTER FORTY-NINE

Fletcher stuck the knife back into the upholstery and used his free hand to pat down his pockets. As expected his cell was missing. One of the women must have claimed it when he'd been under the influence of the Rohypnol.

He coughed as he again tried to free his bound wrist. The action had the same success as before. Namely none. He tried to rip the wrought-iron frame from its mountings with every fiber of muscle he possessed. All he achieved was to soak his body in sweat and induce a coughing fit as he drew the smoke into his lungs.

Around him the room was burning. From what he could make out of the room it appeared to be a former strip club. This wasn't how he wanted to die, chained like a dog and burned to death in a strip club. That was no way for anyone to go.

The Mantis had suggested he cut off his hand and try to escape, but should he go down that route, the gasoline coating his body would be sure to ignite as he tried to get out of the room. Even if he was overcome with the fumes from the burning upholstery, that would see him coughing and choking until unconsciousness took him. He could use the knife to slit his throat, or stab himself in the heart. By comparison to the other options, they'd be quick and painless ways to go, but the idea of giving up and surrendering to death wasn't one he'd ever entertained in the past and he sure as hell wasn't ready to go down that route yet.

A series of crackles filled the room as the fire took hold of what used to be the bar. The one slight benefit of the room being ablaze was that the fire was providing light. The counterpoint to this was that the upper parts of the room were filled with acrid smoke that had nowhere else to go.

Fletcher half remembered a conversation with a firefighter buddy about the combustibility of gasoline. In its liquid form the vapors it gave off were highly combustible, but when it dried on a surface it was far less likely to ignite. To remove as much of the gasoline from his body as possible, he unbuttoned the cuffs of his shirt and tore the buttons off his chest. Next he shrugged it off and rammed it down his tethered left arm. A brief attempt to cut it free with the knife was abandoned in favor of tearing motions. The Mantis hadn't lied; the knife was dull and unable to cut the damp cloth.

His boots and jeans came off next, although his boots went back on as soon as the jeans were off. He could feel the heat from the fire on his skin, but his thinking was that he'd rather face the prospect of burnt skin without wearing gasoline-soaked clothes to give the fire fuel. He was working on the principle the heat from the fire would dry the gasoline on his skin before it got close enough for there to be any vapors to ignite. It was a risky strategy, but it was better than taking his chances with gasoline-soaked clothes.

The dullness of the knife was a kick in the nutsack he could have done without. As unthinkable as the idea might be, cutting off his hand would always be his preferred option. He'd live his life one-handed if needs be—that was a whole lot better than dying.

With a sharp knife and no pain meds other than a folded belt to bite on, the removal of a hand would be an excruciating ordeal. To hack through flesh and cartilage, and to separate tissue from bone with one as blunt as the one he had, that would be a descent into a hellish agony.

With the fire creeping ever closer, the necessity to choose a course of action was upon him. In a final act of desperation, he surveyed the railings, the handcuff and his wrist, looking for a weak point he could exploit so he didn't have to cut off his hand.

Fletcher picked up the knife and gritted his teeth in preparation for what he was about to do.

CHAPTER FIFTY

For all she'd offered the cabbie a bribe and shown her badge, he was still driving at a law-abiding speed.

"Please, drive faster. I'm an FBI agent and I guarantee that you'll not be getting any tickets."

"There's no need to hurry, lady. Angels shut down five years ago. Ain't no urgency needed here."

"Yes, there is, damn you."

The cabbie didn't respond. No words fell from his mouth. No increase in pace. Just the same sedentary journey. Traffic was light. He could easily add twenty miles an hour to his speed without risking an accident.

The cab was a basic yellow taxi like they had in New York. There was a meter, a dividing partition and the hint of body odor competing with a worn air freshener. Quadrado had made a thousand cab journeys, and this was by far the most infuriating.

She had to find a way to get this guy to speed up. To this end she opened her purse and pulled three hundred bucks from her wallet.

"Here, do you see this?" She fanned the bills and held them up so he could see them in his rearview mirror. "This is yours if you'll just stop dithering and speed up."

"Not going to happen, lady. I'm not falling for it. Minute you see me speeding you'll arrest me for it. Try your tricks elsewhere, but not in my cab." He flicked the stalk and went to pull over. "This is about as far I'm taking you. Not going to play me those games. Oh no, no way."

As he drew up by the sidewalk, Quadrado stuffed the notes back into her wallet and resorted to plan B. This wasn't who she wanted to be, but the cabbie's refusal to follow her instructions had left her with no option.

The barrel of her pistol was slid through the gap in the divider for passing money back and forth. Its aim, the back of the cabbie's neck.

"Hey." This time there was no pleading in her tone; she was in full command mode now. She spoke to the cabbie as if he was a suspect she was taking down. "Keep driving and drive a hell of a lot faster. You got me?"

"I got you."

The cab picked up speed and veered back to the center of the road. The cabbie's previous sluggishness replaced by a desperate need to comply, although he was muttering something to himself as he drove. Whether he was praying or cursing her out didn't matter to Quadrado, the cab was moving at a good pace and that's all that was important.

"How far is it to Angels?"

"A half mile." The cabbie's voice was tight with fear. "Look there's an intersection coming. I need to turn left and to do that, I'll have to slow down. Please, don't shoot me."

As predicted, he slowed for the intersections, but the traffic stops were kind and he still managed to get round the corner at enough pace to squeal the tires.

This street was the least salubrious Quadrado had encountered in Las Vegas. Some buildings were boarded up and there were weeds growing in places they shouldn't be. Altogether it was a gloomier and darker part of town than the glitzy Strip.

Ahead of them a wide, low building stood apart from others. Its parking lot a mess of weeds and abandoned items. Smoke was creeping out from several openings around doors and windows. Quadrado knew before the cab stopped by the building that it would be Angels.

She dropped the Glock back into her purse, shoved some bills towards the driver, yelling at him to call the police and fire department, and leaped out.

CHAPTER FIFTY-ONE

Fletcher's wrist ached as he strained to get the tip of the knife where he wanted it. He was at full stretch, but he was able to get the knife's point lodged into the screw fixing the wrought-iron frame into a support post.

Stretched as he was, it wasn't easy for Fletcher to apply the necessary pressure to the knife to both keep it seated in the screw head and to rotate it. The heat in the room was making his hands slick with sweat, and it was all he could do to make a quarter turn at a time.

After ten turns, the screw was showing a half inch of its threads. Another twenty turns had it loose enough for him to move onto the next. This one was lower down, so he vaulted the frame and set to work.

As he stretched and strained to get the necessary force onto the knife, he kept his head low where the clearer air was. His eyes streamed from the smoke, and the bouts of harsh coughs that wracked his body were becoming more frequent as he inhaled the various poisons in the smoke.

The second screw was loose so he turned his attention to the next pair. They were closer to his end of the frame, which made it easier, but when he tried to turn the first one, it was stubborn and resisted all his attempts to break free.

He moved to the second screw. It too was stiff, but he managed to get it rotating. With one slow turn after the other, he loosened it enough to take it between his fingers and twiddle it free.

The frame was now held by the one stubborn screw and the two first ones he'd loosened until they were hanging from their holes. With the time for any hint of finesse long past, Fletcher rose to his feet, clamped the frame with both hands and gave it a hard pull.

It came free, but only to a point. The one stubborn screw didn't give in any meaningful way. Fletcher pulled harder, his muscles bulging as they gave every shred of their power to his cause.

The frame rotated as if on a hinge. The one stubborn screw holding so fast the frame was bending under his movements. That wasn't good; he needed the frame loose, not broken or twisted.

To apply pressure in a different way, Fletcher adjusted the frame in his hand until it was laid flat like a tray. Now he pushed forward, using the edge of the post the stubborn screw was fixed to as a fulcrum to increase the pressure he was applying.

Even above the roar of the fire, Fletcher could hear the squeal as the screw protested at being drawn from its home. A coughing fit engulfed him and he fell to his knees until it had passed.

By now he could hardly see for the thickness of the smoke and the tears it had streaming down his face. Every movement was an exercise in pain management as the fire crept ever closer. His skin felt scorched and he knew things were going to get a lot worse before they got any better.

Before repeating the movement, Fletcher lifted the knife from where he'd stuck it into the seat back and jammed its handle in the gap he'd opened up between the frame and the support post.

One mighty heave and the frame dropped to the floor, dragging Fletcher with it. He picked himself up, grabbed the frame and hauled it upright so he could easily take it with him.

The next thing on his agenda was getting out of here. The entranceway where the Mantis and Iris had exited was ablaze and impassable to all bar a fully clad firefighter.

That left him searching for other options. The bar's appearance was that of a strip club, complete with poles and stages. Therefore there would be changing rooms, an entrance where the dancers could come and go without walking through the main bar. There would also be a back office and a storeroom somewhere. Each of these may have a door, and Fletcher was sure there had to be a fire escape somewhere.

In the end, it was the fire that made the decision for him. The entire area by the bar was ablaze, and there was no way he was getting through it without picking up some serious burns, or bursting into a fireball if his theory about dried gasoline was incorrect.

Off to one side of a stage there was a doorway. The door was closed but that wasn't an issue for Fletcher. Whether boot or shoulder were needed to open that door, it would be opened.

To get to the doorway, he had to pass the ring of fire. Had to get past the waist-high flames and survive the experience. How the gasoline that had been sloshed on his body would react to the licking flames was unknown, but he couldn't wait where he was for the smoke or the fire to take him.

As he neared the flames, he wrenched the metal frame around, lay the leading edge flat on the floor and used it as a bulldozer to drive away the burning material as he passed by.

Four purposeful strides got him to the door and it opened as soon as he turned the handle. As he'd suspected, it was a changing room.

CHAPTER FIFTY-TWO

Quadrado ran around the former strip club looking for a way in. She didn't find one that looked anything like obvious. All the doors were clad with metal sheeting, and she could see the hinge pins which told her they opened outwards. The windows were all barred, with the bars set into the masonry frames.

She tried giving one or two of the bars a pull, but they were set fast.

Her first thought was to use the grip of her pistol to break a window so she could shout in to Fletcher. It was an idea she dismissed as soon as she had it. The breaking of a window would allow air into the building. This would oxygenate the fire, breathe gusto into it. If Fletcher was in there, she had to find a way to get in and save him, or at least help him to escape.

As she passed each door, she put her hand against it to check its temperature. The double doors at the front were giving off intense heat before she even made contact. As did one of the two other doors. It was the third she concentrated her efforts on. A pair of narrow double doors that were undoubtedly an emergency exit.

Because they were designed to be an emergency exit and open outwards, there was little chance of her being able to kick the doors in. That didn't mean she didn't try. Five times she kicked out at where the doors joined. Five times her foot did nothing more than propel her backwards when it slammed against the door.

She tried taking a couple of steps back and then running at the doors and throwing her shoulder against the join. The net result of this was a yelp as she bounced off. The door unmoved by her feeble attempts to break it down.

To get through the doors she needed a battering ram and people who knew how to use one. It took her four precious minutes to summon the fire brigade. She spent the time on the phone circling the building to double check her initial assessment.

As she dropped the phone into her pocket, she returned to the doors that had thus far resisted her efforts to break into the building.

With her failed attempts to get in having been about brute strength, Quadrado knew she'd have to change her tactics. Instead of relying on muscle alone, she'd have to find a way to pry the doors open.

In her mind she tried to picture what the inside of the doors looked like. As a pair they would be identical. There would be the waist-high railing that operated the locking mechanism that prevented people entering from outside. It would be connected to a rod that ran from top to bottom on the open side of each door. The ends of the rod would be housed into the floor and the return of the doorway. She didn't need to open both doors, just one.

Quadrado fumbled in her purse, found a credit card and slid it in the gap between the two doors. It went in about three quarters of an inch and then refused to go any further. It was as she'd suspected: the doors were lapped to prevent drafts and easy break-ins.

She turned and cast her eyes across the empty parking lot in search of something to pry one of the doors open. A fire ax would be ideal, but there was no chance of finding one there. Her eyes landed on lots of items, but few of them were of any actual use. Trash blowing in the wind wouldn't pry a locked door open. Nor would a pizza box, a discarded stroller or a supermarket's shopping cart. It was as she was about to give up, that she spotted something that might work.

It was the head of a shovel. Rusted and abandoned to its fate, it felt sturdy as Quadrado picked it up. If it still had its handle it would have been far more use, but it was the best she had.

She sprinted back to the doors and began to assault their join with the point of the shovel head. If she could do enough to release the mechanism, she'd be able to get in. The first thing she knew she had to do was identify which door lapped the other, so she wasn't trying to prize open the wrong one.

CHAPTER FIFTY-THREE

Fletcher wasted no time in the changing room. It was devoid of anything but smoke. The other door opened inwards, but before he grabbed the handle, he took the precaution of putting the palm of his hand against the wood.

It was warm to the touch. He hauled the wrought-iron frame after him as he swung the door open and stepped forward.

There was no fire on the floor or walls of this part of the building, but the ceiling was a series of fiery beams. The floor was littered with drywall that had fallen loose, no doubt from an unfixed leak in the roof.

Step by careful step he kept moving forwards, the frame he was cuffed to an inert hindrance that seemed to snag on everything it could. The smoke was as dense in here as everywhere else, and he struggled to see more than a few yards ahead of him.

Fletcher would have crawled on hands and knees, but the frame snagged enough things as it was without laying it flat.

A series of loud cracks above him made Fletcher increase his slow progress forward. He was too late. The cracking increased in tempo and was followed by a whooshing crack as one of the beams was no longer able to support its own weight.

The beam fell beside Fletcher, missing his body by a fraction. He was relieved as it passed his shoulder only to be drawn towards the fallen beam when it landed on the frame.

Fletcher's bare shoulder was on the burning lumber. It hadn't fallen all the way to the ground. The end nearest the bar rested on the frame while the other end was still housed in its original place atop the wall.

There was no time to think about what to do. Instinct and training kicked in as Fletcher twisted the frame so the end of the beam slid away from his body before it ignited any of the gasoline with which his body had been doused.

There was no woof or whoosh as the gasoline ignited, so Fletcher assumed his firefighter buddy had been right about gasoline being neutralized when it dried. All the same, his shoulder got burned and he could smell the hairs on his legs and chest burning.

The beam still lay on the now flattened wrought-iron frame, so he had to twist and haul to free it. As he did so he could hear the other ceiling beams cracking as the fire burned through the ends that were closest to the bar.

Fletcher picked up the end of the frame he was tethered to and charged ahead before any of the other beams came down on him.

At the end of the hallway were two doors. One opened into a small, shelved room that had obviously been used for storage.

The second led to a space he figured was once an office. There was another door in the office, so he made his way towards it as fast as his latest coughing fit allowed.

The door was cool, but when he opened it he found it led to a hallway between the main public area and an emergency exit.

The emergency exit would have been a glorious thing to find were the doors not chained together and padlocked.

CHAPTER FIFTY-FOUR

Fletcher's boot collided with the crash bars at the center of the emergency exit doors. They cranked open a fraction then stopped.

He put his shoulder to the doors and heaved at them. Again they only opened as far as the heavy chain allowed.

A sliver of face appeared in the inch and a half crack between the doors. "Fletcher, is that you?" Quadrado's voice. Somehow she'd managed to find him.

"Yeah. The doors are chained and padlocked."

"Are you okay?"

"Bit cold, if I'm honest." Even over the roar from the fire he heard Quadrado's intake of breath at his dark humor. The ability to joke while in extreme danger was something he'd learned in Helmand and it had never left him. "Have you got handcuff keys with you? If you have, pass them to me."

"One second."

Fletcher threw a glance over his shoulder. The fire was feeding off the air coming between the doors. It wasn't the biggest opening, but he could feel the sucking as the fire drew new oxygen in to feed its flames.

He needed to get out of here fast, as the fire was getting ever closer. All the same he kept a knee against the doors to maintain the gap. The keys he'd requested flew in and hit him on the chest.

Rather than go to pick them up, he focused on Quadrado's next gift. It was her pistol. "I'll get out of the way. Shoot the padlock."

His old instructor had never advocated shooting locks. According to him, the round either jammed the mechanism or a ricochet took down the shooter. Fletcher didn't have the luxury of trying an alternative method, so he gave Quadrado the count of five to get to a safe place and took aim at the padlock from a distance of two inches. He aimed at an oblique angle so any rebounds would be deflected away from him.

Twice he squeezed the trigger, and twice the padlock jumped under the onslaught of a bullet. The padlock was damaged but when he rattled it against the chain, it held firm. He fired another pair of shots into the padlock with the same lack of results. It was now a misshapen lump of metal whose moving parts would be jammed solid.

Fletcher fed the gun back out to Quadrado and lifted the handcuff key. He fumbled them into the lock and released himself from the frame. The key got dropped to the floor; it had served its purpose and doing anything else was a waste of precious time. Behind him there was the creaking crash of a falling beam and a cloud of sparks filled the room. Each one that touched his skin setting off a vicious sting than made him fearful the dried gasoline would ignite at any point. For all the theory about dried gasoline not igniting might be correct, it was one thing knowing something, another staying calm when it was your skin the gasoline was on when surrounded by fire.

With the frame in his hands, Fletcher eased it backwards and then with a scything swing, directed one of its corners at one of the vertical bolts running down to the floor. There was a metallic clang and a sudden vibration that carried back to his arms with enough force to judder his upper body.

Fletcher didn't hesitate in repeating the swing. The first blow had knocked the bar sideways a half inch. The second drove it free.

Fletcher's hands wound around the bar and he hauled it towards him. As intended, the bar eased away from the door and started to bend outwards near its central fixings. As soon as the bending began, Fletcher released the bar and reached for the frame again.

To help, Quadrado was trying to feed the shovel in to use as a crowbar, but every time she exerted any pressure the rusty shovel buckled and twisted.

He now had enough of a gap to feed the frame between the bar and the door. Once he'd pushed the frame through until it was butting against the bar on the other door, Fletcher hauled the frame backwards.

There is always a way to increase your power by using your head as well as your muscles. By having the frame positioned the way it was, Fletcher could exert far greater pressure on the bar than he ever could by pulling on it alone. The only goal he had now was to remove enough of the emergency exit mechanism from one of the doors to allow it to open.

With the heat from the fire threatening to scorch his back, Fletcher didn't waste any time tensing his muscles or taking a deep breath. He just hauled the frame backwards intent on popping the set of screws.

Instead of the mechanism pulling loose, it gave an inch and then locked solid. So mighty was Fletcher's heave on the frame, there was still a lot of energy and momentum unspent. With the mechanism holding fast, the power of his muscles just bent the frame until there was a forty-five degree kink at its end.

Fletcher wasted no time trying again. He simply hoisted the frame until it was level with his head and drove it at the top part of the vertical bar. Such was his desperation, his first attempt was sufficient to separate the upper part of the bar from the door.

His next target was the horizontal crash bar that operated the mechanism. He slid a corner from the straight end of the frame behind the end of the crash bar furthest from the chain and padlock.

It took five mighty attempts before the end of the crash bar came free.

Fletcher's hands gripped the loose end of the crash bar and hauled it towards the padlocked end. It twisted until it was at a right angle from the door.

But no matter what Fletcher did there was no way he could release the chain.

However, the various damage he'd done to the mechanism meant the chain was no longer as tight as it had been, and the gap between the doors was now roughly a foot wide.

Fletcher took a step back from the door, the sweat drying from the fire's heat as soon as it exited his pores, dropped the frame to one side and launched himself at the gap between the doors in a low dive, twisting onto his left side as he flew through the air.

Both ears grazed a door on the way through, and as soon as his head was out, he was looking round for Quadrado. She was a half pace away and moving forward to him.

Fletcher's arms were still extended above his head. "Grab my hands and drag me out."

Quadrado did as she was told without argument. Fletcher was doing all he could to propel himself forward, flames singeing the remaining hairs on his legs. His chest, the bulkiest part of his body, was jammed between the doors. The one thing he had going for him was that he was pushing in the right direction between the part-open doors. If he'd been trying to go the other way, they would have scissored in on him, trapping him with no hope of ever getting through.

To Fletcher it felt as though Quadrado's tugs would remove his arms from their sockets, but he knew it was working. He could feel the progress he was making from the scrapes his back and chest were picking up from the doors.

Inch by painful inch, Quadrado dragged him to a point where he felt the constriction of the doors lessen. "Let me go. I've got it now."

Fletcher's brain was working on a different plane as he hauled his body free of the doors. His first thought was his locket. Once he'd checked it was where it should be, he cast his eyes around, looking for the Mantis or one of her sidekicks. Would they be watching? Were they skulking in the shadows, waiting to dispatch him if he managed to get out of the impossible situation he'd been left in?

He reasoned not. If they were around, Quadrado would be dead by now, and so would he. All the same, he wasn't going to take any chances. As much as he wanted to let the cool air flow over his body, to drink in sweet breaths of clean oxygen, he knew he had to stay alert.

The sound of sirens rent through the night air and he knew he needed to act. To move.

He rose to his feet and gripped Quadrado's shoulders as he looked into her eyes. "I have to get out of here. Have to get away from this fire." Her reaction made him recognize how desperate his tone must sound. That didn't matter, the only thing that mattered was getting away from the building as soon as possible.

CHAPTER FIFTY-FIVE

"This way. There's a twenty-four-hour store along the street. We can get you some clean clothes."

Fletcher let Quadrado lead him to the store and then ducked round the back while she went in and got him a pair of jeans, a shirt and jacket. New York might be the city that never slept, but from what Fletcher had observed so far, it didn't appear that Las Vegas so much as snoozed, as he'd noticed there were stores that were open at all hours of the day.

The fact he'd managed to escape the inferno was beginning to affect his body as the adrenaline spike vanished and left him trembling. He didn't want Quadrado to see him shake. He knew there was no shame in natural human reactions, but he had his pride, and there was no way he wanted her to think of him as afraid.

The few minutes she'd be gone would give him a chance to regain control of his body, assess the injuries he'd picked up and most important of all, give him some thinking time.

Fletcher's injuries were plentiful, but while there was a lot of stinging from minor burns and scrapes, none of the injuries were serious. There were no second- or third-degree burns, no broken bones and no torn muscles. Every limb worked as it should, just more painfully than usual. Pain was something he could handle, being unfit to continue wasn't. The Mantis had tried to kill him in a horrific way; now, the case wasn't just about stopping a deadly killer, it was about settling a score.

Along the road three fire trucks jerked to a halt and discharged firefighters who went about their job with a smooth efficiency that spoke of experience and practice.

Footsteps indicated Quadrado's return. As well as the clothing, she'd gotten a bundle of first aid supplies, some bottles of water and a few high-energy bars.

"Thanks." Fletcher drained one of the water bottles without ever removing it from his lips. He'd not recognized how thirsty he was until the water was in front of him. He took another bottle and emptied its contents over his head and used his hands to swirl the liquid around until he'd done as good a job as he could of washing off the soot and debris from his head, face and hands. He reached for the shirt next and used it as a flannel to complete the clean-up operation.

What he didn't want was to draw attention to himself. That's why he wanted to get away from the burning building as quick as he could. For as long as possible, he wanted the Mantis to believe he was dead. He'd seen her real face. Could describe her to the FBI. They could do facial composites and get an artist's impression of her. Or at least they could if he told them. The question uppermost in his mind was how the Mantis had found them with such ease, and the only way he could think she'd been able to do that, was she had an informant in the FBI office, the mayor's office, or Soter was playing two ends against the middle.

"How did you know where I was?"

"I got Soter to trace your cell phone. Is it worth getting him to run traces on other cells in the vicinity?"

'It's worth a shot, get them to cross-reference the location of the bar where they approached us to weed out any false positives."

He pulled on the clothes. They weren't a bad fit. More troubling than their fit was the way they aggravated every one of his many wounds. He pushed the pain and discomfort aside and faced Quadrado as he bent to tie the laces of his boots.

"Which way is the Strip?"

"That way." Quadrado used a bob of her head to give the direction.

Fletcher set off walking, knowing Quadrado would fall in beside him. "We need to get after the Mantis."

"How?" Quadrado flapped her arms out from her side. "We don't know the first thing about her. Anyway, shouldn't you rest? Go to the emergency room and get your wounds treated?"

"I'm fine, there's nothing wrong with me that won't heal itself in time. And we know more than you think. She was wearing a disguise in the bar, but she removed it."

"Why would she do that?"

"Because she was gloating when I told her she'd be tracked for abducting me."

"Okay, I get it. We'll get on with artists' impressions. Digital composites. The whole works." Quadrado pulled her cell from a pocket, so Fletcher stopped her before she could make a call. "Come on. We can get you in front of a screen. You've seen her and may spot her in one of the files."

Fletcher held up a hand in the halt gesture. "Slow down a second. As soon as I step inside the FBI building, or you start requisitioning the files for me to look at, we'll be sending a message and I don't think that's a good idea. We've already made too many mistakes as it is."

"What message? What mistakes?"

"The only way she can know about us is through either the FBI or mayor's offices or Soter. If they all think I'm dead, that'll be the information the Mantis has too. The longer she thinks I'm dead, the more time we have to catch her."

"That's the message. What are the mistakes?"

"Getting captured and almost killed twice in one day." Fletcher fixed her with a stare. "We let ourselves be fooled by the Mantis. She was right under our noses and we let her go. Not just let her go. She damn near killed me, and if she hadn't wanted me to suffer an agonizing death, I'd be dead right now. That was her mistake. I made another one though. A big one." Fletcher felt as if he should be toeing the ground like an errant child at this next admission. "I should have picked up her wig and the pads she used to puff out her cheeks. I didn't though. We could have used them to get DNA samples and they might have identified her, which in turn would have given us a chance of catching her."

Quadrado cast a glance at the former strip club. He knew she'd be thinking; decimated as it now was by fire and the water being pumped at it by the firefighters, there was no chance of recovering any possible evidence.

"Wouldn't that have meant going to the FBI and or Soter anyway?"

"Yeah, but DNA is much more accurate than a groggy memory. Plus we didn't have to offer it up right away. It could be turned in tomorrow. You could even say you found it in the wreckage of the fire."

"So what do we do now, then?"

"I saw a matchbook in the Mantis's purse when we were all at the table. At first I thought it odd because she didn't smell of cigarette smoke. Then I dismissed it as something she'd picked up as a memento. I know why she had it now. It's what she used to start the fire."

Quadrado's nose wrinkled a little. "I'm guessing you're mentioning this because you saw something on the matchbook."

"Correct. It had the name of a motel on it. The Santa Fe Lodge to be precise."

Again Quadrado pulled her cell from her pocket. "I'm calling this in. We can get a SWAT team, every agent available and catch them in their beds."

"No way. We do this ourselves. If you get a tactical situation like that, one of several things could happen. Number one: everything works perfectly and she gets captured with no loss of life or injury. Number two: she gets killed in a shootout. Remember she's damned good at what she does, so it's likely she'll kill a few of the SWAT team before she gets taken down."

As they reached the Strip, Quadrado again used her badge to hail a passing cab.

"Number three: the Mantis may well be up to something else just now, and if she returns and spots the agents or the SWAT team you want to whistle up, she'll slink away and we'll lose her trail. Number four: the Mantis isn't actually at the motel and it's a waste of time. How do you think Thomson will like that? Number five: our mission is to find and kill her, not to call it in. How long do you think Soter will keep me out of jail if we start disobeying him? Number six, and this is the big one for me: I've never liked the idea of killing a woman, despite the fact she's an assassin, but after what she tried to do to me, after hearing about how she callously killed a kid with Down syndrome, I want to see her die. I want to be the one who puts her down."

The cab drew to a stop in front of them.

Quadrado looked back at him as she opened the cab's door. "We check out the motel, but if we see her, I'm calling it in. I'm not having you getting into a public gunfight with her."

CHAPTER FIFTY-SIX

For once luck was on their side. The motel was opposite a row of various stores and bars. It wasn't the best area of Las Vegas, but it was by no means the worst.

They found an all-night diner and set themselves up in a booth that gave them a chance to look across the street and monitor comings and goings from the motel.

As was his way, Fletcher had selected a booth where they'd be able to observe both the motel and the door. Quadrado's gun was in his waistband based on three theories. The first being that if the Mantis should walk into the diner, he didn't want to waste time identifying her to Quadrado. The second less complicated, yet more pragmatic: Fletcher was prepared to shoot the Mantis dead in front of witnesses and Quadrado wasn't. The final reason was straightforward. Fletcher was the better shot.

The server schlepped over to them, her feet scuffing the floor with every dragged step. She dumped a plateful of ham and eggs in front of Fletcher and refilled his coffee for the second time without saying a word. She had a face that was more squatted in than lived in, and there was defeat in her every movement. Whether she hated her job or her life the most was a moot point, but even as beat up as he was, Fletcher found himself feeling sorry for the woman.

A pair of women wandered towards the motel, but unless the Mantis and her cohorts had fitted a new disguise, neither of them were likely candidates. The Mantis and her cohorts had all been of a similar size give or take an inch, and one of the women he was looking at was a head taller than the other, which, when Fletcher thought about it, proved they weren't the women he was looking out for.

Despite the industrial-strength coffee he was mainlining, he could feel himself flagging under the twin assaults of the comedown from extreme danger, and the fact he'd had four hours' sleep in the last forty.

He took a gulp of coffee and lifted his knife and fork. Protein from the food would help. There had been a stack of pancakes on the menu, but he'd opted against a favored dish and chosen what his body needed most.

As he ate he kept his eyes on the two points where they needed to be. The motel and the door.

The food didn't help him with the drowsiness he was feeling. Nor did the coffee.

Twice he nodded off only to be awoken by an elbow in the bicep from Quadrado. Each time he came to with a start and checked his vantage points first before giving her a sheepish look.

There was nothing but sympathy in her expression. "You're exhausted. I've heard nothing from Thomson, which suggests that the Mantis is resting for the night. She's had her hit for today. And she's had a go at you. She'll be tired too. You rest up. I'll wake you if I see anyone who even remotely resembles your description of the Mantis."

"You can't have heard from Thomson. He hasn't got your cell number." Fletcher shifted in his seat to find a less uncomfortable position. "And you've lost your laptop. One of the other women had that. You need to call this whole thing in to both Thomson and Soter, but make sure that you use a payphone when you call Thomson. Tell them about me being taken, but not that I'm still alive." He tried his best to give a supportive smile. "Thomson will try and rip you a new one. You're going to have to deal with that."

"If I can deal with you, I can deal with him." For all Quadrado was smiling as she spoke, the smile never got anywhere near her eyes.

CHAPTER FIFTY-SEVEN

Quadrado typed the email to Soter without looking at her cell. It was a skill she'd long had and barring a quick check for grammar and punctuation errors, she had no need to see what she was writing.

Outside the motel a group of young men wandered towards the entrance. They moved with all the grace of drunks the world over. They stumbled and lurched, whooped and hollered as they went. The two largest of the group brought up the rear, a smaller man held between them, his toes scraping the asphalt as they got him home. Other than them, there was no activity on the street.

The diner itself was quiet with only one other table occupied: a young couple who were interested only in one another. Their obvious love for each other made her think of Xavier. She missed him. Yes, it was still early days in their relationship, but she could feel herself falling for him.

A scan of the diner for a payphone came back empty. She considered walking along the street to find one, but gave up on the idea as soon as it entered her mind. To leave her post would be reckless in the extreme. Besides, with all her FBI training she'd grown used to a hierarchal structure. Her instincts were to wait for Soter to respond. He was her direct boss on this, and although Thomson was in charge of Las Vegas, Soter clearly outranked him.

Quadrado knew she was ducking the issue. Soter wouldn't be pleased about their failure, and Thomson would use Fletcher's alleged disappearance as a stick to beat her with. The loss of her

FBI laptop would be a nail driven through Thomson's stick. Above any other emotion, she was ashamed that she'd taken her eye off the ball to take a personal call. The idea that Fletcher had almost died because she was chatting with her boyfriend snarked her professional pride. To counter the shame, she was determined to make amends. To get a decent lead on the Mantis and, along with Fletcher, bring her down.

An email ping had her snatching her cell from the Formica-clad table.

DISAPPOINTING TURN OF EVENTS. FINDING FLETCHER IS YOUR TOP PRIORITY. IF FLETCHER DEAD, YOU RETURN TO NEW YORK AT ONCE. IF ALIVE RESUME MISSION. NEW LAPTOP AVAILABLE AT LVFO

The email was typical of Soter. Blunt and to the point, the only hint of human emotion was the first word. After that it was all straightforward instructions. She'd need to get the laptop from the Las Vegas Field Office to continue the mission, but doing so would bring her into contact with an irate Thomson, who surely wouldn't miss the opportunity to throw some criticism her way.

The one saving grace about it all was that she'd managed to keep to Fletcher's plan. Other than herself, no other law enforcement officer in Las Vegas knew he was still alive. That would give them a slight advantage and hopefully keep the Mantis off their backs.

Another thought that had plagued her since getting Fletcher out of the burning strip club was that it could have just as easily been her who'd been left to burn. She'd been absent by chance, and while there was a part of her that thought the Mantis had spared her, the majority vote was that she was alive down to dumb luck.

All of this knowledge was fuel to the inferno roiling in her gut. Never before had she experienced the desire to kill someone. With the Mantis it was different. She knew that if she ever got the woman in her sights, she wouldn't hesitate to pull the trigger. The same went for her two cohorts. There would be no second thoughts about right and wrong if she encountered them. No moralistic reasonings, just a squeeze of the trigger. There would be a recoil bucking the Glock into her hand, a spread of blood from the bullet wound, and the world would become a safer place.

Now, for the first time since they'd got this case, Quadrado could better understand Fletcher's rationalizations when it came to the taking of a life. The people she wanted to kill were vermin; they took money to end lives. She was aware enough to recognize a counterargument to this line of thinking was that she and Fletcher were little better. That line of thinking didn't stand for her, though: they were on the side of the righteous. Their mission was to exterminate vermin, not to deliver death for dollars. Like Fletcher, the murder of young Frankie appalled her. He'd offered no threat to the Mantis, yet he'd not been spared. No quarter had been given by the Mantis, and Quadrado was damned if she'd show the woman any mercy if she got a bead on her.

A flicker of movement across the street had her elbowing Fletcher in the ribs. He woke at once and followed the finger she was aiming in the direction of the Santa Fe Lodge.

Three women were approaching the motel. Quadrado didn't recognize them, but the way Fletcher had drawn the Glock from his waistband was all the confirmation she needed. They'd found the Mantis's base.

CHAPTER FIFTY-EIGHT

A half hour had passed with no sign of any of the women, so Fletcher ordered the stack of pancakes he'd forsaken earlier. The nap had revitalized him enough that he could now stay awake with ease. When in the Royal Marines, he'd learned—as had everyone else—to eat, sleep and crap whenever the opportunity arose. He'd slept, didn't need the bathroom and wasn't sure when he'd next get the chance to eat, hence the stack of pancakes.

Fletcher was wiping the last dribble of maple syrup from his chin when a woman exited the reception of the Santa Fe Lodge. She was one of the Mantis's cohorts. The one they'd met who'd worn the lace top: Iris.

The sliver of attraction he'd felt for her was long extinguished, but its memory shamed his professional and personal sensibilities.

As Iris set off along the street, Fletcher rose from his chair. "You get a new laptop sorted out. I'm going to follow her. When you've done that, swing by our motel and pick up two more pistols and a handful of magazines." He held out his hand. "Give me your cell and pick up another burner. Drop me a message with your number, and I'll keep in touch if there's anything to say."

"On it."

Quadrado's voice was strong, but there were heavy bags beneath each of her eyes. Where he'd had an hour's sleep, she'd stayed awake. He wanted to suggest that she get her head down for an hour, but there was no time to rest. Things were coming to a head; she could get all the sleep she wanted when the mission was over.

With nothing left to say, Fletcher left the diner.

For all he was a trained soldier, Fletcher didn't know much about following people. That was the domain of gumshoe detectives and law enforcement surveillance teams. What he did know he'd learned from books and internet tutorials.

Since being forcibly recruited by Soter, Fletcher had recognized there were gaps in his skill set that may cause him issues or compromise the missions he expected to be given. To counter these holes, he'd tried to envisage every possible scenario he'd encounter, identified his weaknesses and then learned techniques that may one day save his life. The art of following someone, spotting a tail he'd picked up and losing tails that may be put on him were subjects he'd studied extensively.

He'd spent a fair amount of his spare time practicing these skills on unsuspecting civilians. At first he'd been spotted by the men he'd tried following. He'd made a point of only following men, as if he was spotted, he didn't want a woman thinking he was a stalker. More for her sake than his, but by protecting the women he was also protecting himself.

One of the things he'd learned: it was a lot harder to stay inconspicuous without losing the target than he'd first thought. Too close and you got spotted. Too far and the target could be lost in a crowd. All the research he'd done on the subject had eschewed single persons as a surveillance team. They advocated a team. Changing over at random and leapfrogging ahead. The tails would change their jackets, add glasses or a hat, but never would they use the same look twice.

He stayed across the street from Iris. Maybe seventy yards back. Her white dress making her easy to see. To make this tailing job harder, his target knew what he looked like. She might think him dead, but if she did spot him, she'd certainly recognize him. That would be a double negative.

The Mantis would learn that he was still alive, but worst of all, she'd do all she could to shake him off. There was no doubt in Fletcher's mind Iris would lose him. He'd only been following her for three hundred yards so far, but he'd seen her execute some of the countersurveillance measures he'd learned. To combat this he walked a little slower to increase the distance between them. When she was walking straight forward, he whipped his jacket off and put it on inside out. The different-colored lining wasn't much when it came to changing his appearance, but it was the best he could do.

Iris stopped in front of an electrical store as if browsing. The fact it was 5:00 a.m. made a lie of her attempts to look like a shopper. Fletcher kept walking. There was nothing to duck behind, so doing anything except continuing would draw attention to himself.

There was a side street, so he turned into that, his pace measured and consistent. Once he was out of sight, he whipped off his jacket, stuffed it into a trash can and turned around. His bald head was a giveaway, but there was nothing he could do about that.

Except there was. A store was opening up fifty yards in front of him, the storekeeper wheeling out various carousels holding the cheap kind of stuff that can be found at any tourist destination.

The closest carousel to Fletcher bore an array of hats and baseball caps. Fletcher patted his pockets. It was a pointless exercise. His wallet had been in the clothes he'd stripped off when escaping the fire. He had not a cent on him. Even if he had, by the time he purchased a hat or two, he'd have lost Iris.

All the same, the idea of changing his look appealed. He lengthened his stride until he was in a full run. Fletcher's arrival at the store coincided with the storekeeper returning into the shop for the next carousel.

Fletcher snagged a black beanie and a white baseball cap, then turned to run back the other way. To steal like this went against every last one of his principles, but there was nothing he could do about it in this moment. Once the Mantis had been apprehended and stopped, he'd return to the store and pay for them. Any storekeeper whose day started this early wasn't making a lot of money. They'd be working long hours for little profit. Were the store a national chain, he'd feel less guilty about the theft, although he'd still come back to pay for his goods. With this store so obviously under private ownership, he felt like he was taking money directly from the owner's pocket.

As he neared the corner, Fletcher slowed his pace lest the still, early morning air carry the slap of his footsteps.

He jammed the baseball cap onto his head and stuffed the beanie into a pocket. When he rounded the corner, he was confident that his appearance was sufficiently changed for Iris to not recognize him as the same guy who'd been on the street earlier.

She was now two hundred yards ahead. She'd stopped walking and was looking into the window of another store.

Fletcher kept up a steady pace as he closed the distance between them. Not so fast that he'd pass her when she set off again, yet not so slow as to make it look as if he was dawdling.

Iris resumed her way along the street. As he trailed her, she cut around a block then returned to the same street the motel was on.

The more she showed her skills at running countersurveillance, the more Fletcher worried she'd spot he was tailing her. He was figuring whether or not he should just snatch her, drag her into an alleyway and force her to give up the Mantis's exact location and room number at the motel, when she entered a club.

CHAPTER FIFTY-NINE

Iris's decision to enter a club left Fletcher in a quandary. He didn't believe she'd gone there to dance and hook up with someone, not at 5 a.m. when surely it would be about to shut. It was part of her countersurveillance. She'd either exit via a side door or stay inside, waiting to see who followed her in.

The club wasn't one where Fletcher would fit in without looking like a dirty old man. Even from where he stood on the street, he could hear its techno-infused hip-hop beat. His first instinct was to wait until she exited, but he was sure there would be a back entrance she could leave by. It may require her to bypass a few staff members or a locked door or two, but he didn't believe either of these obstacles would slow her for long.

An extra reason not to wait on the street was the nagging feeling she'd not just made him as a tail, but had full-on identified him. This meant she could be holing up in the club, to keep him in one place until the Mantis and the third member of their team could join her. If that was the case, there would be no elaborate plan to kill him. It would be a knife through the ribs as he loitered on the street, or a blaze of gunfire from a passing vehicle that cut him down like a cornstalk going through a thresher.

As much as he doubted the wisdom of doing so, he knew he had to enter the club. He crossed the street. There wasn't much traffic at this time of morning. Something he was glad of, as now he had the idea of a drive-by shooting in his head, he found he was looking at every vehicle with suspicion. If he saw one coming his way with an open window, he was ready to take whatever cover he could find.

The doorman who stood square in the doorway was a Scot with an average face and a burring accent. Fletcher could tell the doorman was sizing him up as an opponent; he could guess the guy's thought processes. The doorman would be running him through his database of experience. Fletcher was older than the majority of customers in a place like this. This would place him in one of several categories in the doorman's mind. By being alone, he could be anything from a predator looking to prey on young and drunk women, to a father come to extract a teenage daughter with a fake ID and disliked boyfriend. The fact Fletcher was sober would go against him. Had he been showing signs of drunkenness, or giving off the stink of booze, he might be assumed to be someone looking for one last drink.

He saw all these calculations in the doorman's eyes.

"What brings you here?" The question seemed innocent, but Fletcher understood its real purpose. The doorman was letting him know that he wasn't their usual type of customer and that it had been noticed.

"I just got off a hard shift. Been called out to two fires and a suicide tonight. The music you're playing in there reminds me of my daughter. She used to listen to that stuff all the time. Couldn't stand it when she was at home, but now, now she's gone to college, I miss her." Fletcher pointed at the door. "I can't believe it myself, but I miss that damn music too. All I'm gonna do is sink a couple of beers and think about her and my shift before I go home and crash."

The doorman gave Fletcher an understanding nod as he stepped aside.

As he took his first steps into the club, Fletcher realized there was a lot of truth in the line he'd spun the doorman. He would miss Wendy when she left for college. He might not miss her choice of music, but he wasn't confident that he wouldn't miss everything about her regular presence in their home.

The club was rammed with people who were sitting, drinking and dancing. Inside, the music was as loud as a howitzer and, in Fletcher's jaded opinion, just as hazardous to health.

His eyes were scanning every inch of the room in rapid succession. They scoured booths, seared into groups of people and slid across the dance floor. Iris's white dress was distinctive, but he saw no sign of it until his eyes lit on a rear entrance and exit. There were a group of women exiting and they were all wearing white. He saw a couple of sashes on them, and one had a bridal veil sitting on top of her head. It was a typical bachelorette party. The kind that takes place all over the country.

Iris was in the middle of the group, and while they were all interacting with each other as they walked along the street, Iris kept herself to herself.

To the casual observer it was a great piece of camouflage. To Fletcher who'd been tailing her for a half mile, it was an amateurish move that had trapped her; she was now unable to run her countersurveillance measures without making herself obvious.

So far as Fletcher could work out, Iris couldn't have spotted him, as if she had, there was no way she'd have cocooned herself in a group of strangers.

As they arrived on the Strip, the women of the bachelorette party broke into their third rendition of "Going to the Chapel." A vocal coach's studio might have been a wiser choice of destination, but they were having a good time and Fletcher didn't grudge them that.

As he walked along the Strip after the knot of women, Fletcher felt the phone in his pocket vibrate. He pulled it out and saw a message from Quadrado. It just said her name, but that was enough. He stored the number into the contacts as he trailed the women. Across the street were some of the casinos he'd grown familiar with. The Strip itself had lost whatever luster he'd had when first arriving, but that didn't mean it wasn't thronged with others of a less cynical nature.

The women approached a crossing at a stop sign and halted. Not Iris; she'd slowed until she was at the back of the pack, and she slipped away from the other women and continued along the Strip. None of the bachelorette party noticed her leaving their group. Whether she'd asked if she could walk back to the Strip with them for safety's sake, or had remained silent didn't matter. She'd gone her own way now, and after everything he'd learned about the Mantis and her cohorts, Fletcher was sure something was about to go down.

This suspicion only deepened when Iris walked into the Gold Mine casino, the home of J.B. Ronson and his gang. It was the one Fletcher was most convinced would be a target and this was all the confirmation he needed.

The card with Ronson's number on it had been in his wallet and had therefore fallen victim to the fire. At this time of night, there was no way he'd be able to get anyone to believe he needed to speak to J.B. Ronson.

He looked around at the guards, hoping to see a familiar face who'd be able to carry a message to Ronson. Either Len or Bald-and-Not-Very-Undercover would be the perfect man for the task.

CHAPTER SIXTY

Iris had dropped all her attempts at countersurveillance when she joined the bachelorette party, and they remained dropped as she made her way around the Gold Mine. Fletcher could see she was keeping her wits about her, but gone were the double backs, the looks in reflective surfaces and the other less obvious measures she'd used.

From being silent and unnoticeable in the midst of the bachelorette party, Iris was now working her femininity. A sway had developed in her hips and from the way men were smiling at her, Fletcher could imagine that she was flashing them a wide smile. The dress now made sense to Fletcher: like the spotter she may have been yesterday, she was dressed in a way that was designed to be conspicuous.

She stopped and played the slots a couple of times. Not with any great intensity, just a few coins fished from her purse and fed into the machine. At one point she approached a roulette table, but hung back as if watching. As always with the casinos, there's no way of knowing the time of day without looking at your watch. The extra oxygen pumped into the room and the constant artificial lighting blend night into day and day into night. The passage of time is something that happens elsewhere. To other people. In a casino, everything is focused on the next card, the next spin of a wheel or the pull of the slot's handle.

Fletcher was certain Iris had a purpose in being here. That her every move in the casino had a specific reason. He glanced around her and weighed up her surroundings from an objective point of view.

She was in a cluster of roulette tables, to her back was a section for blackjack and other card games. To her right was a booth for exchanging and purchasing casino chips, and to her left the rows of slots.

If her mission was to be a robbery of any description, the booth would be the prime target. It wasn't a robbery, though, it was a hit. What Fletcher had to work out was why Iris had positioned herself where she had.

He thumbed out a rapid message to Quadrado, telling her where he was and urging her to bring weapons, body armor and spare ammo as soon as she could.

As he pressed send on the message, he again let his gaze wander around the vicinity occupied by Iris. Sometimes a break away from a task, even one so brief as he'd just had, was enough to restart his thought and observation faculties.

Now when he looked, he was seeing different things than before. Instead of looking at the furnishings and layout, he was looking at the people. No matter how often he scanned the room, he didn't once see a face he recognized. Maybe Len and Bald-and-Not-Very-Undercover were off shift or in a different part of the casino altogether. Wherever they were, he couldn't see them.

He did see five security guards within eyeshot of Iris. The closest a tall fellow with an obvious affinity for the gym and male grooming.

Fletcher paid him a little more attention without getting close to Iris. The security guard's eyes moved all the time, scanning the crowd, but Fletcher twice caught his gaze following a passing woman rather than sticking to the task he was being paid for.

Tall-and-Groomed was a potential weak link. Did the Mantis and Iris know about his wandering eyes? Was he part of their plan, or was Fletcher imagining it?

Iris moved and destroyed all of Fletcher's theories regarding the security guard. Coincidence should never figure in his thinking, but it had here, and had almost sent him down the wrong track.

Rather than moving far, Iris was now overlooking the nearest blackjack table to where she'd been. Her move from point to point had been a slow sashay that was akin to a bird displaying its plumage. Every movement from her was sensual and seductive in its intensity. A glance at Tall-and-Groomed showed his head was turned to follow the direction of her travel. Only when she stopped moving did he resume his sweeps of the area.

Two minutes after Iris moved to the blackjack tables, the five security guards all moved round one space counterclockwise. Now Iris was within five feet of Tall-and-Groomed. Except she'd maneuvered herself first so he was coming to her.

Like so many of the Mantis's hits, this was clearly well researched in advance and planned to the minutest detail.

Iris bent her knees forward in turn. The action making her butt wiggle as she stood still. Fletcher could see Tall-and-Groomed's attention was on her and her alone.

The dereliction of duty from the guard disappointed Fletcher, but it didn't surprise him. For the most part, his job would be boring and monotonous with days, perhaps weeks, of just standing around looking, with the odd spike of excitement when someone needed to be ejected. It was human nature to switch off a little. A young man who cared about his appearance, spending many bored hours in a place where there were attractive women—it would only end one way. His eyes would wander. He'd temper the long shifts with a little eye candy. Perhaps once in a while he'd get an offer, or at least that's what would be his constant hope, if the way he was ogling Iris was any indication. A true professional wouldn't allow himself to be distracted, but there weren't many true pros left.

With the guard distracted, one of two things could happen. Iris could use seduction to get the guard to let her into a rear area, or she would simply be a distraction that allowed the Mantis to penetrate the casino's security.

Iris moved off and circulated an area of the casino where the next guard was surveying an area by the slots. Servers were coming and going through a set of service doors. They carried trays of food from the kitchen, drinks from the bar, and empty dishes and glasses back.

Another rotation counterclockwise put Tall-and-Groomed near Iris once more. She gave him a lascivious smile that reddened the back of his neck and ears. Tall-and-Groomed spoke into his radio for a few seconds then abandoned his post. Fletcher guessed he'd made an excuse of some kind, like needing the bathroom, as the four other guards in rotation with him all shuffled round a little to cover for him.

Tall-and-Groomed approached a door marked "Private," took a look around and then waved Iris over.

It was at this point a new theory hit Fletcher. Maybe Tall-and-Groomed was a stooge of the Mantis's instead of a randy young man. If that was the case, he was taking a huge risk crossing his bosses at the casino.

CHAPTER SIXTY-ONE

The laptop bag slung over one shoulder was cumbersome enough, but Quadrado was also weighed down by a bag containing two sets of body armor. She hadn't wanted to put it on until she knew she was entering a battle zone. Walking around Las Vegas in body armor would draw the wrong kind of attention. Especially for someone with brown skin. Yes, she might have an FBI badge in her pocket, but that wouldn't help her if some weekend warrior decided to make a preemptive strike on what they believed was a terrorist.

By dint of its purpose, body armor isn't light. It's designed to stop bullets and, as such, has to have a certain heft, otherwise it would be less than useless.

For the first time since arriving in town, there wasn't a cab to be seen anywhere. She jogged as best she could with the two bags buffeting her body as she went. Again, she recognized that she might be deemed suspicious by the less tolerant members of society, so her eyes were always on the move, looking for threats.

A pair of elderly women, dressed in velour as they took an early morning walk, wasted no time in getting out of her way. One turning to the other with a shocked expression on her face. In her mind, Quadrado could imagine the woman getting ready to tell a juicy story about the young female terrorist whom she'd seen in Las Vegas. The story would receive increased embellishments with every retelling until it bore not even a semblance of the truth.

The Gold Mine casino was maybe a half mile away when she heard a beep from her phone. It could only be Fletcher. He was the only person she'd given the number to. Not even Xavier had it yet.

She fished the device from her pocket and picked out the message as she trotted forward.

HIT IS GOING DOWN NOW! SUMMON SWAT TEAM TO GOLD MINE ASAP. GIVE DESCRIPTION OF ME TO THEM. DON'T WANT TO BECOME A FRIENDLY FIRE STATISTIC.

Not good. Not good at all.

Quadrado slowed until she was in a fast walk. Because the phone was new and she'd never had a moment to herself since she'd got it, she hadn't yet programmed any numbers into it. The phone she'd given to Fletcher had Thomson and Forbes as contacts, as well as the FBI office's number. This one didn't.

She was tempted to call through the switchboard at Lake Mead Boulevard, but she knew that would be a slow process. For all she could introduce herself as an agent, she would still have to jump through all the hoops designed to trip up the prank callers. That would take time. More time than she had.

Quadrado tapped out a message to Soter. He had incredible pull; it was time for her to utilize it.

With the message sent, Quadrado put in the call to Lake Mead. For all Soter might be their fastest option, she knew from experience that he was potentially ruthless enough to deny them the SWAT team.

By the time she got to the Strip, the Gold Mine was still two blocks away. As tempting as it was to break into a run, she continued with a fast walk, wanting to conserve her strength, as well as not arouse suspicion.

Another reason for caution was the operator she was speaking to. The woman was professional enough to not be condescending, nor to let doubt enter her voice, but Quadrado knew she was going to have a hard enough time getting the SWAT team without panting and gasping down the phone.

One block to the Gold Mine. The sun hadn't yet risen, but there was more than enough neon and other artificial lighting to make the Strip seem bathed in sunlight.

A man lurched across the street in front of her. Quadrado's first thought was that he was going to tackle her, but it was a drunken stagger rather than an attempt to intercept. She rounded him and kept going, her calves burning from the long strides as she speed-walked forward.

Quadrado was in good shape. She ran four miles at least twice a week and swam a minimum of a mile each week. Her stamina was good and there was little excess weight on her, yet despite all this and the cool morning air, there was still a sheen of perspiration on her brow when she arrived outside the Gold Mine.

In an ideal world, the call would be finished by now and she'd be able to go in, hand over what Fletcher needed and then support him as he hunted the Mantis. This wasn't an ideal world. Quadrado paced back and forth outside the casino. She would have continued inside, but there was no way she was taking the risk of having this conversation overheard.

CHAPTER SIXTY-TWO

Fletcher approached the door Tall-and-Groomed had used by following another of the guards. He suspected the man was on his way to recall Tall-and-Groomed, but that wasn't any of his concern. Upon seeing the guard leave with Iris, he'd already bidden the man goodbye. To leave him alive would be an unnecessary loose end, and so far the Mantis and her team had left not even the tiniest thread to pick at, much less an entire loose end.

The first order of business for Fletcher was to get through the door and deal with the guard. For this, timing was everything. The guard swiped his pass, clasped the door handle and swung the door wide. Fletcher was ten paces away. He had to get through that door before it closed, but without making a scene that would have other guards swarming his way.

As the guard opened the door wide and lifted his foot to step into the rear of the casino, Fletcher set off. Long fast paces became powerful strides forward. By the time he was four paces from the door, the guard had stepped through and the door was closing behind him.

Fletcher upped his pace and crashed his left shoulder into the door a half second before the latch could click into its housing. From a psychological standpoint, the timing was perfect. With such entrances and exits being weak points in the security, the guard would have relaxed a little, believing he'd gotten through without incident. He'd also be distracted with thoughts about

Tall-and-Groomed. His focus wouldn't be where it should, and that would cost him.

The barge through the door caught the guard by surprise. He half wheeled in time to see Fletcher's sudden presence. There was a split second of indecision, then his hand went for his gun. He was a lifetime too late. By the time his hand was moving to his waist, Fletcher's palm strike was a quarter of an inch from the guy's chin.

The palm strike lifted the guard onto his toes then dumped him on his butt. He was a long way from consciousness and would be dining with a straw for weeks to come.

For Fletcher there was no sense of guilt at what he'd done to the man. If he'd been on his game, he'd have seen what was going down with Tall-and-Groomed and Iris. If he'd been on his game, Fletcher should never have gotten through the door. On the other hand, he'd gotten lucky. If Fletcher was the Mantis, he'd be dead by now.

The gun on the guard's hip marked him as different. Most of the guards Fletcher had seen weren't carrying, so the one he'd just felled must have been a supervisor, team leader or whatever management term was appropriate.

There was an old-fashioned bolt at the top and bottom of the door to back up the modern electronic locks. They looked new, which suggested they were extra precautions brought about by the Mantis's killing spree.

Fletcher slid both bolts closed and dumped the guard against the door. It was only a matter of time before one of the security detail investigated. If he'd been seen entering the door, they'd already be on their way. The guard's key card had fallen to the floor, so he lifted the card and planted it into his shirt pocket. He also claimed the guard's gun and a spare magazine. Better to have and not need, than to need and not have. There was a night stick on the guard's belt, but Fletcher left it where it was. When he came into contact with the Mantis, he wanted a gun in his hand, not any other kind of weapon.

As he moved along the hallway, Fletcher was trying his best to remember the schematics of the hotel element of the casino. He'd studied so many since arriving in Las Vegas, the details had begun to blur together. He found plenty of anterooms used for storage. Whether cleaning products, spare slots or just hotel equipment like tables and chairs, there were plenty of dead ends for him to run into.

The fourth door he opened led into another hallway. Like the first, there were untreated block walls and a sense of functionality. Also like the first, there was a security guard. The man was brushing crumbs from the front of his shirt. Like the guard at the door, he went for the weapon on his hip, a night stick.

Fletcher already had a gun in his hand. Admittedly it was his weaker left hand, but the guard didn't know that.

"Hands on your head and don't even think about moving." Fletcher put dominance and surety into his voice so the man would comply.

The guard was old enough to be experienced at his job. This meant he was also old enough to have picked up some life experience. He did as he was ordered.

"Don't shoot, buddy. Whatever you're here for, I ain't going to stop you getting it."

Fletcher closed the fifteen paces between them in a series of rapid steps.

"Easy, buddy. I'm not your enemy."

"No, you're not." Fletcher's right elbow crashed into the side of the man's jaw, causing him to slump into a disheveled heap at Fletcher's feet.

The hallway ended in a junction. There were stairs at one side and an elevator door at the other.

Fletcher always preferred stairs to an elevator. They offered freedom of movement, a better element of surprise and less chance of being ambushed. His foot hit the staircase at the same moment he heard voices. They were coming down the stairwell. He was a stranger here. He had no uniform, and no reason for being here. The guards he'd felled would soon come round and raise the alarm. Thoughts of the Mantis executing a hit at any moment were enough to spur him onwards in terms of being active, although he didn't want to encounter any of the hotel staff who might be using the stairwell. It was one thing dealing with a guard or a henchman, but there was no way he planned to harm any innocent civilians. All the same, he swapped the gun to his dominant right hand.

With his eyes and ears on the stairwell, Fletcher backed away towards the elevator. Of the two ways of getting to the higher floors, it was now the better option.

He was still focused on the stairwell when the elevator doors opened.

There was no informative chime, just a hissed whisper as the doors slid open. Fletcher whirled round, his gun coming up as he turned. There were three young men in the elevator. Each one an obvious henchman. Fletcher had faced worse odds than three against one on many occasions, but only a few times without room to move or the element of surprise to aid him.

As good as Fletcher might be, the henchmen had the advantage of numbers and, without room to retreat, Fletcher had to face them down. Easy to do when you've got a gun in your hand pointing the right way, not so easy when the weapon is pointing the wrong way.

The biggest of the three men rushed him. Fletcher was bowled away from the elevator and slammed face first into the wall. Strong hands gripped his gun arm and kept it directed away from anywhere it could achieve anything that would help Fletcher get free.

CHAPTER SIXTY-THREE

Fletcher knew he had perhaps one, one and a half seconds before things got out of his control. His gun was useless to him, but the desperate way strong hands were trying to tear it from his grasp was very informative.

First it told him that he was dealing with unarmed men. Had the three henchmen been carrying guns of their own, twisting one in his ear would have left him no option but to release the weapon. Second, the fight over the weapon told him he was dealing with instinctive thinkers not analytical ones. A smart opponent would have dropped heavy punches into each kidney or banged his head against the wall until his grip loosened. They'd come around to that way of thinking, hence the fact Fletcher knew he only had a small window in which to act.

The problem with being pressed against a wall is that you can't get any leverage into your blows. There can be no backswing to increase the power of any offensive move. And when your face is pushed against a wall, you also have the disadvantage of not knowing your opponents' exact positions. But what you do have is something invaluable: a hard surface that you can lever yourself off.

Fletcher allowed the hands fighting for his gun to pull him to one side. This moved him out of the way of the henchman pressing on his left shoulder. He now had one henchman at his back and one grappling either wrist. Not an ideal situation, but one he could deal with.

While the henchman on his right wrist was fighting for the gun, the one on his left was doing nothing more than trying to restrain Fletcher. A wise opponent would have pulled the arm straight and applied any one of a variety of locks. This would have applied a balance to the man trying to yank the gun from Fletcher's grip.

Fletcher used the henchman's poor tactics to his advantage by bending his arm at the elbow, planting his hand on the wall and pushing. This levered his body away from the wall. All three henchmen had the same instinctive reaction and tried to flatten Fletcher back against the wall.

As Fletcher thudded into the wall a second time, he dragged his left hand downwards and free of that henchman's grip. With the hand free, it was time to go on the offensive.

The closeness of the wall meant he couldn't deliver a meaningful blow, but that didn't mean he couldn't attack. Because Fletcher's hand was now at his side, there was only one target within close proximity. His fingers grasped the henchman's groin and squeezed until the man howled in agony. To add insult to injury, Fletcher gave a final sharp twist before releasing the man.

With the henchman nursing his crotch, Fletcher squirmed his free arm between his gut and the wall as he hauled on his gun hand. The combination of the moves spun him so he was side on to the wall, and the henchman who'd been attempting to take his pistol was being hauled towards him. Because he'd planned the move, Fletcher was ready for the henchman's arrival and had already cocked his head back to throw a vicious headbutt that was timed to perfection. The henchman's nose splattered as he staggered back, groggy and unsteady on his feet.

The third and final henchman had enough sense to grab Fletcher's wrist and try to control the gun. With room to move, Fletcher countered the man's attempts to twist the gun free, went under his arm and when the man's arm was straight, dropped the gun and grabbed the henchman's wrist. A simple rotation through ninety degrees had the man in a perfect armbar.

Now it was time to take him and his buddies out of the fight. Fletcher's elbow crashed into the henchman's. With the henchman's elbow already being hyper-extended by the armbar, there was only ever going to be one result.

The henchman sagged away, doing what he could to support the hinge Fletcher had just broken.

Fletcher was on the move as soon as the blow was delivered. His next target: the henchman with the crushed groin. The man had already straightened and was winding up a punch that would fell an elephant if it landed.

That was the problem with going for a single punch that would end a fight. To get the necessary force, you had to wind it up and put everything into it. If the punch landed, you won. If it missed, you were exposed.

The henchman's punch missed Fletcher by a clear four inches. Fletcher's uppercut landed square on his opponent's jaw. Like his buddy's elbow, the jaw broke as the henchman's eyes rolled back.

Now there was only the groggy one left. He was shaking his head to clear the wooliness and wiping his eyes to rid himself of the involuntary tears a shattered nose causes. He was in no state to defend himself, and Fletcher was in no mood to show too much mercy. Fletcher wasn't sure the man even saw it coming as he landed a thunderous punch square on his temple. Two seconds after impact, the third henchman lay on the floor beside the other two.

Fletcher picked up his gun and checked the one tucked into the back of his jeans. Had any of the henchmen the slightest intelligence, they would have frisked him as soon as he'd been slammed against the wall. That they hadn't had the sense to do it marked them as amateurs. With their intellect, it was unlikely they'd rise far, and this is why Fletcher had chosen not to retrieve his second gun. In his mind, the henchmen deserved a harsh lesson, but they weren't deserving of a final one. That's why he'd left them unconscious and broken, rather than dead or dying. They were nothing more than three guys doing a job, even if they were doing it badly.

The sound of heels pocking on concrete stairs filled the air now the fight was over. Rather than get caught like a puppy beside a wet patch, Fletcher ducked into the elevator. The alarm would be raised soon enough when whoever was coming down the stairwell found the defeated henchmen. What Fletcher didn't want, was to give them a chance to describe him to whoever they reported the attack to.

The lift doors closed before anyone appeared. Fletcher pressed the button for the floor above and made sure to have both pistols in his hands and aimed out of the doors when they opened. He needn't have bothered. There was nobody there to worry about. The two henchmen on the floor were in no state to offer a threat. Both had a pair of bullet wounds. Heart and left eye. A signature as sure as a calling card. And proof the Mantis didn't share his merciful attitude towards rubbish henchmen.

She'd been here. Recently, if the blood still trickling down one of the henchmen's chests was anything to go by.

Fletcher stepped forward, his entire being in full battle mode as he surveyed the room over a pair of gun sights.

CHAPTER SIXTY-FOUR

Fletcher crept forward as fast as he dared. He knew he was on the trail of the Mantis, had to exercise caution. But if he dallied too much, he'd never catch up with her.

She was in the building, and she didn't know he was still alive, let alone that he was so close behind her. That gave him an advantage, an advantage he planned to press fully home.

Step by step Fletcher moved forward. Corners were rounded quickly with fingers curled around triggers. His eyes seeking out threats and dismissing the mundane objects he encountered. The fact he'd found the two dead henchmen was enough to indicate he was wrong to think that J.B. Ronson's quarters were on the top floor. Rather than the penthouse suite, he'd taken a lower floor room. Fletcher was sure Ronson's suite would be every bit as luxurious as the penthouse, but there was no escaping the business logic that by taking a lower floor, he was leaving the higher tariff rooms for paying customers.

The boom of a gunshot was followed by two more cracks as the shooter loosed off further rounds. Fletcher's muscle memory had him diving for cover long before the second shot sounded.

He'd seen nothing, but there was a junction between the hallway he was on and another and, from what he could tell, the shots had come from the left. They were followed by a pair of coughs and the unmistakable sound of a body falling to the ground. The rustling of clothes, the thuds as knees, arms, head and torso made contact with the ground was a familiar noise to Fletcher. He'd caused it plenty of times himself.

That the first three shots were unsilenced indicated a henchman or guard had spotted the Mantis and had fired at her. The two muted coughs of a silenced pistol proved the Mantis was unhurt, and still able to deal out death with accuracy. He was on her trail; her back would be to him. An advantage he could have exploited, had the guard not pulled his trigger. The shots he'd fired were sure to have been heard by someone. The Mantis would be prepared for others to come running. For threats to approach her from every angle.

All of this meant Fletcher was close, real close. He had to force himself not to grip his pistols quite so tight. A firm grip was good, but one so tight it caused a quiver could affect his accuracy and that wasn't something he could allow to happen. He guessed he'd get one clear shot at the Mantis. That shot would have to be right on target. It would have to kill her, or cause such damage she couldn't return fire. Getting into a shooting match with someone like the Mantis was foolish in the extreme. She was a deadly assassin, used to creeping into places, executing her target and leaving. She'd be accustomed to snap shots. His forte wasn't this kind of cat-and-mouse game. He was a blunt instrument designed to bludgeon opponents into submission through greater force. His specialty was shock and awe, hers stealth and accuracy.

Shock and awe was out; any noise from running would attract gunfire long before there was any chance of him picking out his target. Fletcher stepped out from the corner into the left hallway, his guns trained forward, seeking out any hint of a female form.

The hallway opened out into what resembled a waiting room. It was maybe ten yards by twelve. A row of cream sofas formed a horseshoe around a coffee table.

The Mantis was at the far end of the sofas, her back to him, and her attention forward. Fletcher was fifteen yards away. Close enough to take a shot and feel confident about hitting his target. He would have pulled his trigger but for one thing: his mission wasn't just to neutralize the Mantis, it was to find out who her paymaster was and take them down too. The easiest way to do that was to get her to talk. To shoot her from this distance would mean he'd have to aim for center mass to be sure of hitting her. His shot would either kill her or inflict grievous injury. She might not be fit to speak if he only injured her.

Fletcher had no qualms about killing her. She deserved it. But it would be far easier to fully complete his mission if he could extract information from her. That's why he was stepping forward as silently as he could. Once he got within seven or eight yards of her, he was confident he could put a bullet into her shoulder or arm that would nullify any threat she posed, yet still leave her alive and able to talk. After that he'd be able to get his answers.

He got within ten yards without issue. The Mantis's entire focus was on the doors ahead of her. A gun was held in each hand, and they were trained at a pair of doors that led from the waiting room.

Except it wasn't the Mantis. He could see that now. It was Iris, the woman he'd been attracted to when she'd worn the lace top. The one he'd followed here. That attraction was long gone, and the strategy he'd planned hadn't changed. Disable and then question was still his plan.

Iris now wore a pair of black leggings and a tight black tee. It was the outfit and the shape of her body underneath it that had tipped Fletcher off to her real identity. She was a little bulkier than the Mantis, and that bit closer to curvaceous.

Two more steps and he'd be able to pull his trigger. The problem with doing that was the shot would attract attention. As would any screams of pain. Either from the wound his bullet inflicted, or his attempts to coerce her into talking.

There's a difference between male and female screams of agony. Feminine screams are higher, shriller. Not only would any of the casino's henchmen hear the shots and the subsequent screams, the Mantis might, too. The henchmen and J.B. Ronson he could deal with easily enough if he had the Mantis at his mercy. They'd point their guns for a while, but when they realized who he'd shot, they'd not pull their triggers if he handed her over. Iris was almost as deadly a killer as the Mantis herself, so things might pan out differently. If she claimed Fletcher was with her, things could turn bad in an instant.

All the same, he'd have to stick to his plan unless he could get close enough to put his gun against Iris's head. A plan he thought unlikely to succeed.

Another step forward and he was within eight yards of her. He heard the noise at the same time he saw her react to it. The noise was that of a door handle being operated. Her reaction a stiffening in preparation as she kept her guns trained on the two doors leading from the waiting area.

The door opened to reveal a henchman carrying a submachine gun. With Iris crouched behind the sofa, it was Fletcher who first attracted the henchman's attention. The henchman pulled his trigger, the submachine gun spitting a murderous hail of bullets in Fletcher's direction.

CHAPTER SIXTY-FIVE

Geoffrey Elliott couldn't sleep with any degree of success. Like a lot of people in high office he could manage on less sleep than the average person, provided that sleep was deep and uninterrupted. As he'd climbed the greasy pole of promotion to become director of the FBI, he'd learned to compartmentalize things. To know when to worry at an issue, and when to let it go. Yet tonight he'd had the unsettled, broken sleep of a lifelong insomniac. He'd get maybe a half hour at most then his body would jerk awake, his mind filled with sleep-preventing thoughts.

They all settled back to one point: Fletcher was missing, but Quadrado was carrying on with the case. That made no sense, as regardless of how fine an agent she might be, she lacked the skill set to neutralize someone as deadly as the Mantis.

Quadrado could be set on exacting revenge, but he didn't think that was the case. Her psych profile showed little inclination to seek vengeance. Justice, yes. Revenge, no. Other than her admirable stubbornness to complete a job, he could see only one reason why she was still working the case in the way she was: Fletcher was alive and she was keeping the fact secret.

It made sense on many levels, but the thing most perturbing Elliott was that she'd kept him out of the loop. It may be that she didn't trust their methods of communication, that she thought they might have been hacked. If that was the case, she'd have found a way to get a message to him. Ergo, he was the one she or Fletcher had trust issues with.

This was the point currently destroying his sleep. He was no fool. He knew half the people he dealt with on a daily basis didn't trust him. That was all part of the job. He didn't trust them either and was therefore rarely surprised by his counterparts in other government agencies. For all they'd banded together to establish Fletcher as their black-ops man, they each retained separate agendas on other matters.

He could see where the issues had stemmed from. He got it. First there had been that note slipped into Quadrado's pocket. That was a brazen move by the Mantis, and if its purpose had been to unsettle Quadrado and Fletcher, it had certainly worked on Quadrado. From what he understood of Fletcher being taken earlier, they'd been in an out-of-the-way bar. They'd moved out of their hotel and found other accommodation. All their FBI-issued communications devices had been left at the hotel, and they'd not told him where they were staying. He didn't doubt for one minute that Fletcher would be doing all he could to stay under the radar after the note, and yet, the Mantis had still found Fletcher and managed to spirit him away. That spoke of a detailed surveillance on them. Or inside information.

Under the guise of Soter, Elliott was the one person who had inside information and direct contact with them; therefore, it was no great feat of deduction for them to think he was the person who'd leaked their presence and location. Whether they suspected him of being in cahoots with the Mantis or just insecure was immaterial. The fragile bond of trust he'd established with them was, at least for now, broken.

The silence from Quadrado was understandable, frustrating as it might be. It could be that Fletcher was dead. Or that he was locked in battle with the Mantis. Maybe he'd killed her and was currently after her paymaster. That would be the perfect scenario, but there was no way of knowing which, if any, of these scenarios reflected what was really happening.

Elliott closed his eyes and willed sleep to take him. Whatever was happening over in Las Vegas, it would result in a busy day for him tomorrow. The Chief of Staff's threat hung over him. If Fletcher and Quadrado didn't succeed, he would potentially be out of a job.

CHAPTER SIXTY-SIX

Fletcher hit the floor hard enough to drive the wind from his lungs, but feeling breathless was the least of his problems. In the tiny snapshot of time he had before diving to the floor, Fletcher had recognized the shooter: it was Len, the pit boss who'd questioned him a couple of days ago.

Fletcher knew with certainty that Len only had to direct his submachine gun down a few degrees and his body would be riddled with bullets. That didn't account for the fact Iris was in the room and armed. Whether she was as deadly as the Mantis was a moot point. When you're in a gunfight, it's about the number of opponents you're facing, their positions, their fire power and how accurate they can shoot.

For each of the three people in the room, there were two opponents.

Iris had two pistols, the same as he had, so they were matched in that sense. He suspected that she'd be every bit as good a shot as he was, which still left them matched. Len was another matter. His submachine gun far outgunned their pistols. Its rapid-fire rate more than making up for its lack of accuracy and any failing Len may have.

Fletcher was in a direct line with Iris and Len. So far, Len's bullets had flown high, but it was only a moment's task for him to readjust his aim. Fletcher snapped off a shot with each of his guns. His aim was a mile off, but it wasn't his objective to score a hit, more to show some resistance and perhaps force Len into cover, or at least delay his next burst of fire. He could see Iris doing the same thing. Her pistols bucking in her hand as she fired in Len's general direction.

A lightshade shattered, accompanied by a yelp from Len. By peering round a sofa, Fletcher saw his aim had been driven ever higher when he was caught by one of Iris's shots.

With his right hand, Fletcher fired off a couple of shots at Len, winging him again in the same arm Iris hit, and using his left hand he sent another pair of shots at Iris.

Both shots at Iris missed, but they did make her aware of Fletcher's presence. As she sent another couple of rounds towards Len, she flicked a glance backwards at him. Before he ducked back into cover, he saw her eyes widen in recognition.

Len had found cover somewhere. Now all three of them were in hiding. The sofas all extended to the ground, so there was no point in Fletcher trying to peek under them in order to locate either of his foes.

It would be the same for the other two; therefore, it was now about dumb luck and playing percentages. He knew the approximate position of the others, but they were in the same situation. To raise a head above a sofa, or to peer round a corner was a gamble that could go either way. It could lead to a bullet between the eyes or the chance to get the upper hand on his foes. Were this just between him and Iris, he could empty both of his pistols into the lower parts of the sofa she'd been hiding behind, in the hope at least one bullet would incapacitate her.

The presence of Len and his submachine gun made this a moot point. As soon as he realized the sofas wouldn't stop bullets, his superior firepower would win this for him.

What Fletcher needed to do was change the narrative. To force one of the others into making a mistake. He laid down one of his guns and reached across towards the low table at the edge of the room. On the table was a shallow bowl filled with decorative pine cones. He lifted the bowl without making a sound and tensed his muscles ready for action.

Pine cones scattered off the back of the bowl as Fletcher frisbeed it in the direction of where Len had last been.

As soon as the bowl left his hand, he grabbed his gun and propelled himself backwards. A stream of gunfire stitched every wall in the room as Len panicked at the sudden noise. The bullets were maybe four feet high, but as Fletcher was on the floor, they carried no risk to him.

As the submachine gun fell silent, Fletcher popped up and put three bullets into Len. Two in one shoulder and another in his remaining good arm. The man was no danger to him now, and although the henchman had been trying to kill him, Fletcher was content to leave the man as he now was. If he survived the night, he'd face a lot of jail time, unless he gave up Ronson and his men to the FBI.

Iris had different ideas. She popped up and sent a pair of shots at Len that sprouted red mushrooms in the center of his chest. As he died, his finger squeezed the submachine gun's trigger until it emptied the magazine.

Fletcher fired a round from each gun at Iris, and moved his position before she could return fire.

With Len and his submachine gun taken out of the equation, Fletcher and Iris were now engaged in a game of cat and mouse. Fletcher's least favorite situation after a Mexican standoff.

Now it was all about second-guessing each other. From the series of clacks, they both knew the magazine of the submachine gun was empty. What they didn't know was if Len had a spare on him. To get the submachine gun and a spare magazine would swing the advantage in either Fletcher's or Iris's favor.

Two coughs from Iris's pistols bludgeoned holes in the sofa Fletcher was hiding behind. He returned fire with a single shot and moved along to a new position. He was down to his last five bullets. When they ran out, he'd be a sitting duck.

CHAPTER SIXTY-SEVEN

Quadrado had long since grown tired of the obstructive security guard who was refusing to let her enter the rear areas of the casino. She'd pleaded, suggested that he could emerge a hero by letting her in and tried every other method of persuasion she could think of short of offering herself.

The guard had been resolute. Not rude, just immovable in his insistence that she wasn't getting access. There was only one thing left for it: she drew out her badge and showed it to him.

Quadrado loaded her voice with as much authority as she could muster and stared down the guard. "Look, buddy, I'm a federal agent and you're in my way. Now let me back there or prepare to face the consequences."

"Bull. If you are a fed, you'll know that you need a warrant. You're an imposter who's wasting my time, or you're a fed trying to get in via illegal means. Don't matter to me which you are, you're not getting in."

Quadrado took two steps back and rethought her options. The guard was right in what he was saying. If she could find a way to convince him of the urgency of the situation, he might relent and allow her access. She'd expected this kind of reaction to her badge, which was why she'd held it back until she'd exhausted every other option.

Her mind worked through every option she had without finding a solution for the umpteenth time. She wished Fletcher was with her. He'd find a way to get past the guard.

After a moment's thought she realized just what he'd do. "Screw it." Quadrado's hand dove into her pocket and as she stepped forward, it emerged with one of the Glocks she'd got at the FBI office. Before the guard could react, she had the Glock against his ribs. "Do I need to do some cheesy countdown or are you letting me through?"

The guard took a glance around him as he licked his lips. "No, ma'am. Now let's stay cool about this. You good with that?"

"I'm only good with you letting me in back. Anything that doesn't make that happen will see me pulling the trigger. Now get over to that door. You're going to lead me to where I want to go."

"Yes, ma'am." All the previous traces of obstruction were gone from the guard's demeanor. He was now scared enough to be compliant.

The guard moved to the door in steady, measured steps. There was no hint of sudden movements, and Quadrado was confident he wouldn't try to fight back in any way. All the same, she didn't allow herself to lessen her vigilance for possible retaliation.

The door opened to reveal a guard hauling himself off the floor. He was holding his jaw and looking decidedly sorry for himself.

"Lead on. You're taking me to wherever J.B. Ronson will be at this time of night. Once that's done, I'll let you go. Trust me, if you try anything clever you won't live long enough to regret it." The threats she was making sounded off to Quadrado. To her ear they were the bad dialogue of a testosterone-fueled movie rather than things real humans actually said. They seemed to have the right effect on the guard though, so she ignored her misgivings and kept a close watch on him, in case he'd had a plate of heroics for his breakfast.

Quadrado followed as the guard led her through a maze of corridors. When they came to a part where there was a choice between an elevator and a stairwell, Quadrado didn't fail to notice the fresh bloodstains on the floor and walls.

"Take the stairwell."

The guard did as instructed. His legs trudging upwards as Quadrado hung back a couple of steps, fearful of a mule kick that would send her flying back down the stairs.

Rather than lead her to the top floor as she expected, the guard halted on the first floor and pointed along the passageway. "Go along there and you'll be in Mr. Ronson's private rooms." There was fear in his voice, as if he half expected to be killed now he'd served his purpose.

Quadrado pointed back down the stairwell. "Off you go then. And please, don't get any smart ideas about coming back to get me with a bunch of your buddies. You'd be better off calling the cops. There's serious crap going down that you're far better keeping out of."

As the man scurried back down the stairs, Quadrado dropped her bag of supplies and pulled out a bulletproof vest. If she had to go to war, she wanted to have the most protection possible.

CHAPTER SIXTY-EIGHT

Fletcher ducked down to minimize his chances of being hit by one of Iris's bullets. She was far closer to hitting him than he was comfortable with. As he only had three rounds left in one gun and two in the other, he had to preserve his fire.

From the angle of the bullets, he could tell she was moving around the room in the direction of the henchman. She was going after the submachine gun. That either would or wouldn't help her, but not knowing which meant Fletcher had to try and stop her anyway. He picked off a shot that was aimed at the halfway point between where she'd started out and the henchman fell.

It was time for a change of tactics. Time to exert a little pressure. "Hey there, lady. How's this working out for you? I can wait all night. I'm on the right side of this. You, you're gonna have to hit the bricks soon. Either J.B. Ronson's men will come in force, or the FBI will. My colleague has already put the call in, so they'll be here damn soon. How long can you wait?"

"Sounds like the desperate words of a man who hasn't got a lot left in his gun. You been firing off pairs of shots since you got here and now you're picking singles. Sounds a lot like you're saving ammo to me." There was a dragging rustle that accompanied her words. Fletcher could picture her crawling commando-style towards the henchman.

"Or maybe I'm bluffing you into making a stupid move like rushing at me." Another dragging rustle came from across the room. "Bit of a shame you're going to find that he only had one magazine for his submachine gun."

Fletcher got silence as his answer. No dragging, no cocking of a weapon, just complete and utter silence filled the waiting area.

He'd spooked her by pinpointing her goal, by suggesting she'd revealed her position for what may be a waste of time. How she responded would be telling.

All he got was a dragging rustle as she pressed forward. Now was the time to really turn the screw.

"You know, from where I am, I can see his gun. I have my sights trained on it as I speak. Do you think you can get it and back into cover before I put a bullet through your hand?"

Fletcher heard four rapid coughs and saw the end of the sofa he was hiding behind sprout four holes. He let out a low moan as if hit and let one of his guns slip from his grasp so it clattered on the laminate flooring.

"Hah." A one-syllable word rarely carried more contempt than Iris's utterance.

Fletcher drew himself slowly upright to see her legs protruding from behind a sofa as she retrieved the henchman's gun. He put two bullets into her legs and dashed to where he could see her full body. Against hope and expectation, she was tough enough to be raising her guns his way despite the injuries he'd just inflicted on her.

Fletcher had no choice but to shoot to kill. His first bullet caught her high in the chest, the second passed through her throat. As she fell backwards, Fletcher said goodbye to his chance of getting information from her.

CHAPTER SIXTY-NINE

Even before Iris died, Fletcher was on the move. He scooped up her pistols and frisked her for ammo. There was a spare magazine for each pistol, so he stuffed them in his pockets.

A part of him didn't like being so callous to someone he'd just killed, but if their roles were reversed, he figured she'd have shown him neither compassion nor respect as he lay dying. To at least ease her final moments, he fired a shot into her forehead.

His next move was to stuff one of the pistols into his waistband and frisk Len. As he suspected, there was no second magazine for the submachine gun, but he did at least manage to scavenge a vicious combat knife and a Leatherman Multi Tool. Both of these were pushed into a pocket as he advanced towards the door Len had entered the room via. It was the left of the two.

The Mantis was somewhere ahead of him. The questions assaulting his mind were, "where?" and "how far?" He might encounter her on the other side of the door and he might be way behind her.

His best guess was that she'd be quite a way ahead, which meant he had to hustle. His reasoning was that she was sure to have reacted to the gunfight he'd just been in. His pistols and Len's submachine gun had made a serious racket that was unlikely to have gone unheard by anyone in the area. The Mantis was sure to have known Iris's whereabouts, and it was unlikely she'd abandon one of her team. Above anything, the risk Iris might have been captured and forced into giving her up would be a primary reason for her to check out what had happened. There was also

THIRD KILL   269

the ripple effect of leaving a comrade behind. It was terrible for
morale and in a close team like the Mantis's, trust in each other
would be everything.

He heard no sounds of gunfire from the room, which gave
him the confidence to burst through it. Yes, the Mantis may have
silenced pistols, but J.B. Ronson's men wouldn't.

Fletcher's eyes scanned the entirety of the darkened room in a
fraction of a second. It was a boardroom, the kind found in any
office space. There was a water cooler, and a huge central table
that was polished enough to reflect the light from the door onto
the far wall. His own body silhouetted against the paintwork.

On the side wall was a door. He now had a choice: continue
through that door, or double back and try the other door from
the waiting area.

He pressed on. Len had come from here and, as there was
no one else in the boardroom, he figured the Mantis must have
entered via the other door, Len having been missed as he came
through the boardroom.

The door opened to reveal a hallway that ran parallel to the
boardroom. At its right-hand end lay a door that would lead to
the waiting area. He knew what was there: two dead bodies, one
submachine gun and zero ammo.

Onwards he moved. The need to balance stealth and speed
uppermost in his mind as he battled to find a point where he felt
neither was compromised.

The hallway turned left at what would be the end of the
boardroom. He got to the corner quickly and then paused with
his back against the wall before stepping forward.

Rather than using his sense of sight, Fletcher was relying on
sound and smell to inform him of what lay around the corner.
In the ten seconds he waited, he heard no rustles of clothing,
no sounds of movement, nor breathing. There were no hints of
body odor, cigarette smoke from someone's clothes nor any other

scents that alerted him to the presence of an assassin waiting to ambush him.

What he could smell was the coppery tang of fresh blood. It was too much to hope the blood belonged to the Mantis, so he turned around until he was facing the wall and took a sideways step that allowed him to see along the hallway.

His grip of the pistols eased a fraction when he saw a man's body on the ground. Like all the Mantis's victims he'd been shot twice. Heart and left eye.

The man's feet lay in an open doorway. A peek around the corner of the wall showed the room beyond to be empty. The room was a dining room that had a small kitchenette off to one side. The kitchenette had a fridge, kettle, toaster and what looked to be a top-of-the-range coffee machine.

The dining table was a traditional wooden one. Teak, was Fletcher's best guess and it was burnished to the same level a Ferrari in a showroom might be.

Fletcher padded across the room to the door at the far end. Unless he'd completely missed another door, this must be the only way to access Ronson's private quarters.

The next door opened to reveal a box room with four doors. As opulently as the room was decorated and carpeted, it was nothing more than a place where people could move from one room to another. One door lay in front of Fletcher, another was on his left and the remaining doors were on his right.

In his mind, Fletcher mapped out where he was in the hotel part of the casino. His thoughts were on the layout of the building, where the outside walls would be and where he was in relation to them. The dining room was cocooned inside the building, surrounded on all three sides by passageways, and the one wall that had a window only had a limited view of the Strip and Las Vegas itself.

The four doors would probably lead to three types of room: bedroom, lounge and bathroom.

Whatever lay behind the door on the left, Fletcher guessed it wouldn't be a bedroom or the lounge. Unless there was a passage or hallway behind that door, leading to another part of the hotel, it had to be the bathroom, as it was in the heart of the hotel, not the edges.

To follow that line of thinking, the doors on his right would be the bedrooms. It made sense the doors to the bedrooms were side by side.

That left straight ahead as the lounge. At this time of the morning, Ronson ought to be tucked up in bed with his wife, but Fletcher knew enough about casino bosses to know they lived different lives than the rest of the population. They didn't settle down for the night at ten and get up at five or six. They stayed up late to oversee things. After midnight was when the high-rollers hit the casinos hard, and the bosses would be around to deal with any issues, press the flesh if necessary and basically run their business empire. Once the sun came up, they'd get their rest and recharge themselves, ready to repeat the process all over again.

The question remained, though, which of the rooms would Ronson be in? Had he gone to bed yet?

Fletcher went to the bedroom door nearest the dining room. There was no time for ceremony anymore. The Mantis was in one of these four rooms, and the only way he'd encounter her was to go looking.

Thoughts of her lying in wait for him had to be suppressed as he swung the door open and strode into the bedroom.

As soon as he'd recognized there were no threats to his life in the room, he turned his head back so he was watching through the door. If the Mantis went to leave Ronson's suite, he'd see her and be able to get a shot off.

There was a woman on the bed. Her temple was bleeding, and she was immobile other than the rise and fall of her chest. For the first time since getting this mission, Fletcher gave the Mantis a spot of credit for her humanity rather than her skills.

The woman on the bed had been knocked out cold instead of shot. It was a risk the Mantis hadn't needed to take, yet she had. The woman was young, late teens to early twenties. She could be a hooker, Ronson's daughter or any one of a dozen other things that would give her reason to be here. Those reasons weren't important to Fletcher. Catching the Mantis was the only thing that was. Should anyone ever invade his home to attack him, he hoped they would show Wendy the same consideration the Mantis had shown the young woman.

He moved to the second bedroom and found another bed with a woman in it. The woman in this bed was a lot older than the first, a damn sight less pretty, and a damn sight deader. Her prone body showing the two signature bullet holes.

There was still no sign of the Mantis, so he made his way to the lounge door. Unless she'd already fled, she had to be in the lounge.

Like the bedroom doors, this one opened with only the sound of the underside swishing on a plush carpet. As he'd figured it would be, it was a lounge. High-end furniture and a TV screen big enough to rival the one at any football stadium would be the first things most people would notice.

They didn't register at all for Fletcher. All he saw was the Mantis. She was rising from where she'd been sitting in front of a laptop, her right arm, gun in hand, pointing his way.

Fletcher and the Mantis fired at the same time. Because he was already on the move, Fletcher got far enough away from the Mantis's original aim that her bullets did nothing more than graze his arm.

His crashed into her shoulder. The right arm dropping as she turned to bring her left hand and another pistol into play.

From the far corner of the room, Fletcher spied the third member of the Mantis's team. She was bringing up a pair of pistols. He didn't wait for her to get her target. He just kept moving until he was able to duck into cover. As he got himself behind a heavy ornamental chest, Fletcher spotted the three dead men. He could only see one of their faces, and it was J.B. Ronson's. His best guess was that one of the other two would be Zelter.

This wasn't good. He might have winged the Mantis, but she still had one arm operational and a buddy to help her. Where the fight with Iris and Len earlier had been one versus two, the two hadn't been on the same side.

Unless Fletcher could kill one of the women in the next few seconds, it'd take them less than a minute to flank and then kill him.

CHAPTER SEVENTY

Quadrado saw nothing but carnage over the sights of her Glock. The walls were pockmarked with bullet holes, and the rows of sofas were riddled with shredded fabric. One of the women from the bar lay on the floor, her throat a mess of blood.

Quadrado spied the legs of a man poking out from behind a sofa at the other side of the room. Her first thought was that it was Fletcher and he was down, but she recalled she'd bought him blue jeans, not black suit pants, and her heart slowed a fraction.

All the same, her grip on the Glock tightened as she took a sideways step to get a better look at the man. She already had the first two pounds of pressure on the trigger and was poised to add the extra three that would discharge a round at the man should he be armed.

"FBI, lay down your weapons at once."

There was no answer. No verbal reply, no shots fired her way, and no sounds of movement. She added another two pounds of pressure and took another sidestep until she could see the man more clearly.

He offered no threat. Not anymore. A submachine gun was lying at his side and there were enough bullet holes in him for Quadrado not to worry about him trying to shoot her.

Perhaps the woman was the Mantis and perhaps she wasn't. Either way, the Mantis or at least one of her cohorts was still ahead of her.

Quadrado stepped from the room and made her way along a passageway. She couldn't hear anything except her own breathing, which could be a good or bad sign.

She rounded a corner, stepped over a dead man and entered a dining room. A quick scan revealed the room empty.

At the far end was a door. It was open and she could see through the next room into another. In that room she could see a female holding a silenced pistol in either hand. The woman had her side to Quadrado, her pistols aiming off to Quadrado's right. Either the woman was the Mantis, or a cohort. Which wasn't important. All that was important was the double coughs her pistols made when she squeezed their triggers.

Quadrado would have given her 401K for a weapon with a longer range than her Glock. In a firing range she could hit the target nine times out of ten at this distance. In a real life situation, with a racing heart and sweaty palms, it was a different matter. It didn't help that the woman was moving left to right as well. Instead of Quadrado being able to aim at center mass, the sideways stance of the woman meant she had only a third of the width of target she was trained to aim at.

She calculated that she could achieve somewhere between a half and two-thirds success rate if she fired a few bullets at the woman. With anyone other than a trained assassin, she'd fancy those odds, but the way the Mantis had so far eluded injury, capture or death told Quadrado that two-thirds surety wasn't enough.

She had to get closer. Had to narrow the gap and increase the odds in her favor. There was no question she was going to shoot the woman; she just wanted to make sure her first shot did its job and incapacitated or killed.

Quadrado soft-stepped her way forward until she was halfway to the door from the dining room. Once she got to the door, she'd add the final pounds of pressure that would see the Glock spit death at the woman.

The doorway was seven more steps away. Quadrado was shaking inside as she moved forward, but her Glock was rock steady. In the other room, the woman was moving round a large sofa. Two bullet coughs erupted, but the woman's pistols showed no sign of being fired. There must be someone else in the room.

From what Quadrado could see, the woman was doing a flanking move. The problem with that was that she was moving away from Quadrado, and thus opening up the gap Quadrado was trying to close.

Four more steps and she was closer to the woman, but not close enough.

Another two steps and Quadrado could feel the sweat running down her spine.

One step and Quadrado was at the door. This was the point where she'd decided she'd shoot, but the woman was still too far away for Quadrado to be confident of her shot.

"Screw you. You tried to kill me once and failed. You're not getting a second chance."

It was Fletcher's voice. She'd suspected he was the one the woman was shooting at, but now she had confirmation, she felt her stomach twist in fear for him.

Fletcher must have fired back because the woman ducked down.

This was all the opportunity Quadrado needed. She ran forward the eight steps needed to carry her into the other room while the woman was taking cover.

Quadrado arrived as the woman sprang up to shoot back at Fletcher. "Freeze. FBI."

The woman didn't obey Quadrado's shouted command. Instead, she whipped her guns Quadrado's way and pulled their triggers.

Quadrado was ready for such a response, and her bullet caught the woman high in the shoulder. Its impact slamming her hard enough to send her shots above Quadrado's head.

The woman who popped up from behind a different sofa didn't miss. Her first bullet struck Quadrado in the heart, spinning her round and sending her to the floor. The bullet that should have hit Quadrado's eye went through her left bicep.

CHAPTER SEVENTY-ONE

Fletcher knew he had the ornamental chest to thank for the fact he was still breathing. Its thick wooden construction more than enough to stop the bullets that were sent his way. Quadrado's arrival at the final second was just the intervention he needed, and after hearing the gunfire all swing her way, he risked a look round the chest and was rewarded with a golden opportunity.

The Mantis had exposed herself to take a shot at Quadrado. Not by a lot, but by enough to give him a target. He pumped four bullets her way. Two of them passed by her, one thudding into her already wounded shoulder and the fourth plucking a plume of blood from her ear.

All thoughts of taking the Mantis alive for questioning had vanished when triggers started getting pulled. Sometimes you have to shoot to kill and deal with the blood on the floor at a later time.

He wanted to shout out to Quadrado, to ask her status, but whatever her answer, it was better to not know than to share that information with the enemy. Now he was able to look round the corner of the chest, he could again play a part in the proceedings. No longer was he neutralized, unable to risk the acquisition of a target.

The Mantis, the one who'd called herself Chloe in the bar, was back down behind cover, but the third woman was still fully active. He could hear her moving to a new position, and he could hear the pained wails coming from all three women. At least the fact Quadrado was making a noise told him she was still alive.

How active she was wasn't known. From the way the cohort was moving, he didn't think she could be too badly hurt, or else the flanking maneuver would have resumed.

"I'm going to kill you, Fletcher, you son of a bitch. And see when I've killed you, I'm going to Utah. To a town called Vernal, and I'm going to kill your daughter. Wendy's her name, isn't it? You see, Fletcher, I know all about you. The street you live on, where your daughter goes to school, the car you drive. Trust me on this, by the time I'm finished with her, she's going to be begging me to kill her. Begging me, I tell you, begging."

"You tell him, Chloe. That dickwad, his bitch girlfriend and his little girl are all going to die, and I'm going to spit in their dead faces."

Fletcher didn't react. He stayed calm and blocked out the mental images trying to show him harm coming to Wendy. He knew what the Mantis was trying to achieve. She wanted him to burst out from cover and expose himself. Quadrado's arrival swung the odds back in their favor, and she was trying to get him to make a mistake. All the same, he was going to have to make damned sure that Wendy was safe the first chance he got.

"Bad news, ladies. It's you who's going to die. Either by our hands, or via the needle. There are SWAT teams coming. This is the end of the road for you both." Quadrado's tone was pained as she burst the Mantis's bubble, but that didn't matter to Fletcher. Her voice was strong and rasp-free. That's all that counted. She might have been knocked down, but she was a long way from being counted out.

"If I'm going to die, then so be it, Fletcher, at least I'll die knowing I killed you. And that little bitchbag. As for your daughter, she'll get hers in time."

Fletcher snapped off a shot at where the Mantis was hidden and a second towards the cohort. The action as much to keep them pinned down as to help his and Quadrado's situation.

The Mantis and the cohort were able to see each other and communicate via hand signals. He and Quadrado didn't have that luxury.

Again he put a shot towards each woman. If Quadrado was watching, then she'd be able to move into a better position or get a telling shot off of her own.

It was a good plan, apart from one thing: the Mantis and her cohort were trapped animals. They were facing certain death for their crimes if they remained in the room. Therefore the onus was on them to attack.

They moved in unison, the Mantis leaning round a corner of the sofa to send a stream of rapid shots Quadrado's way, while the cohort sprinted sideways to a position where the chest would no longer offer him its shielding presence.

As Fletcher aimed both of his pistols at the cohort, he heard the boom of Quadrado's Glock as she returned fire at the Mantis.

The cohort's wild dash threw off his aim, but he soon corrected it. His first bullet hitting her thigh. The second her wrist. As she pulled up from her injuries, he put a bullet into her head that dropped her for good.

He diverted his aim at the Mantis and saw he needn't have bothered. She was no longer in any condition to be considered a threat. Quadrado had hit her twice, once high in her uninjured shoulder and a second time in the middle of her stomach. Red froth appeared on her lips as she fought to breathe.

CHAPTER SEVENTY-TWO

"You okay, Fletcher?" Quadrado's voice was strained with worry and pain, but the fact she was the first to speak allayed Fletcher's concerns as he stood.

"Yeah, fine. How about you?"

"The evil cow got me in the chest and nicked my arm, but other than the fact I'm going to have a bruise the size of Texas on my boob, I'll live."

When Quadrado came into view, he could see she was already unbuckling the bulletproof vest she was wearing.

Fletcher aimed a finger at the Mantis. "You feel like talking to us, Chloe? I'm guessing that's not your real name."

A cough and some frothy bubbles passed her lips. When she got her breathing under control, it was shallow, but at least bloodless.

"Actually, it is."

"You've been hit bad. Both shoulders will be ruined and from the blood you're coughing up, I'd say the bottom of your lungs may be punctured. They say gutshots are the most painful. That's a bad way to go. Doubly bad if any of your intestines have been hit. They'll be leaking all kinds of poisons into your system. Of course, the SWAT team will be here soon. So will EMTs and a whole host of other people. The EMTs will do their job. They might succeed in saving your life. Then what for you? Years of trials and sitting on death row, waiting until the waiting is over. I'm going to ask you some polite questions, but don't think for one moment that I'm not averse to poking a finger or two into your bullet wounds."

"Screw you." The Mantis's face was tight as she fought to maintain her composure.

Although Fletcher knew the Mantis's real name was Chloe, he had to keep thinking of her as the Mantis, as a formidable predator. To think of her as Chloe was to humanize her, and that would just make what was to come all the harder.

"I reckon we've got about two or three minutes tops before the FBI's SWAT team arrives. So this is very much a one-time deal. You tell us who hired you for this mission, and I'll put you out of your misery. You won't have a slow, painful death, nor weeks of agony if the doctors can patch you up. When it comes to your trial, there's no way you'll get acquitted; there's far too much evidence. You'll end up getting that needle I talked about. I've read up about death row. I found out what happens in Nevada when I got put on your trail. Nevada is a needle state. That means you'll get a lethal injection." Fletcher thought it wise not to mention the last prisoner executed in Nevada was in 2006. "Nationally, most of those who are put to death are glad when their time comes. It's a form of mental torture. Think about it, all those years knowing that one day you'll be strapped to a gurney and will feel the kiss of a needle. There are different schools of thought about using the needle as a form of execution, and one of them is that the muscle relaxant and anesthetic aren't always successful in blocking out the pain caused by the drug that actually kills you. I could tell you the names of the drugs, but time isn't on your side. So, who's paying you to kill all these casino bosses?"

"How do I know you'll keep your word?"

"You don't, but you have to believe me because I'm the only chance you've got. Imagine if you do end up in jail. We'll hunt down your paymasters anyway, and they'll think you've ratted them out. Prison will be even worse for you then, as they're sure to want their pound of flesh from you. Tell me who they are and where I can find them and I'll take all your pain away."

A swallow, followed by a look of resignation. "They're an Armenian gang known as AP18. They're neo-Nazi scumbags, but they pay well. Very well. They have a warehouse on the corner of Thompkins and South Grand Canyon, and plans to rule Vegas for years."

"Why do you do it? Why do you kill for a living? Killing gangsters I can understand, but what drove you to kill innocents?" As he was speaking, Fletcher's thoughts were on the kid with Down syndrome. On Issy.

"I was in the Navy, the US Marines. They taught me how to kill, and I found a way to use what they taught me to make money." Coughs erupted from the Mantis's mouth. Each one sending speckles of blood onto her chin. "Not just a few bucks, but real money. First couple kills were tough and left me feeling guilty, but the third, oh man, the third kill was spectacular. A life changer. It was after the third kill that I admitted to myself that I enjoy killing people. I always knew this day would come, but I made a lot of money and had a ball making it." The Mantis closed her eyes and scrunched her whole face into an agonized knot. "That's everything I have to give you. Do it now, please?"

Fletcher was in the act of bringing his pistol to the Mantis's chin when the top of her head flew off.

Quadrado stepped forward, pushed him aside and put one of the Mantis's guns back into her lifeless fingers.

He got why she'd taken the shot. If he'd taken it, forensic analysis of the evidence would prove he'd assassinated the Mantis. By standing further away and shooting downwards, Quadrado had eliminated the twin problems of gunshot residue and the bullet's trajectory. It was a clever move on her behalf. He'd not considered the implications of shooting the Mantis when she was already down until Quadrado had taken over.

It was a burden she'd carry. He knew her too well to not know that she'd question her action a thousand times over. She wasn't a person who saw herself as judge, jury and executioner.

Fletcher touched her shoulder. "Let's go get ourselves into a position where the SWAT team can see us in plenty of time to not shoot us."

CHAPTER SEVENTY-THREE

Fletcher could see a vein in Thomson's temple pulsing as the Special Agent in Charge swore his way around the room. There were agents in full protective suits, crime scene technicians, photographers and a host of others recording and trying to make sense of the crime scene. Off to one side, Quadrado was having her arm bandaged up by an ashen-faced EMT. None of this was important to him. Wendy was safe. He'd spoken to her. Spoken to his in-laws and told them they and Wendy must go to the police station at once and stay there until he returned home.

"This is your shitshow, Fletcher, and I'm going to make damned sure it sticks to you."

"Bite me." There were a thousand more tactful things Fletcher could have said, but there was no way he was going to be Thomson's whipping boy.

The vein on Thomson's temple twitched again. The man could only be one bout of anger away from an aneurism.

"I beg your pardon?"

For the sake of Thomson's health, Fletcher didn't bother responding; instead he turned and walked back into the lounge. There was something that was off about the timing. When the bullets were flying, he'd not had a chance to think about things, but since Quadrado had shot the Mantis, he'd had time to run events through his mind.

He'd been behind the Mantis by a couple of minutes as she worked her way into Ronson's suite. By the time she'd done her thing in the lounge and the two bedrooms, he should have met her on her way out. Ronson and his men were dead by then, so there was no reason for her to delay her exit. Except that's what she had done.

Fletcher walked his way through his memory of encountering the Mantis in the lounge. She'd been sitting on the sofa while her cohort had been at the other end of the room. On the table in front of her was a laptop. She wasn't actively using the laptop, but she had been looking at it. Because of the ensuing battle, he'd never looked at the laptop, but that's where he was going now.

A technician was busy photographing the area by the sofa, so Fletcher let them do their stuff and stepped forward only when they directed their camera elsewhere.

The laptop's screen had gone black so he pressed a key to bring it back to life. What he saw didn't make any sense to him, so he called Quadrado over.

"Do you understand this?"

She bent forward and peered at the screen. Her eyes narrowing and then widening. "Wow. There's millions here."

"Millions of dollars?"

"Yes and no." Quadrado aimed a finger at the screen. "See this? It's cryptocurrency. Lots of criminal gangs convert their money into it, as it's near impossible to trace."

"Add in that they're probably bringing money from other businesses to their casinos to launder it and there's bound to be a lot of it."

"Sure. But that's not the issue here. This cryptocurrency isn't being bought—it's being transferred."

"Where to?"

Fletcher ignored Quadrado's shrug; it was a foolish question he'd asked. There could only be two possible destinations for the cryptocurrency. Either the Mantis's private account or that of her Armenian paymasters, and it didn't matter which it was.

"Hang on a minute." Quadrado's fingers snapped a number of times as she gathered her thoughts. "Has she been doing this at every casino? And if so, why haven't we heard about it?"

The question only needed a moment's thought from Fletcher. He might not know much about cryptocurrencies, but he knew about human beings, especially those in a macho environment such as a crime gang.

"It's probably happened at the others too. They'd never admit it, not to the cops, nor to other gangs. Having their top men hit by an assassin shows them as weak. To have their money stolen as well would make them a laughing stock. My dollar to your dime says that if the other casinos targeted have also been robbed, they'll cover it up."

"That's a bet I'm not taking."

"Also, think about things in a different way. With most of the hits, it wasn't just the top man who was killed, but also two or three of his likely successors. That would only leave lower-level guys, grunts if you will. What's the odds of those grunts knowing about where the money is?"

"Too low for me to bet on."

Fletcher put Quadrado's new-found glibness down to the fact she'd just survived a gun battle where people had died. He felt the effects too, but he'd experienced the adrenaline rush of survival enough times to be able to control his emotions. Quadrado, on the other hand, would be euphoric for a while, and then when she had time to properly think about the gunfight with the Mantis, she'd realize how close to death she'd been. Then she'd likely be deeply shaken by the memory of the bullet slamming into her chest. For all the bulletproof vest had prevented the bullet from killing her, vests only absorbed a bullet's penetrative force by spreading the impact over a larger area. This force had still crashed against Quadrado's chest, and Fletcher knew from experience that it would be days before the bruise stopped hurting. When you face your own mortality in such a way, it always leaves a trace on your psyche. The question that Quadrado would soon be facing, was whether she could ever get past the natural fear of entering such a situation again after seeing the horror of a life being extinguished. Of dealing with the guilt that comes from ending a life. Even killing someone as deserving of death as the Mantis took its toll.

Quadrado's phone rang. She pulled it from a pocket, showed Fletcher the screen and set off to find somewhere private for the conversation.

It was Soter on the line and that intrigued Fletcher.

How had the mysterious figure known to get in touch at this precise moment? Was he aware the Mantis was dead? And if so, how? Thomson would no doubt have gotten someone to email the FBI director, if he hadn't put in a call on the way here. How that news had gotten to Soter so quickly was the part he was puzzling over.

Was the FBI director aware of Soter? Was *he* Soter? Or was Soter an amalgam of high-ranking people within the FBI and other agencies? That was an issue for another time. Now, the Mantis was dead, and his mission in Las Vegas was all but finished. A SWAT team or seven could round up the Armenians. He was done with Las Vegas.

"Hey, Quadrado, get your scrawny ass back here, I'm not finished with you."

Fletcher stepped in front of Thomson, who was trying to block Quadrado from leaving. "Let her go. Trust me, that's not a call you want to interrupt."

"Just who the hell do you think you are, Fletcher? You can't go telling me what to do. I'm in charge here. Me. Not you, you Neanderthal thug."

Fletcher extended an arm to prevent Thomson from moving aside. Quadrado slipped past as Thomson went to move Fletcher's arm out of his way.

"I wouldn't do that if I were you. I don't care what rank of Feebie you are, if you lay one hand on me, I'll break that hand in so many places that when it gets X-rayed it'll look like a jigsaw puzzle."

Thomson stopped his hand a half inch from Fletcher's arm. His face a mask of hate and impotent fury. The vein in his temple pulsing like a snake's body as it swallowed its prey.

"Fletcher." Quadrado was beckoning him. "He wants to speak to you too."

Thomson didn't step aside; instead he glared at Fletcher, daring him to bump him as he moved to join Quadrado. It was a dare Fletcher was happy to take, but now wasn't the time. He stepped around Thomson with exaggerated strides, to make a fool of the man, and strode along the hallway until he could take the cell from Quadrado.

"The Mantis is dead. I'm going home. The Mantis said my daughter is at risk and nothing you can say will trump that."

"Have your daughter go to the nearest police station. I'll have her under armed guard long before you can get there."

"I want a SWAT team. Nothing less. If anything happens to her, I'll hold you personally responsible, and you can imagine how that will end."

"There's no need to threaten me. I know how precious your daughter is to you. Think of the future she can have if you do as I ask. I know the stakes involved in keeping her safe. I promise you that she will be safe and if, God forbid, anything happens to her, I swear that I'll hand myself over to you." As always, Soter's voice was distorted by some electronic gadgetry. "This AP18, they're bad news. They are an offshoot of Armenian Power, who are bad enough in their own right, but AP18 are something else altogether."

"How so? I'm guessing the one and eight are numerical representatives of the alphabet, for the initials of Adolf Hitler. The Mantis said they were neo-Nazi scum, so I'm guessing it's something to do with that."

"You're bang on the money. What you don't know, is that Interpol have reported over a hundred members of AP18 have left Armenia and are making their way to the States. My guess is they're reinforcements for the guys who are already here. There are three heads of AP18, the Oganesyan brothers, and they're in Vegas. I want them dead, and it's you who will kill them. Intelligence has the brothers at the warehouse the Mantis told you about."

"That place will be heavily fortified. I'll need support. Why aren't you sending in a SWAT team?"

"I can't tell a SWAT team to just murder people with zero official evidence. But I can tell you. May I remind you that your original brief was to neutralize not just the Mantis, but also her paymasters? These Nazis are still alive, so by my calculations your job is only half done. These are bad men, Fletcher. They hired a killer who was willing to shoot a kid with Down syndrome. Don't tell me you think they won't leave many more innocents dead before they get what they want."

"The Mantis was supposed to be one person. Instead she turned out to be a three-headed dog like Cerberus. Now you're telling me her paymaster is also a triple threat. And God knows how many of their own men will be at the warehouse with them. It's a job for a SWAT team, not a single man."

"A SWAT team couldn't be given a kill order. You can." A moment of silence came down the line and was followed by a slow exhale. "In recognition of the risk you'll be taking, I'll double your fee for this mission."

"Once again, there are three of them. I want triple. I also want you to make sure that Thomson gives me whatever I ask for with neither question nor delay. And I want this to be my final mission."

"I can't promise that. But on the fee, okay. You drive a hard bargain."

"One other thing, what about the henchmen, any lower-level thugs I might encounter. What am I supposed to do about them?"

"You do whatever you need to do to get past them and kill the Oganesyan brothers. Thomson will facilitate your every desire. I want those brothers dead before the sun comes up." His instructions given, Soter cut the call.

Before Fletcher could even tell Quadrado about the conversation, Thomson's cell began to chirrup.

CHAPTER SEVENTY-FOUR

Even in the early morning gloom, the warehouse where AP18 ran their business from didn't look as if it was the hideout of a gang of neo-Nazis. This was a good neighborhood, with well-kept buildings, intact fences and no obvious graffiti.

As a place for a gang to hide out, it was ideal. The fact there were active businesses around it just added a further layer of camouflage. A sign above the door gave a company name: 28 Day Logistics. Logistics was a catch-all term that could be used to describe so many different things. It would also allow for vehicles to enter and exit the premises at all hours without there being any undue concern among those who might see them.

Fletcher was in the back of a panel van driven by Quadrado. He was clad head to toe in black, and wore body armor on every part of his body that it was made for. Even with all his experience in the Royal Marines, he'd never before worn as much armor. He knew that should he have to move quickly at any point, the heavy armor would sap his strength before he'd traveled far. All the same, there was no way he was undertaking this mission without the armor. He had a Glock pistol on either hip, an MP5/10 submachine gun—all with suppressors fitted—in his hands and enough ammunition to deal with whatever numbers he might face. He also had a wicked fighting knife, several grenades and a helmet that had a pair of video cameras on it. In his left ear there was a bud that allowed Quadrado to communicate with him. She was to watch the feed from the video camera that was filming behind him. If she saw a threat, she could warn him.

Thomson was in the back of the van with him. The FBI man had been silent the whole time they'd been in motion. His face grimmer than usual, but there was also a hint of empathy about him that surprised Fletcher. Maybe the man wasn't too bad a person when the strain was lifted off him. He was pleased Thomson had kept his mouth shut. He needed to steel himself for battle, not deal with any of Thomson's posturing, or worse, an inane pep talk from someone who'd never faced what he was about to.

He got why Soter wanted the Armenians dead. Understood why he wanted that to happen before sun up. With over a hundred reinforcements on their way here, Soter would want the problem solved before it could become a war. By eliminating the Oganesyan brothers, he'd be removing the gang's leadership.

Fletcher was under no illusions, Soter was using him in the same way the Mantis had been used by AP18. For all he might be on the side of the just, this mission was nothing less than a triple assassination. Soter had given him permission to use whatever force was necessary when dealing with any guards he might encounter, but that didn't mean he was going to cut people down like the hero in an action movie. It was one thing to cut the head off a serpent, another altogether to gun down men just because they were there. If the henchmen he encountered forced his hand, he was comfortable with using deadly force, but only if they gave him no other choice.

The van drew to a stop as close to the warehouse as it was possible to get without crashing. Thomson slid the door open and patted Fletcher's back as he stepped out. "Good luck."

CHAPTER SEVENTY-FIVE

Thomson raced from the van with a pair of bolt cutters and snipped the chain securing the gates before making his way back to the van. Fletcher trotted through the gates and hustled towards the warehouse as fast as the armor allowed.

One thing the light surveillance hadn't spotted was the Armenians' security measures. They knew the Oganesyans were inside and there were reports of up to a dozen of their henchmen, but what they hadn't been able to pick up was if the Armenians relied on human or electronic security. No lookouts had been spotted, which suggested electronic systems, but that wasn't a certainty.

For all Fletcher knew, a henchman on guard duty might well be arranging a welcoming committee as he fiddled with the lock of a side door. Thomson had raised an eyebrow to the middle of his forehead when Fletcher requested a set of lock picks, but he hadn't uttered a word of criticism and had supplied them along with everything else Fletcher wanted.

With the lock picked, Fletcher swung the door open and stepped inside. The area was in darkness, meaning all he saw were shadows. He'd considered wearing night-vision goggles, but had opted against them. As good as they were in the dark, when someone switched on a light, as superior forces were likely to do, they became blinding to the wearer.

Fletcher heard no signs that his entry had been detected. There were no shouts, no running feet and, best of all, no alarm sirens. It was possible there was a guard patrolling, so Fletcher used precaution as he moved forward, the layout of the warehouse etched in his mind.

From where he was, there was a large storage area. At the other end of the building, there was an area sectioned off into various offices. It was in these office areas he expected to find the Armenians. A faint light came from the office end of the warehouse.

The floor of the warehouse was stacked high with various boxes, crates and pallets of goods. A pair of panel vans were parked in front of a large roller door, and the walls were metal shelving laden with smaller boxes. As he scanned the areas for any threats, he saw the various boxes bore labels of cleaning chemicals. There were glass-cleaners, floor polish, detergents and a dozen other products. 28 Day Logistics would be a front that would allow the Armenians to travel all over town. They'd have their men delivered to all the casinos, hotels and bars. Everything they learned about the premises would be fed back to the Oganesyans and used to further the AP18 cause.

Fletcher's nose twitched as he approached the corner of a high stack of boxes, his rubber-soled boots soundless on the polished concrete floor. It was the unmistakable scent of cheap cigars. As he flattened himself to the corner, he saw a faint glow as the smoker sucked on the cigar. From where he was, Fletcher judged the man must be close, as the glow from the cigar wouldn't carry far.

Above all else, he had to take the guard down without making a noise. If the guard managed to get out a shout, or alert his buddies in any way, Fletcher would end up facing far more enemies than he could handle.

Two quick steps got him round the corner, the MP5 aimed ready to intimidate or kill. The guard was facing the other way and turning back to investigate the noise made by Fletcher's rapid steps. His chin was an easy target for the stock of the MP5, and Fletcher wasn't someone who'd look a gift horse in the mouth. The man crumpled with only a faint moan. He'd be out for at least five minutes.

Fletcher slipped a plasticuff from one of his many pockets and bound the guard's hands behind his back. By the time he came to and shouted for help, noise would no longer be an issue.

With the MP5 leading, Fletcher continued on his way across the warehouse. There were no more guards to trouble him until he approached the offices. As he teased his way around a corner he saw the office areas. There were three doors at ground level and a metal staircase that led to an upper office.

The upper office had a large window, presumably designed so the owner or manager could oversee the warehouse. There was a light on in the office, although it was muted by blinds.

Worst of all was the presence of a guard at the foot of the stairs. He was a big brute. Six foot plus, he was a mass of muscle. He stood with his arms folded and a bored expression. There was a gun in a hip holster, but the guy looked big enough to throw the warehouse, so Fletcher guessed he would prefer hand-to-hand combat over a gunfight.

From his vantage point there was little chance the guard would see him, but Fletcher didn't want to take the man down from where he was. The only way he could do so was with a bullet, and to ensure the man's silence, that bullet would have to be a lethal one.

The problem with killing the guard was that there was no telling how much noise he'd make as he fell, and then there was a chance those in the upper office would hear and raise the alarm. There was also the fact that enough people had died, or would die, because of the Armenians' power grab. While Fletcher was comfortable with the idea of killing legitimate targets such as the Oganesyan brothers, he didn't want to add to the death toll any more than was necessary.

To get to the guard, Fletcher had to navigate his way around boxes and then confront him from a distance of fifteen feet. That could go a number of different ways, few of them in Fletcher's favor.

Fletcher pulled back from his vantage point and crept forwards. He had the beginnings of a plan and, while it wasn't a brilliant option, it was the best he could think of.

When he was on the other side of the boxes from the guard, he bent down, put one of his pistols on the ground and stood again. With the MP5 aimed at the corner the guard would have to come round, Fletcher put his foot on the Glock and scratched it across the ground.

The scraping noise seemed like a foghorn in the still of the warehouse. To make sure the guard heard it, Fletcher repeated the move twice and prepared for the guard to investigate. He was gambling the man would trust in his muscly physique and would keep his gun in its holster. He'd met enough muscle-bound men to learn they often had an overconfidence in their abilities that was down to the knowledge of their superior strength. If the guard came round the corner with his gun drawn, Fletcher would have no option but to shoot him dead.

Fletcher used his toe to nudge the gun on the ground against the leg of a shelving rack. It made a muted metallic clatter that couldn't be ignored.

"*Ov e ayntegh?*"

The words didn't mean anything to Fletcher, but he guessed they'd be the Armenian equivalent of "who's there?" The bored tone in which they'd been delivered was good. He'd not shouted or raised an alarm. For all Fletcher had made a noise to attract the guy, he'd made one small enough to pique interest rather than raise an alert. He was banking on the guard's sense of machismo to deal with the noise himself. The guard would know there was another person standing guard. He'd think it was him or perhaps a rodent he'd heard. The last thing he'd want to do would be to raise an alarm for nothing.

The guard came round the corner, hands by his sides but held ready for action. He was good; Fletcher approved of the way the man had taken as wide a route as possible as he rounded the corner. It created distance and thereby made ambushing him harder.

All the same, he was now face to face with Fletcher. And more pertinently, to Fletcher's MP5. There were six feet between them. Too far to try anything stupid and too near for there to be any chance of Fletcher missing. Fletcher's left hand was in front of his chin, forefinger extended up over his lips. The guard might not speak English, but he'd know what the gesture meant.

The guard's mouth twisted enough for Fletcher to add a pound of pressure to the trigger. With his left hand he signaled the guard get down on his knees. There was pure hate on the guard's face as he did as he was told.

Fletcher understood the guard's position. He'd be trying to work out if complying with Fletcher's instructions was a way to make it easier for Fletcher to kill him, or whether doing as he was told would save his life. To this end, Fletcher never let his gun waver nor his expression soften. He had to make the guard believe compliance was the only option.

Something in the guard's eyes shifted, leaving Fletcher with no choice. By now the guard was on his knees, but his right hand was a mere six inches from his gun. Fletcher could easily put half a dozen bullets in the guard before the gun was drawn and aimed his way, but that wasn't what he wanted. Instead, he stepped forward as the guard made his move and crashed the MP5 into the guard's temple. Unlike the first guard he'd encountered, this one didn't go down with a single blow.

As Fletcher wound back to strike again, the gun was being drawn from the guard's holster. Fletcher got to the peak of his backswing at the same moment the pistol exited the holster. It was now about who was quicker: the guard at getting his aim, or Fletcher at bringing his gun against the guard's temple a second time.

Fletcher won the race, but it was a lot closer than he was comfortable with. In his fear of being shot, he'd put extra power into his swing and the collision between the MP5's stock and the guard's temple was hard enough to break bone.

Again, Fletcher slipped plasticuffs onto the guard's hands. The gun was slid far enough beneath the nearest shelving to be inaccessible, and the Glock he'd used to create the noise returned to its holster.

His next move was to grab a pair of wooden-handled mops. The handles had a metallic end with a screw thread, so he removed the mop heads, leaving himself with two five-foot poles, each an inch in diameter.

As he rounded the corner ready to head to the upper office, the left-hand door opened and a bleary-eyed man stumbled out of the room. He was wearing nothing more than a pair of shorts.

The man opened the next door along and with the door open, urinated nosily into a toilet bowl.

Fletcher crept up behind him, the two mop handles in his left hand, and with one violent sideways thrust, crashed the man's head against a hand dryer. A second later, the man was on the floor, a puddle of urine still spreading.

With the man incapacitated, Fletcher moved to the left-hand door. It was partially open and he could see six cots. Five were occupied, and there were the usual snores and smell of farts that accompanies any group of sleeping men.

He pulled the door closed and snagged the latch as quietly as he could. His next move was an old prank that had been played many times during his time in the Royal Marines. The first mop handle he placed vertically behind the door handle. Then he moved its base outwards so the top was touching the door and the bottom protruding out. The second mop handle he slid behind the first, but horizontally so it rested against the walls on either side of the door. Next he raised the horizontal mop handle until it was as high as it could go. The first was now pinioned between the door, the door handle and the second door handle. From inside the room, it would be impossible to open the door, as the inward curve of the door handle would jam against the braced piece of timber. No amount of pulling would free the door unless the men inside the room could free the door's latch without opening the handle.

Fletcher padded his way to the metal stairs and climbed them two at a time, his feet close to the edges to minimize any possible creaks they might make. In his ear he could hear Quadrado breathing, but so far she'd not spoken, although there had been a small gasp as the second guard had been reaching for his gun.

The time for stealth had now passed. He could go with his favored method: shock and awe. This part of the plan was simple: he'd storm in, shoot the three brothers, a double tap each, and then make his exit. Anyone else in the room would be shot in the leg to stop them following.

By the time the occupants of the makeshift bedroom had woken, realized they were trapped and then smashed their way out of the bedroom, he'd be long gone.

He burst through the door, his aim already picking out the first target. Thomson had furnished him with pictures of the Oganesyan brothers, and he could see they were all in the room. The problem was, they weren't alone. There were four young women and an older guy also in the room. How they were located meant Fletcher couldn't easily take out his targets without hitting any of the possible innocents.

CHAPTER SEVENTY-SIX

From the way the women were dressed and so much younger than the Oganesyans they were draped over, it was obvious to Fletcher they were prostitutes. To him this marked them out as non-targets. Had they been wives of the Oganesyans, he'd probably still not have thought of them as targets, but he'd have been less worried about them catching a bullet by accident.

In a hostile situation like this, he ought to just strafe the room to ensure his own safety, but with a minimum of four innocents in the room, that wasn't an option. Instead of collective fire, he'd have to pick off his opponents one by one.

His first target was Hakob, the youngest brother. He was far enough removed from the woman for him to be an easy hit, so Fletcher put two bullets into his chest and moved on to the next target.

To get there he had to skip past the older man, onto Vahan, the eldest Oganesyan. He remembered what he'd learned of the three brothers. Hakob was the most brutal, for him violence was a hobby not a by-product of his Nazism. Samvel was the middle brother and the real brains of the outfit. Fiercely cunning, he was credited with the rise of the Oganesyan empire. Vahan was a fanatical neo-Nazi and the credit—or blame, as Fletcher saw it—for the gang's extreme right-wing propaganda lay with him. Vahan didn't care about money; he just wanted to create a master race.

Vahan had a swastika tattooed onto each cheek, and they contorted as he dragged the nearest hooker in front of him as a shield.

Fletcher snapped off a shot at his head to keep him in stasis while he moved onto Samvel.

The middle brother was a step ahead. The hooker nearest him had been on her feet and, rather than cower behind her, he'd planted a foot in her gut and propelled her toward Fletcher.

There was a gap of nine feet between Fletcher and Samvel, too far for the hooker to be carried by the force of Samvel's push, yet not so far that she didn't end up between them. As he stepped to one side so he could get a bead on Samvel, Vahan produced a gun and started firing his way.

His first shot was wild, but the second caught Fletcher in the midriff. The bullet may have been stopped by the body armor, but that didn't mean that it was without consequence. To Fletcher it was as though he'd been kicked in the gut by the winner of the Kentucky Derby. He doubled over, only for a shot to his chest to push him back upright.

As he kept moving sideways, Fletcher managed to get a shot off that caught Samvel in the gut. He yelped in pain, but kept lifting the gun he'd had under a cushion. Now that the hooker was between him and Vahan, Fletcher put a single shot into Samvel's face that blew out the back of his head.

There were a pair of booms from Vahan's gun, and Fletcher saw the hooker dropping to the floor. She had a through-and-through wound in the right side of her chest. Fletcher had seen enough similar wounds to know that, at best, she had minutes to live.

Fletcher dropped another couple of shots Vahan's way, but he didn't get close enough to even make the man duck. As well as the hooker, Vahan had reached across her and dragged the older man across as well, so he was totally shielded from Fletcher.

Twice more Vahan's gun boomed. For all the man's vision was impaired by his human shields, his shots were eerily close to Fletcher. One skimmed off the side of his helmet, leaving him with a ringing in his ears and a fuzziness to his vision. A crackling in his ears told him that comms from Quadrado had been cut by the bullet.

The hooker and the old guy were squirming to free themselves, but Vahan's grip was too strong.

Fletcher managed to put a bullet into Vahan's foot that caused an agonized howl and what Fletcher suspected were Armenian curses from his lips.

The woman was able to free herself by clawing at Vahan's arm, but the Armenian was also on the move. Despite his injured foot, he'd risen to a standing position and had secreted himself behind the older guy.

Another shot came Fletcher's way, this one catching him on the unprotected forearm above the left wrist. Now it was Fletcher's turn to howl in pain.

A huge boom sounded from below and there was another pair in quick succession. Fletcher recognized them as being from a shotgun, and if his suspicions were correct, his improvised barricading of the bedroom door had just felt the attentions of a shotgun. Time was no longer on his side, as the other henchmen would now all be pouring out of the bedroom and getting ready to charge up the stairs.

"Please." The older guy's hands came up. "Don't shoot."

There was nothing left for him to do, so Fletcher aimed at the older guy and pulled his trigger.

CHAPTER SEVENTY-SEVEN

Both of Fletcher's bullets slammed into the older guy's legs. He dropped at once, and as Vahan fought to support him to maintain the man's shielding ability, there was a moment when his head was exposed.

A bullet from Fletcher's MP5 entered Vahan's eye and exited the back of his head. As he fell his fingers squeezed the trigger one more time, his bullet catching one of the hookers in the shoulder.

Fletcher didn't waste time assessing what state the others in the room were in. The imminent arrival of at least five henchmen was uppermost in his mind. He pointed his MP5 at the window that overlooked the warehouse and fired until the magazine was empty.

Once the magazine was replaced with a full one, he pulled a pair of flashbangs from his belt and tossed one out of the window in a way that would see it land at the foot of the metal staircase.

Next he grabbed the low table from the center of the room, stood it in the doorway and pushed the top of it forward. The table fell as predicted, its legs hooking over the middle rail of the protective railing that flanked the metal stairs.

Fletcher primed the second flashbang and sent it after the first.

His legs pumped as he dashed to the back wall of the former office and then drove him forwards and through the door. Like an Olympic jumper hitting their mark, Fletcher's right foot planted itself on the angled table and thrust him upwards as he dove over the railing.

As he flew through the air, Fletcher corkscrewed his body in a vain attempt to protect his now useless left arm. He was aiming to land on the nearest pile of boxes. From there his momentum would roll him off the far side or at least close enough that he could drop down without a significant delay.

He achieved his aim of landing on his right side, but in his desperation to distance himself from the upper office, he'd over-cooked his thrust from the table and he bounced once then fell off the other side.

Despite his best efforts to twist enough to land on his feet, the ten foot drop wasn't enough to allow such a maneuver. He landed hard on his left side, his injured arm slapping against the unyielding concrete with enough force to bring a torrent of swearwords to his lips.

Even as he cursed, he was hauling himself to his feet and aiming his MP5 at the corner of the boxes, where he expected the henchmen to come charging around. He emptied the magazine and tossed the weapon aside. The shots had been nothing more than a delaying tactic. He wasn't prepared to get into a gunfight with the henchmen. He was outnumbered and could easily be flanked. If he was fully fit it would be a tall order—with a smashed forearm it was little more than suicide.

His next move was to slide his final flashbang towards the corner. It wouldn't do the recovering muscle-bound guard a lot of good, but then again, it wouldn't do him that much harm either.

Rather than wait for the flashbang to go off, Fletcher turned and sprinted towards the door he'd entered via. The first guard he'd knocked out was shuffling along, slug-like, so he grabbed him by the scruff of his collar and dragged him like a heavy sack. Before he exited the door, he tossed the guard outside and then rolled an incendiary grenade under one of the shelving racks.

Fletcher was ten feet from the building when he heard the whoomp of the grenade exploding. The fire it created would prevent the henchmen from following and, by the time they found another route from the building, they would have had enough time to realize that distancing themselves from the warehouse was far wiser than seeking revenge on him.

All the same, he kept a Glock tucked under his left armpit as he dragged the guard away from the burning warehouse.

At the gates he could see Thomson waving him across and a worried-looking Quadrado at the wheel of the van.

CHAPTER SEVENTY-EIGHT

Quadrado helped Fletcher stow his bag in the trunk of the sedan she'd borrowed from the FBI pool and climbed behind the wheel.

As was typical of him, he was on his feet waiting for her when she'd pulled up at the hospital. His left arm was in a cast from wrist to elbow. According to the doctor, he'd been lucky to escape serious and permanent damage, although it'd be a while before his arm was fully healed. How he was dealing with the knowledge the Mantis had been a US Marine wasn't a subject Quadrado planned to broach unless he brought it up. Fletcher's own background was in the Royal Marines, and he was sure to feel a sense of betrayal, as she knew how highly he thought of all Marine corps.

"How many do you think I have this time?"

"I'd say plenty." Whenever she and Fletcher met after one of his missions, there were always a number of questions he needed answers to before he could move on. "I'm not going to put a number on it though."

"Chicken."

His tone was light, so Quadrado took no offense at the jibe. "You're the one with the broken wing. Want me to catch you up?"

"That'd be good." Fletcher wriggled in his seat and dropped the sun visor down.

"I'll go chronological. First off, the laptop from the casino: we gave it to one of our IT guys. Because it was still running, we managed to trace the account where the cryptocurrency was going. It was going to a similar place as the payments from the Armenians."

"So the Mantis was running a sideshow as well as collecting for the hits. That was one smart lady."

"Not just smart but deceitful. It was into a separate wallet, as crypto accounts are called. Our best guess is that she was ripping off the casinos exclusively for her own benefit and that money wouldn't be shared with her cohorts."

"So she wasn't just a killer who was screwing over her paymasters with a bit of side action. She was also screwing over her team. Wow, that's one cold lady. Did you find out who she really was?"

"Yep, we've got them." Quadrado gave a tight smile. "We ran her DNA and fingerprints, and those of her two accomplices. We tracked down an old boyfriend of Iris's, and he told us the whole story when we threatened to leak his identity as the person who'd hit the AP18 warehouse to the remaining members of the gang. Chloe and Iris really were their names. The third one was called Kristen, and she was Chloe's cousin. All three went to high school in Montana, where they became best friends. After high school, Chloe joined the Navy and the other two went off to college together." Quadrado took a deep breath. "Kristen and Iris were sexually assaulted by a group of frat boys one night. Apparently, when Chloe learned of this she took revenge and targeted their attackers and killed them all. By the time she'd moved onto the last ones, the other two had sussed what Chloe was doing and called her on it. She'd not just admitted to killing their rapists, but she somehow recruited both Iris and Kirsten and got them to help her with the final two kills. According to the boyfriend, as soon as Chloe could leave the Marines she did, and then she trained the other two up to her standards and started taking contracts. They were making millions. It would have been hard to turn their backs on that, I guess."

"How did the boyfriend know all this?"

"She got loaded one night and confessed everything to him."

Quadrado paused with her report as she navigated her way across a busy intersection, so Fletcher asked a question that had been nipping at him. "What about the various gangs? Have they all stopped knocking lumps out of each other?"

"So far so good. As soon as Thomson left us, he and Forbes and a couple of other senior agents visited all those affected or involved and told them it was over. That they had to go back to business as usual, otherwise he'd throw everything he had at them."

"I'll bet they were quaking in their Guccis."

Quadrado ignored Fletcher's barb about Thomson. For all the man was a poor communicator, he was still FBI, still part of her tribe.

"Now, the warehouse. It was partly destroyed by the fire, but other than one of the call girls and the three Oganesyans you killed, everyone else survived."

"Good. I'm pleased the body count wasn't too high. Even the henchmen. They were low-level grunts, even if they worked for Nazis. I suppose they might pop up somewhere else, but after their plan turned to crap, they'll not bother anyone for a while."

"Thomson had them all rounded up. I didn't know it until after the fact, but he had five SWAT teams two blocks away. As soon as you came out of the warehouse, he called them in. It was them who rescued the women and the older guy." Quadrado cast a quick look at Fletcher. "I'm surprised you've not asked me about the older guy."

"I know that if he's important, you'll tell me about him in due course. If he's not important, then you not telling me about him isn't important."

Quadrado couldn't keep the smile from her lips or her tone. "Turns out he's very important. He's none other than Henry Young the Third. The chair of the Nevada Gaming Commission."

"Interesting." Fletcher pulled a face as he scratched at his uninjured arm. "He was at a warehouse party with hookers. The party hosts were a criminal gang who are trying to muscle in on Las Vegas casinos. Would I be right in saying he's dirtier than a sewer-dwelling rat?"

"You'd be very right." Quadrado's nose twitched. "And thanks for the mental image. Young was a rising star and was tipped to run for governor. In fact, Thomson told me this morning that Young had gone to college with the FBI director."

"Now that is properly interesting." Fletcher's fingers drummed on his leg as he leaned back until his head was on the headrest. "In a way it answers a different set of questions that've been plaguing me."

"What questions?"

"How did the Mantis find us? How did she know about us to begin with? I thought there was a leak in Thomson's office, but now I'm not so sure."

"Why not?"

Fletcher lifted his head off the rest and twisted it Quadrado's way. "Roll with me here. After we'd killed the Mantis and her minions, we spoke to Soter. During that call, Soter gave me the mission to wipe out the Armenian bosses. Remember how I told him that I'd need Thomson to play ball. Well, one minute after I finished speaking to Soter, Thomson was on a call and I heard him address the person on the other end of the line as 'director.' That suggests to me that the FBI director is very close to Soter. Maybe he's having his string pulled too, or maybe he is Soter. In the bigger scheme of things, me knowing who Soter really is satisfies my curiosity and does nothing else; it won't release me from his grip. And if I was dumb enough to call him out over it, he'd have me killed or jail me for what went down in Georgia."

"You're right. Now let me get this straight, you think Young was getting information from his old college buddy, *the director of the FBI*, about us? That suggests Soter actively sold us down the river, or the director did."

"Not intentionally. The director couldn't know Young was mixed up with the Armenians unless he was too, and that's not something I can believe. I think that to maintain his cover, Young contacted the director about the killings. All it would take was a loose comment along the lines of, 'don't worry, I've sent a pair of specialists in to sort it,' and that's Young and the Armenians tipped off about us. After that it's about basic surveillance."

Fletcher was right. As usual.

Quadrado turned into the drop-off bay of McCarran International Airport and pulled to a stop. "Want me to carry your bag to the gate?"

"I wouldn't want your boyfriend getting jealous."

"How do you know about him?" Quadrado felt heat on her cheeks as she tried not to meet Fletcher's eye.

"When I got taken by the Mantis, before it happened, you got a call that made you do a goofy grin. Only love makes someone grin like that. I'm pleased for you. Everyone needs that kind of excitement in their life."

"It's not love. Not yet. It's too soon. We've only been out a few times." Quadrado realized she was gabbling and tried changing the topic. "Anyway, I asked a question. Do you want me to carry your bag to the gate?"

Fletcher didn't bother answering. Instead, he gave one of the shrugs that infuriated Quadrado. He'd know she was offering company and friendship rather than her services as a pack mule, but he was easy about it. Fletcher would go on just fine whether she carried his bag and kept him company, or whether she left him to his own devices.

For now, it was time to go home.

A LETTER FROM JOHN

I want to say a huge thank-you for choosing to read *Third Kill*. If you did enjoy it, and want to keep up to date with all my latest releases, just sign up at the following link. Your email address will never be shared and you can unsubscribe at any time.

www.bookouture.com/john-ryder

One of the key points in my mind when I set out to write *Third Kill* was that it had to be set in an urban environment after Fletcher's first two adventures took place in rural and small-town settings. Rather than look to sprawling metropolises such as New York or LA, I thought it would be great fun to bring the worst sin to Sin City. Las Vegas has long fascinated me, as it's truly a rapacious beast intent on devouring every possible dollar and is, or certainly was, famed for its underworld links in ways few other cities have been.

When it came to creating a baddie to go up against Fletcher, I'd already decided to pit him against a trained assassin, but I still had to create that assassin. The Mantis was born in the dark recesses of my mind, and arrived pretty much fully formed, although the addition of her cohorts didn't germinate until I was plotting the novel out. Female assassins are quite rare, and I loved the idea of a small, tight-knit group of them working together. It also ramped up the stakes and difficulty for Fletcher and that's never a bad thing.

What happens next for Fletcher is anyone's guess, but I do know one thing, trouble won't need a GPS to find him.

I hope you loved *Third Kill* and if you did I would be very grateful if you could write a review. I'd love to hear what you think, and it makes such a difference helping new readers to discover one of my books for the first time.

I love hearing from my readers—you can get in touch on my Facebook page, through Twitter, Goodreads or my website.

Thanks,
John

JohnRyderAuthor

@JohnRyder101

johnryderauthor.com

ACKNOWLEDGMENTS

As always I'd like to end with some hearty thanks to those who've helped, supported or just kept out of my way when I was writing this book. My family have always been incredibly supportive and I'm hugely fortunate to have them in my lives.

I'm also very lucky to have many friends in all areas of the publishing world and so many of them give help, advice and support in so many ways they don't even know how awesome they are. My Crime and Publishment gang are a bunch of stars and their friendship is immeasurable to me.

Whenever writing a book there's always a need to reach out to specialists for expert opinion, and friends Nigel Adams, Fire Investigator, and Toni White, Pathology Lab Manager, gave detailed advice freely, and any mistakes in the interpretation of it are mine and mine alone.

I'd also like to thank the wonderful peeps at Bookouture, specifically my eagle-eyed editor, Isobel Akenhead, whose pedantry, logical mind and point-blank refusal to let me make up words improves my writing every time she picks up her red pen. She's ably backed up by an even more logical copy editor, Janette Currie, who does a fantastic job of keeping me right. Noelle and Sarah are the kind of publicists every author wants on their side and I'm damned lucky to have them on mine. The whole backroom team who manages the audiobooks, and marketing and promotion of books and authors are all superstars and industry leaders at what they do.

Finally, my readers are the reason I keep on writing. Without them, I'm nothing more than a typist who's not very good at typing.